The Hard Road Home

By
H. W. Hollman

Dedication:

I would like to dedicate this book to my daughter, Jessica. Because of her I would not have written this tale about my great-grandfather.

Chapter One

IN THE SHADE of an old sycamore tree, smoke drifted from a mud brick chimney of a small house. Timeworn branches began to show their first signs of life with the warm mid-February weather. It was going to be an early spring this year.

It was peaceful and quiet at the Hillman's homestead, but things were busy as I was getting ready for spring. In the field across the dirt lane that led to my house, I fussed with my stubborn mule. The animal, clearly resisting my efforts to steer him in the right direction, stretched out his neck and disturbed the stillness of the morning air with his loud braying.

"Get up there!" I called to the obstinate animal. I wanted to break ground and get the field ready for seeds. If the weather was good this year and we didn't get too much rain, we might make a little money from our crops to put aside.

A movement on the road caught my eye. A wagon and a few riders were coming down the lane that ended at my house. They must be looking for me.

"Whoa," I called, pulling on the reins to stop the mule. I watched for a moment to make sure the stubborn animal stood still and didn't wander off. Satisfied, I wrapped the bridles around the plow's wooden handle and made my way across the freshly turned rows to the fence.

When I arrived, I took off my hat and wiped the sweatband with my handkerchief. Looking over my shoulder and seeing the mule wasn't straying, I turned my attention back to the three riders. They stopped with their wagon on the opposite side of the fence from me. I didn't recognize any of these men on horseback or in the wagon.

I pulled my hat back onto my head. "Warm day for February, ain't it, boys? Sa-boys, what y'all doing here? Y'all want a drink of water or something?"

One rider eased his horse closer to the fence. He smiled. "Thank-ye kindly, sir, but I figure we are fine as we are. Could you help me?" He pulled a piece of paper from the inside of his jacket. He looked back at me. "We're looking for a man named Riley... Riley Hillman. Do you know where we might find him? Is this his place?"

Smiling back at him, I replied, "Yep, you found him friend. Yes, sir... that's me, all right."

The rider leaned back in his saddle, still smiling. "Well... glad to make your acquaintance, Mr. Hillman. We are here to congratulate you. You, sir, have been selected to serve the Southern States of America in its glorious cause!"

Confused, I narrowed my eyes at the stranger across the dry, gray railing of my fence. "What do you mean, serve?"

He folded the paper and stuffed it back inside his jacket. Watching me, still smiling, he continued. "Sir, you are hereby notified that you have been selected to serve in the Confederate States of America's Army for as long as your government should see fit."

My heart pounded in my chest. I was getting nervous. I'd heard there was some kind of fighting between the people living in the South and the ones in the North. But that was far away from here... in Virginia. Not anywhere close. It didn't make much sense to send armed troops into your own country to make people see things the way they wanted you to see it. Didn't make sense at all!

I remembered a while back, they were taking volunteers at the Rapides Parish courthouse, if I wanted to join up. They were raising a regiment of soldiers to go to Virginia and fight. I declined the invitation. I had enough work around here. I didn't have time to traipse around the countryside playing soldier-boy, naw, sir.

I did hear that both of Mr. Moore's boys who lived down the road had joined up. I really liked those boys. I grew up with them under the same roof.

There seemed to be a difference of opinion between these riders and me. I didn't know if this was a bad jest or not. I looked hard at the rider. "Hey, I can't be going anywhere. I got too much work to do around here, mister. Spring's coming and I have got to get my ground plowed and ready for planting. I ain't got time to go off and *serve*. Naw, sir, you must be mistaken and have the wrong man. I ain't going nowhere but right here."

The rider, still smiling, rose in his saddle, looking around. Seeing I was alone, he took off his hat. As he wiped his face on the sleeve of his jacket, he slowly drew his revolver and laid his hat over the gun as he rested it on the saddle horn. I heard the hammer cock and I froze.

I ain't never had a gun pointed at me, and I can tell you right now, I was scared. My left thumb worked my index finger like there was no tomorrow. It worked quite a bit that day in fact. Lucinda always laughed at me when I rubbed my fingers together. She knew I was thinking or worried about something. I kept looking back toward the house to see if she saw what was going on. Thank God she didn't come outside.

The rider, the smile now gone, looked down at me. "Sir, I truly apologize for the inconvenience, but your country needs you. Therefore, I think you will be coming with us, Mr. Hillman. Yes, sir, I do believe so."

I swallowed hard. "Hey... lookee here, mister, I have got to get the plowing done and my wife... my wife is about to deliver our baby; our first. I really can't go with y'all and leave her alone right now... really, I just can't do it. Not in her condition."

"Again, sir, I do apologize for the inconvenience. I truly do, but I don't think you understand. You are needed! You, sir, will be going one way or the other, makes no difference to me which way. But like it or not, you will be going, Mr. Hillman. You might as well get use to the idea.

"I'll give you time to go over and say your goodbyes to your wife there, sir, but that's about all the time I'm giving you. So, go on to the house yonder and say your goodbyes. I'll go along with you," he said, motioning me toward the house.

I walked in front as he eased his horse behind me. He remained mounted, covering me with the pistol hidden under his hat. I guess he wanted to make sure I didn't lose my way to the waiting wagon.

I stood in front of the porch and called to Lucinda. The barrel of a scattergun eased itself out the window next to the

3

door. A voice from inside called out to me, "Riley... Everything all right out there?"

I smiled to myself and nodded. "Yessum, everything is fine. Lucinda, these men are here to take me away to serve in the army."

The woman's voice said, "Is that so?"

I looked up at the rider who had turned a shade whiter and holding both hands in the air, showing his hat in his left hand and his pistol in his right. I said to the man, "You'll have to excuse my wife. She don't take to strangers to well. You see, she's full-blooded Cherokee and she ain't got no sense of humor. So if you act right, so will she."

He nodded, and I called into the house. "It's all right, Lucinda. Put away your scattergun. The man only wants to talk."

As soon as the rider's revolver was placed into its holster, the door to the house opened. My wife, a lovely young Indian maiden with long black hair tied behind her head and a swollen belly large with child, came outside with a shotgun slung over one arm.

The rider's eyebrows rose in surprise. I'm sure he thought all Indian women were short, fat, and ugly. He wasn't prepared to see such a beauty living off the reservation. He looked down at me and said under his breath, "Lucky man."

To Lucinda, the rider bowed in his saddle, placing his hat across his heart. "Beg your pardon, ma'am. I am so sorry to bring bad tidings at such an inconvenient time as this, but our government has commissioned me to do its bidding. I am here to recruit the men listed on my orders here in my pocket and bring them to Camp Moore for training. Make no mistake, madam, he will have to come with us peacefully or I can come back later and take him by force. Either way, ma'am, he has to come." He patted his jacket where he kept his papers to emphasize his duty.

I knew if I didn't go with them they would come back. I could fight them, but I wouldn't win, and Lucinda might get hurt. I couldn't live with that. Naw sir, I had to tell her I had to go.

Before Lucinda could say a word, I cut in and said, "Honey, I can't stay. I don't want any trouble with these government men. So it's best I go with them now. It looks like I

4

don't have a choice in the matter anyway."

The rider nodded. "He's right. He has no choice. He has to come with us, but don't y'all worry none, ma'am. He should be back in a few months or so. Just as soon as we whup those Yankees and win this war; shouldn't take too long."

Lucinda, not smiling, turned her dark eyes to the rider and said, "Uh-huh." She turned to me. "You be careful, Riley. You go on and do what you're supposed to do and then you come right back here. You hear?"

I took off my hat, worry eating at my stomach. I said softly, "Yessum. I'll be back, just as soon as they let me. Will you be all right here alone?"

She nodded, standing in the doorway. I turned to go and then stopped. Turning back to her, I took her into my arms and hugged her close to me, whispering into her ear, "I love you. Be safe, Lucinda. Let Mr. Moore know what's happened and see if you can stay at their place until I come back. I'm sure he won't mind and his girls will love to have you there."

I released her, my heart heavy, and walked toward the waiting wagon. At the back side of the carriage, I hopped in with the other men already seated there. The driver turned his team of mules around and headed down the road which it came.

As we were leaving, I heard my mule braying loudly. I looked to where he stood, still hitched to the plow, standing patiently in the field where I had left him. I had forgotten all about him. I guess Lucinda would have to take care of him. There was nothing I could do about it now.

As I sat there on the back of the moving wagon, I watched my house as it disappeared behind clusters of trees. Lucinda stood in the doorway holding her scattergun still in the crook of her arm then I lost sight of my place.

While we traveled the dusty road of dead grass, we made a few more stops, picking up more *volunteers* until the wagon was fully loaded. Never knew I had neighbors living within ten miles of me. No, sir, I did not know that.

We joined four other wagons in Rapides near the Red River at the army depot. Not long after, five wagons pulled out and traveled in a caravan down another dirt road, heading southeast following the river.

After leaving Rapides, I was quickly lost. As long as I

could remember, I had never been south of Rapides; this was all new country to me. As I jostled in the back of the wagon along with the other men, my thoughts reached back to my little homestead and my little Lucinda. God, I wanted to go home and hold her in my arms. Feel her body next to mine and hear her breathing at the crack of dawn before she wakes.

After a week of slow moving, bumping around in that crowded wagon, we passed through small towns where the folks there didn't speak English. Someone said they only spoke French. When the people down there talked, it sounded like little birds spewing noise a mile a minute.

One rider who knew the language turned in his saddle and proudly announced. "Welcome to Acadia, boys." I didn't understand anybody in that part of Louisiana, but they sure were friendly. I just kept smiling and nodding my head as if I understood what they were a saying. This seemed to make the people living there happy.

At one town, the wagons stopped and women folk brought us very fine food and drinks they had prepared. The soup was spicy and tasty. They seemed to have put everything into that soup: okra, tomatoes, chicken, crawfish, shrimp, and other meat I couldn't identify, but it was mighty tasty indeed with a kick to it. They called it *gumbo*.

We thanked them kindly, and after eating our fill, we loaded back into the wagons and kept on moving south. We never stopped in one place long. Always trekking in that southeasterly direction; following the river.

After a few more days in the French part of Louisiana, we got to towns that spoke English. I was so happy to hear them. Although the English spoken there did sound different from what I was use to. Some of the words I didn't understand, but they did seem familiar. I understood enough to get by and that was good enough.

We finally reached our destination. The wagons turned off the main road and stopped at a gate that blocked our path. In the distance, I heard men shouting and smelled campfires--lots of campfires.

The leader of our small caravan rode forward toward a man standing by the closed gate. The man was dressed in the prettiest gray suit I had ever seen. Our leader stopped his horse at the gate and raised his right hand to the brim of his hat. The stranger standing by the barrier did the same to the brim of his kepi looking up at the rider.

Our man then reached inside his coat and pulled out a piece of paper and handed it down to the man. The man looked at the paper for a moment before folding and handing it back.

Both men went through the same ritual of raising their hands to their foreheads and snapping them down. The rider turned in his saddle and waved for the wagons to move forward. The man in the pretty, gray suit opened the gate and let us through.

As soon as we passed into the camp, we saw men everywhere. Everyone wore the same suit as the man at the gate. I turned to the fellow sitting next to me. "Sa-boy, I hope we get those nice looking clothes to wear. They sure look pretty."

The man I spoke to was called Turner... Joseph Turner. He nodded as he looked around the camp and then leaned over the side of the wagon and spat a big wad of chewin' tobaccy onto the ground.

Chapter Two

AND THUS BEGAN my training as a southern soldier.

Our wagon bounced and jostled toward a large building sitting next to another fence. When we stopped, a soldier with stripes on the sleeve of his gray jacket walked along the side of the wagons, banging a short club against them, shouting at us with his mouth full of tobaccy.

"GET OUT! GET OUT, YOU LAZY SONS OF WHORES! GET DOWN OFF THOSE GODDAMN WAGONS AND FORM A GODDAMN LINE IN FRONT OF THAT THERE GODDAMN PORCH, MOVE... YOU BUNCH OF LAZY ASSES, GODDAMN IDIOTS! GODDAMN YOU, I SAID MOVE YOUR GODDAMN ASSES! MOVE'EM NOW, YOU SONS OF BITCHES! NOT GODDAMN TOMORROW! GODDAMN IT, I AIN'T GOT ALL GODDAMN DAY!"

Tobacco juice spewed out his mouth and he pointed to the building with the long porch on one side. Then he turned and took off at a run, back to the first wagon, waving his arms in the air and cussing more. When he reached the first wagon, he swung his short club, striking everybody and thing within reach not moving fast enough.

I didn't know to what make of this lunatic and his club. What made that man so mad at us? We had just gotten here and I was moving as fast as I could. Ducking under the club he swung at me, I ran to the spot he had pointed to and got into a line before he had a chance to beat me.

Once everyone was lined up, he calmed some. He stood in front of us, now smiling, clutching his short bat with his hands behind his back. In a pleasant voice he said, "Now, that wasn't too hard...was it?"

Well...I thought he was talking to me, so I said, "Naw, sir."

His face turned dark and the smile quickly vanished as he rushed to stand in front of me. He leaned forward, grabbed a handful of my shirt and pulled me to him, placing his nose against mine. He was so close I could smell the tobacco on his breath. His whiskers brushing against my chin tickled and caused me to smile, and that seemed to make this lunatic even madder.

The man commenced to scream in my face, spraying tobacco spit all over me. "GOD DAMMIT, WHO GAVE Y'ALL PERMISSION TO TALK? YOU GODDAMN SORRY EXCUSE OF A MAN! SON, DO YOU HAVE SHIT FOR BRAINS? YOU DON'T TALK UNTIL Y'ALL ARE TOLD TO TALK AND NOT BEFORE, YOU GODDAMN STUPID CLOD HOPPER! WHY ARE YOU SMILING AT ME, SON? I AIN'T YOUR GODDAMN FRIEND! HELL...I DON'T EVEN LIKE YOU, YOU GODDAMN IGNORANT BASTARD!"

He released my shirt and moved away, looking at the other men standing in formation. He said loudly so everyone around could hear, "I am your sergeant and you will address me as so! Do I make myself clear?"

Afraid to make this angry man madder and scared he was going to use that club on me, I said, "Yes, sir, Mr. Sergeant." My left thumb rubbed furiously against my index finger next to my pant leg.

I realized pleasing this man was going to be hard work. I didn't know what his problem was or why he hated me so much. He didn't even know me but it seemed he focused all his anger at me personally.

The man's face turned dark again, moving quickly to where I stood. He pressed his face against mine again, nose to nose, eyeball to eyeball, wearing the ugliest scowl I had ever seen, and screamed, spraying tobaccy juice again. "WHO TOLD YOU TO TALK, BOY? ARE YOU SOME MORON? I JUST SAID, NO TALKING IN RANKS, YOU GODDAMN STUPID SON OF A BITCH! NOW, UNLESS I SAY SO, YOU KEEP YOUR GODDAMN MOUTH SHUT! YOU GODDAMN IDIOT! JESUS H. CHRIST! God Almighty, give me strength!"

He quieted and whispered into my ear, "I'm gonna keep my eye on you, boy. I can see right now that you are going to be a troublemaker, ain't ya, boy? Boy, if you and I are gonna get alone, you had better watch your step with me. You understand me, boy?"

He released my shirt, pushing me away. He walked up and down the line of men, still wearing that scowl on his face. "I will tell y'all when you can talk. I will tell y'all when you can eat. I will also tell y'all when you can sleep and when to wake." He stopped his pacing and turned to us and smiled for the first time. "Hell, boys… I'll even tell y'all when you can take a dump. Now, you can answer by saying *yes, Sergeant*."

As a group, we called out loudly, "Yes, sir, Sergeant."

The sergeant's face turned that deep shade of red again as he grabbed hold of the first man he could reach and screamed in his face. "DON'T Y'ALL EVER CALL ME SIR, Goddamn you… I ain't no goddamn officer! Only officers will be addressed by sir! You goddamn ignorant people. Do I make myself clear?"

In one voice every one said, "Yes, Sergeant."

The sergeant smiled and leaned forward placing his left hand next to his ear. "That's better, but I can't hear you!"

A little louder, we shouted, "Yes, Sergeant!"

Leaning closer, he yelled, "GODDAMN, YOU NINNIES! I still can't hear you, you sons of a whore! Grow a pair of balls and let me hear you!"

We screamed as loud as we could, "YES, SERGEANT!"

Satisfied, he smiled and huffed, "OUT… STANDING!" Now as pleasant as he could be he bowed and waved one arm toward one of the two doors to the building. "Now, ladies, if y'all don't mind, form a single line and one at a time go through that there door over yonder."

We quickly formed a line leading up to the porch as fast as we could, and I noticed as we stood waiting, more and more wagons came into camp. Sergeants moved around meeting these newcomers the same way our sergeant met ours. Banging on the sides of wagons and yelling as they unloaded and formed lines.

My turn, I walked through the door and found myself in a large room filled with all kinds of things. A long table ran almost the length of the wall with men in gray uniforms on one side shoving clothes and things into our arms. We were told to keep moving. "If it doesn't fit, trade it with someone who it will fit."

At the end of the line we were handed a cartridge belt, a beautiful rifle, blanket, and a canvas bag with straps. The man in uniform behind the table called it a *haversack*. They said this was to keep our possessions in.

By the time we left that building, our arms were loaded. We all had gotten a pretty gray suit of clothes, a fancy kepi, and a new pair of shoes... one size fits all. The shoes were made to fit either the left or right foot so I couldn't get it wrong if I tried.

We were ushered out the back door where our sergeant waited with another wagon filled with canvas packs to make our tents. We weren't allowed to ride on this wagon, no, sir. He had us follow the cart on foot, far out into the field. Once we stopped, the sergeant lined us up in front of him, our arms still loaded with everything.

Using his short club as a pointer, he aimed at the ground beneath his feet. "This here, ladies... this is your new home for the next three weeks. Unless you get sick and die or I kill you first. Now..." He pointed to a stand of trees farther out from us. "I want a straight line of tents set up, starting here and ending over there by that grove of saplings."

When he dismissed us, we got to work setting up our campsite the best we could. For someone who never had a tent, I thought we did a pretty good job of pitching and getting them in a straight line.

When we finished setting up the tents, the sergeant took one look at them and shook his head. He didn't think much of the way it looked. In disgust, he mumbled a few curses under his breath. Then he tore through our campsite, pulling up stakes, kicking down tents, and throwing equipment left and right.

Madder than a wet hen, he cussed loudly calling us names we had never heard before. Some I still don't know what they mean to this day.

We spent the rest of that afternoon and well into the night making and remaking, and remaking, that campsite until he was satisfied. During that time, more men and wagons kept coming by and unloading.

By the time we got our campsite the way our sergeant wanted, the moon was well above the tree line. I sure was tired when I was able to finally lie down and sleep.

Lying there, out in the open, looking up at the moon in the sky, I had time to think about Lucinda and home. I wondered what she was doing at that moment. Was she asleep or looking at that same moon, thinking of me. I wished she were here under my warm blanket and I could feel her body snuggled against mine. I sure missed her.

I found myself dreaming of her when I was awakened by this god-awful racket. Someone was walking through our campsite beating on a washtub with a club and yelling, "GET UP! GET UP, GODDAMN YOU, AND FORM A LINE!"

We jumped up, scrambling in the darkness, grabbing our new clothes and quickly getting dressed. We didn't know what to think. What was going on and why was someone making such a ruckus so early in the morning. I heard one man over to my right cry out, "My God... what time is it? What the devil is going on out here?"

Someone called out of the darkness nearby, "Time to get up, ladies... daylight's burning! Get up, get dressed, and form a line!"

Daylight? I thought, looking at the moon. From what I could judge, it was around three o'clock in the morning--way too early to get up. And what in the world were we gonna do at this hour of the morning anyway? It was too dark.

There was an awful lot of moaning and groaning coming from the fellers as we dressed and lined up in front of our tents.

There was a different man with stripes on his sleeves waiting for us this morning. Once we lined up, he called out in a pleasant voice, "Well good morning, ladies! I hope y'all slept well! You have fifteen minutes to get your tents squared away, and then I want you nice ladies to line yourselves back up here in front of me again... right here."

Surprised at someone telling us to do work in the dark, we didn't move at first, wondering if he was serious. The sergeant slapped his short club against the flat of his hand and shouted, "NOW, LADIES...MOVE YOUR SWEET LITTLE ASSES! Time is a wastin'!"

We scurried around, tripping over tent stakes and each other as we cleaned up the campsite as fast as we could. After straightening up nicely, we fell back into line and waited for the sergeant to return. As we stood there waiting, we observed him and three other men in uniform talking together.

After a moment the four men with stripes on their jackets walked over to us. The sergeant that woke us this morning called out to us. "Listen up, men. I want you ignoramuses to form new lines, four abreast. For the real stupid people among you, that means I want four to stand here in front of me side by side facing me. And then I want four more of you ladies to stand behind them and so-on and so-on until all of you are lined up. Is that clear?"

This time knowing what to say and how to say it, we shouted together, "Yes, Sergeant!"

The sergeant smiled and grunted. "You fellers catch on quickly, don't y'all?"

After we lined up, they showed how to stand at attention and at-ease. After those two drills, they let us rest for a moment. The sky in the east was beginning to lighten. With the coming of day, we could now see there must have been hundreds, maybe thousands, of men moving around in that large field. I ain't never seen so many people in one place at the same time. I'm telling you, it was something to behold.

The sergeant called us to gather around him and kneel. He motioned for the other three men in uniform to come over and stand with him. "Men... my name is Sergeant Cole and these are Sergeant Perkins, Sergeant Guardner, and Sergeant Tifton who you met yesterday. We will be training you at Camp Moore."

When I heard the name of Sergeant Perkins, I got excited for a bit. My wife's name was Perkins. I looked around at all the sergeants but none of them looked Indian so I guess he was not related.

As we listen to the sergeant's talk we didn't say a word because they didn't ask for any response. My stomach started to make an awful noise, rumbling and growling like a bear. I wondered when we were going to eat. But no matter how hungry I was, I was not asking the sergeant when breakfast was. Naw sir, not me. I didn't want a taste of that club of his. I wasn't the only one hungry either. I heard the other fellers around me, their stomachs growling loudly too. We waited for him to finish.

Sergeant Cole either didn't hear or chose to ignore the complaining stomachs because he continued talking. "The four of us are gonna get you boys ready to fight them Yankees when they come. Y'all will be part of the Louisiana 27th regiment. Colonel Leon Marks is your commanding officer.

"There will be ten companies in this here regiment. You will be the third company, Company C. That's Charlie Company, and since you boys are from Rapides Parish, y'all will be known as the Rapides Terribles. Y'all will be terrible indeed to behold when y'all come against the Yankee horde advancing into our homeland as we speak.

"We are gonna drive them damn Yankees out of the south and when it's all over, we will go home in a few months and carry on as we did before with our lives. Now-- I know you boys are getting hungry, so form your ranks again and we will march over yonder and get something to eat."

After his little speech, we lined up and marched to where they were serving food out the back of a couple of wagons. We grabbed a tin plate and cup and had cornbread and beans and drank a cup of hot coffee before going back to drilling.

Chapter Three

I THOUGHT IT was funny that the name of this camp was the same name of the family that I was bonded to when I was younger. It made me think back to when I was a young boy. Back to when I was given to a young family there in Slagle; sold to them to earn my keep. I worked for the Moore family and they fed and clothed me. My family didn't have much when they moved there from Alabama.

Times were hard back then. My family didn't have enough to feed and take care of all the mouths they had, and they were-a fixin' to pull up stakes again and move on over to Mississippi where they could find work.

Many newcomers to this country bonded either themselves or their children out to families who were better off so the rest of the family could make a living. You can't do that no more, naw, sir. People just don't understand being bonded to someone. They think you are abandoning your children or selling them into slavery.

Me? Hey... I didn't look at it that way at all. I was happy in my bondage. Yes, sir. They were good Christian people and took good care of me. I never went hungry and I always had a roof over my head.

They had children of their own, Mister Moore and his wife, but not enough to run their farm properly. Everybody worked... everybody. Mister Moore, his wife, and later on when their children got old enough they worked too. Their two sons and two little girls were like brothers and sisters to me. I was their big brother as far as they were concerned. I was always treated as one of them. But everybody worked hard. From before

15

the sun came up until it went down at night and there were no Sundays to rest neither, naw, sir.

When I turned twenty-four years old, my fifteen years of service was up and I had finished my contract with their family. I was now a free man and ready to have my own place. Mr. Moore had lots of land, some he would never use. I sat down and talked with him one day and said I would stay on and work another five years for him free if I could have the twenty acres of scrub land west of his place that he wasn't going to use. He agreed, so we shook hands and I stayed.

I had no money at that time. I didn't need any. I had a bed, plenty of food, and a good roof over my head. What did I need money for? There was nowhere to spend it anyway. The nearest town of any size was east, over twenty some-odd miles away in the seat of Rapides Parish along the Red River.

I had one year left on my agreement with Mr. Moore when I met my wife Lucinda. Ah... She was such a lovely young Indian girl when I first laid eyes on her. She had been abandoned herself when she was three or four years old. She was full-blooded Cherokee. Her mama had left her in the care of a white family near where they camped on their way to the reservation. They promised to return and get her once registered and settled into their new home in the Oklahoma Territory.

Her family was being forced to relocate by the government along with the rest of the Cherokee nation to some scrub land. They were given worthless ground no white man wanted. The government wanted all the Indians to be located in one place so they could keep track of them.

When Lucinda's mama returned for her a few years later, the white family they left her with refused to give her up. There were no courts or lawyers at that time, and I didn't think any court would have judge in favor of any Indian. Don't know how they settled it, but they did. The white family kept the child and raised her as their own.

Her adopted family's name was St. John. I don't rightly know why she didn't take their name, but she didn't. She took the name Perkins as her last name. Nobody knows why, and as far as her age...nobody knew exactly how old she really was.

There was a revival going on at one of the neighbor's farm and Mr. Moore wanted the family to go. I hitched their plow horses to their wagon and they loaded everyone onboard. They had fixed up picnic baskets of food and placed them in the wagon.

I came along just to see what was going on and because of the picnic baskets. I didn't care one way or the other about no revival. I did hear those gatherings sometimes had a lot of people and lots of good food. I thought it would be real nice to mingle with many people at one time.

I first met Lucinda at that picnic. The preacher was having one hell-fire and damnation speech that day. I found out I didn't like being around so many people determined to save my soul from hell. I was ready to leave until I saw that lovely dark skin Indian girl sitting by herself. She sure was pretty. Yes, sir-ree.

I walked up and stood in front of her. That's when I discovered my mind had left my head and ran off somewhere leaving me brainless and stupid. I don't know what happened. I must have looked like an idiot, standing there, tongue-tied. I had never met a girl, other than Mr. Moore's daughters, that is.

Well, I stood there like a fool, with my hands cupped up under my armpits, swaying back and forth, not knowing where else to put them. When I did talk, the only thing I could think to say was, "What's yo name, girl?"

She looked up at me with those dark eyes of hers. "Lucinda... Lucinda Nash Perkins." I thought to myself, *hey... that's a strange name for an Injun.*

She sure was pretty. I thought she was just about the prettiest thing I had ever seen in my life and she looked to be just about the right age to get married too. So I asked her, "Hey... how old are you, Lucy?"

She furled her brow at me, her dark eyes flashing like lightning, and she looked at me real irritated. "My name is Lucinda, not Lucy, and I am old enough to make my own decisions, thank you, sir."

I smiled and thought to myself, *yep... she's sure was just the right age, yes, sir-ree, boy.* Gosh I was young and foolish back then. I was so nervous around her that I didn't know what to say after that. And when I got nervous my thumb rubbed against my index finger. It's a habit I got into when I was young.

I gazed into those dark eyes of hers and my mouth went

completely dry. I was at a total loss of words. I just stood there... like a bump on a log.

She put her hand up to her mouth, giggling as she watched me, smitten by her, and I saw something else in those mysterious eyes. I don't rightly know how to explain it, but I got this funny feeling deep in my gut when she looked at me a certain way. Whatever it was, I wanted to be near her, take care of her, and protect her for the rest of my life.

We were married by one of those traveling preachers who rode by every now and then. Once my last year of work for Mr. Moore was up, he gave me the title to the land he had promised, along with ten dollars in silver to buy me a mule and some seeds. That was 1859.

We weren't married very long when we heard rumors that war was coming between the northern states and the states here in the south. It was supposed to be a war over state rights. Each state had their own laws on how their government should be run. The northern states didn't like the way we did things here in the south.

In the south, we believed each state had the right to govern its own people the way that state government saw fit. Laws made for people living in their state.

Now, those northern people didn't see it that way. They thought we should do things the same way throughout the country, with one central government controlling all the states.

I just didn't understand. How in the heck would somebody living thousands of miles from us know what we needed here in Louisiana? Can you tell me that? It just didn't make any sense to me, naw sir.

It seemed this difference of opinion was what caught in our craw--having someone who didn't know us from Adam to say, "No... we think y'all should do it this way."

Hey... it was too much for us southerners to swallow. So, war did begin that very next spring in Virginia. I heard the northern states were having a fit about slavery. I didn't know anything about that. I didn't have any politics on the subject, and I wouldn't fight for them one way or the other. But letting someone who didn't live here tell us how to live, then you will have a fight on your hands. And that's what was going on now.

I figured it would be over any day. I was waiting for them

to come by and tell us we could go on back home.

Chapter Four

AROUND THE FIRST of May, a young lieutenant on horseback rode by and stopped where we were practicing bayonet drills on straw dummies in the pasture. He motioned for our sergeant, Sergeant Cole.

We were glad for the break. The weather was a hot and muggy for May. The lieutenant seemed excited. He kept smiling and leaning down from the saddle of his horse, patting our sergeant on the shoulder. I turned to the soldier next to me. "Maybe the war's over; they said it wouldn't take too long."

He grunted with a smile.

I was hopeful when the lieutenant and the sergeant finished talking by themselves. The sergeant quickly stepped back a pace and saluted the lieutenant. The young man on horseback returned the salute and touched his spurs to his horse, galloping off to another part of the field.

Sergeant Cole didn't move at first. He watched the lieutenant for a moment before walking back to where we stood waiting. His eyes gleamed with excitement. He called to the company, "Ah...ten...shun! Men..." he paused, looking down at his feet for a moment, thinking. He then looked up and slid his focus from face to face. "The day has come," he started and then stopped again, removing his kepi, glancing down at it as he rubbed his hand along the inside sweatband. He turned his piercing eyes back on us.

We were familiar with that look. From the glow on his face, he must have received some awfully good news from the lieutenant. Something was going on. Pockets of soldiers, here and there, were erupting in loud cheers all around us.

Whatever it was, we were about to find out. I was so hoping he was going to say the war was over and we were all going home. That would be good news indeed.

"The day has come," he began again, "sooner than I expected or wanted, but it has come all the same."

I thought to myself, "Yes! I was right... the war was over."

"Tomorrow," he paused, glaring at us with pride, "we will move out and head for Vicksburg."

"What!" I screamed in my mind, trying to control my emotions.

Sergeant Cole placed his kepi onto his head and pulled it down, his eyes glistening under its brim. "We're gonna be moving fast and there won't be any trains available. So, we're gonna have to do it on foot. Let's break camp, boys, and get ready to move out in the morning. We will march at first light."

Vicksburg? Hey... wait just a damn minute here. What about home? All around me men went wild with the news. Some screamed the Rebel Yell and tossed their hats into the air. Sergeant Cole didn't seem to care if the men hooped and hollered. He stood and beamed with pride.

Well, shucks... my hopes were dashed. I swallowed my pride and celebrated with my fellow soldiers anyway. I didn't want others to think I didn't like the idea about moving to another place, and I didn't want them to think I was a afraid, because I wasn't. I only wanted to go home, that's all. I figured one of these days this war would be over. I would be able to go home... someday.

WE BROKE RANKS and spent the rest of the afternoon taking down camp and loading wagons. Canvas covered carriages clogged the entrance to the grounds, waiting their turn to get onto the road traveling north to Vicksburg.

As the last of the sun's rays dropped behind trees west of camp, wagons were still lined up as far as the eye could see up and down that road beyond the fence line. The same road we would be marching in the morning. All that was left in the vast field was us, our blankets, and rifles.

The camp now looked empty as the last wagon faded into

the evening darkness. The field looked sad, deserted, with no tents, horses, or mules. Everything was gone. Everything but men and small campfires scattered throughout the large pasture.

That night we ate food left for us and filled our canteens from the well for the last time. We slept under the star-filled sky on the hard ground with only our blankets to cover us. I think most of us didn't sleep much that night, wondering what tomorrow would bring.

I lay on my back, hands tucked behind my head, looking at the moon and stars. My thoughts turned to home and Lucinda. Every now and then, a shooting star skimmed across the blackness overhead. I wondered if she was seeing the same stars and thinking of me too.

I wondered how she was getting along without me. Did Mr. Moore take her in and let her stay with them? I knew he would help her while I was gone because he was that kind of person. Good to a fault.

And the baby she carried. She must have had the baby by now. Was it a boy or girl? Did the birthing go well? Would he or she look like their mother or me? I sure wished I was home with her and the baby instead of here on this hard ground and being in the army.

THE BUGLE CALL came early. Long before the sun shone light in the east. We got up, already dressed since we slept in our uniforms and quickly formed up ranks, munching on cold leftover biscuits. Around me were familiar sounds of men moving about in the darkness, some coughing, some clearing their throats while others cussed as they stumbled or tripped over objects in the dark.

The regiment didn't waste time. As soon as the twilight's dim light glowed, the sergeants quickly gathered their men on the road. As soon as the companies were formed, they moved out at a fast pace, marching quickly in the direction the wagons had taken the day before.

First out was D Company. They camped nearest to the road so they led the way. Our company waited until almost last. A thousand of us marched down that dusty lane that day. One long, gray line stretching as far as the eye could see. Men were swaying back and forth in a long gray line as they trooped in unison. A red cloud of dust rose around their feet from the clay common to this part of the country.

Our marching steps sounded like thunder, the dense forest on either side of the road amplifying the stomp of our feet a hundred times over. Our tramp, tramp, tramp echoing all around us as we headed for Vicksburg...headed for glory.

After a few hours on the road, my enthusiasm for glory had marched out of my system. My rifle, cartridge belt, and even my haversack, were awfully heavy. Sweat ran down my face, getting caught in my lashes. I kept wiping my eyes with my jacket sleeve to keep the water away and wished to God we could stop and rest a bit.

But there was no command from our sergeants to halt as they drove us ruthlessly down that road to Vicksburg.

We began to see bodies, dressed in our beautiful gray uniforms, lying along the roadside in the ditches, passed out from exhaustion. At first it was only a couple here and there. As time passed, I saw more and more bodies of worn out, drained brothers-in-arms lying on the side of the road. I hoped this wouldn't happen to me and my fellow soldiers in our company as we marched along as fast as we could on this forced journey.

Sergeant Perkins turned and marched backward, barely breathing hard. He looked like he was on a leisure walk. He shouted, "Steady, men! You men are better than the rest of those other sorry-ass slackers! Remember who you are. We are the Rapides Terrible and we are the strongest and the meanest company in the 27th. NO ONE is going to pass out and lay on the side of this here road from our company, now, ain't they?"

We yelled our reply as loud as we could, "NO, SERGEANT!" Our voices echoed in the trees around us. Up ahead, another company commenced to yell like wild Indians. I think they were looking for anything to take their minds off the march.

The sun was sinking behind the tree line when we caught the smell of food and coffee. Around the bend in the road, we spotted a couple of parked wagons.

Our sergeant called us to halt. As one we stopped. We stood in place, every man breathing hard, but none of us had fallen this first day... not one. The command of "rest" was given and we relaxed, some reaching for a handkerchief to wipe the sweat from their faces. I saw the pride in our sergeants' faces that we had done well today.

After a few moments, our sergeant called out, "Company C... ah-ten-shun!" Like the sound of thunder, we snapped back to attention. The sergeant dismissed us to fall out and get in line to eat. I was so hungry, and the smell of cooking food made my cotton mouth salivate. We were so tired after that first day's march we had no problem sleeping that night.

I overheard Sergeant Perkins telling another feller that we did almost twenty-five miles, and if we could keep it up, we should be in Vicksburg in about three or four more days. That is if we kept the same pace and the weather held.

We rested wherever we could find a spot. Our company relaxed next to the road that night and every night on that march to Vicksburg. Some men slept on the open road itself and some slept propped up against sturdy trees nearby. We remained fully dressed in our uniforms with our rifles stacked close so we would be ready for the next day's march.

Four o'clock the next morning came way too early. I'm glad I didn't get picked for guard duty. I needed every minute of sleep they would let me have. When I got up, my feet were sore, my shoulder was sore, my neck was sore. Jesus, I was sore all over. I prayed silently as I loaded myself down with equipment: *Lord... please get me through this next day, amen.*

Once more we ate cold biscuits left over from the night before for breakfast. Company B was called to lead today. The wagons that fed our supper last night fell in line to the rear of the troops and followed. Since it was empty, it was used for an ambulance for the more seriously hurt men who were marching. The slackers who thought they could get a free ride if they fell out by the side of the road were helped along by a squad of soldiers carrying clubs.

After a few miles, my sore feet and stiff body loosened and I felt better. We marched by a large plantation with fields on both sides of the road. It was a big farm. Biggest I've ever seen. Hoooo... wee! I'm a telling you, boy.

We saw off in the distance a large two-story house with a wraparound porch and grand white columns. I ain't never seen a house like that before; Naw sir. There must have been an awful lot of people sleeping there at night. Sure was pretty. Whoever it was that owned that big house and land must've been rich; mighty rich.

Marching along, I noticed a multitude of black people working in the fields. I was amazed. I ain't never seen so many colored people in my life. Where did they all come from, and where did they all live? They sure were working hard. Some were hoeing, others plowing. And then I saw something that made my blood turn cold.

In one of the fields, a white man beat one of the workers with a cane. The worker was tied between two poles, stripped to the waist. I ain't never seen anybody treated like that; Naw sir. Where I came from, people would not stand for that.

Well, I got myself riled up and tried to break ranks to have a few words with that feller. Maybe show him a thing or two on how to treat another man. My friend B.R. Tatum marching next to me jerked me back in line and growled, "Get in step, Riley. That's none of your business over there, just leave it alone."

I yanked myself loose from Tatum's grasp and started to say something when Sergeant Guardner yelled, "Quiet in the ranks!" I glared at Tatum, nodded, and fell back into step again. I was mad, but Tatum was right. That wasn't any of my business. Just leave it alone.

That was my first look at real slavery. I was never treated like that by Mr. Moore; Naw sir. I would not have put up with that by him or anyone.

I didn't understand why all those slaves would put up with it either, unless that man was a real bad feller. The one who was tied to those poles there. That must have been it. He must have done something really bad to be treated that way.

On our march to Vicksburg, we passed through many towns. Many of them were small communities where people would come out of their houses and watch us as we marched by. They would cheer and wave little flags and we'd stick out our chests, wave and cheer back. It made us feel good, made us feel important, like we were somebody special.

On the fourth day of May, we heard the riverboats' whistles on the Mississippi River. Tall pine trees blocked our view of the water but we would catch a smell of water or mud as we marched.

Later that day, we saw tall rooftops and steeples jutting over distant trees on the hills surrounding Vicksburg. Tired from our steady marching, we made our way around to the back side of the city, stopping near a cemetery on the northeast side of town.

Looking around the graveyard our sergeants picked for us, I said to Tatum. "I don't like this place. Hey... I have a bad feeling about sleeping next to the dead. I'm a telling y'all, I don't like it, Tatum; Naw sir, not one bit."

Several of the fellers nearby laughed at me. One man named Sims called over. "Old gloom and doom Riley. You sure are a superstitious soul, boy."

I frowned. "Hey... I'm just saying. I just don't like it. Mark my word." I shook my finger at him. "This here is a bad sign from above." They laughed and picked on me a few more minutes before we settled in to pitch our tents.

About the time our company was squared away, Sergeant Tifton came by looking for volunteers. He grabbed a bunch of the fellers standing around doing nothing. "You men there, come with me." He took them to a wagon with shovels and pick-axes loaded in the back end. "Everybody grab a tool and follow me."

Grumbling, the men picked a tool and trailed him to the crest of the hill. The sergeant stopped and looked at the slope. He dug a small hole with the heel of his shoe and pointed to it.

"This here is the spot. I want a trench dug," he motioned with his arm, "from this hole, all the way to those cannons there, behind that there stack of logs." He pointed to men placing artillery behind a wall of tree trunks sank into the ground.

Looking at his feet, he continued. "I want it deep and I want it straight and I want it to look real pretty. If I'm not happy, then we will have to cover it up and start over again. Do I make myself clear?"

"Yes Sergeant!"

"Good. Get to work."

The men fell in line and started digging. Nearby, a company of men hard at work near our campsite dug their own trenches. I think they were a Mississippi regiment. Nice bunch of boys, real friendly.

I thought I was lucky, getting out of the work detail. Even though I wasn't chosen, I made myself look busy. Sergeants love nothing better than taking someone who looked like they had nothing to do and finding something to keep them occupied. Sergeant Perkins said *an idle soldier was an unhappy soldier* and he made it his personal duty to see we were as happy as we could be... all the time.

That night I was chosen for picket duty. I walked a portion of the hill looking for any sign of trouble while the men who worked the rifle pits slept. I didn't mind this detail. It gave me time to think of home and my wife. I would always glance to the west because that's where home was.

Chapter Five

THE CANNONS WE took to Vicksburg looked like toys compared to the larger naval siege guns placed on the bluffs overlooking the river. In our spare time, what little we had, we would go to the other side of town and watch the Union gunboats on the water try to get past the city's fortifications in a running fight.

Great plumes of water swelled where shells from our guns landed around the Yankee ships. Some ships lay dead in the water, burning where they were hit. Others not damaged fired back, their shots falling short; ineffective because of the distance from their targets.

The deep booming of our big guns was heard on the other side of the city where we camped. We heard them, off and on, throughout the daytime and sometimes at night if we paid attention. We listened as we dug our rifle pits and set up our gun emplacements near the cemetery road on the hills that protected the backside of the city.

At that distance, however, their reverberations reminded me of thunder. Every now and then I heard their boom as they fired. Often when the noise reached our side of the town, someone working on this side would stand and look towards the river or at the sky. At first, I looked many-a-times myself. Always wondering what was going on across the way.

At night, the flashes from our big guns lit up the skies as if a lightning storm approached. It was quite a show. It was hard to fall asleep at first, but like real lightning and thunder, after a while, you lose interest and pay it no mind.

When we were not working on our defenses, we spent

time drilling. We practiced running to our trench and down the ramp to get into position on our firing line. We also drilled with loading and unloading rifles.

The part of training I hated most was the hand to hand fighting. I didn't like the idea of hitting someone or hurting them. Sergeant Perkins pulled me aside and said, "Private, there are no rules when it comes to killing a man. It is either you or him. He is not going to hold back because you don't want to hurt him. Hell, son, use whatever you can get your hands on, whether it's the butt of your rifle, the blade of a knife, a stone, or even a stick. All are good for killing or maiming the enemy. Just remember, he's gonna try his *damndest* to kill you."

In June of that year, 1862, rumors were going around camp that the Yankees were massing on the other side of the river. No one knew for sure. Our spies said they were digging a canal so they could go up and down the Mississippi without having to run past our guns.

Then in July, it got quiet. All shooting stopped. No thunder came from the guns on the river side. Someone said the Yankees had gone away. They had packed up everything and left; just vanished. The weapons on the bluffs sat silently while church bells rang throughout the city.

We thought, maybe that was it. Maybe we had won the war. No more Yankees, no more fighting, no more digging and working on these dang ditches. I thought to myself... *that was awfully easy*. I mean beating the Yankees and all. I never got a chance to even fire my new rifle at them.

During the bombardment, most of the citizens of Vicksburg moved into hillside caves dug for protection. Now with the silencing of guns from the Union flotilla, they moved back into their houses. All that week they celebrated with parades and parties. We dressed up in our pretty gray uniforms and marched up and down the streets for the folks living there. It was good times again.

Two days after the shooting stopped, the officers of our army and the town officials had one heck of a gala. I hoped to get picked for detail at the party. Well... I was picked, but instead of watching pretty ladies in lovely gowns dancing and having fun, I walked a small section of the hill outside our company campsite, watching the stars in the heavens... again.

I did hear later that the party was something to see, by the soldiers on guard duty at the ball. They said the officers were dressed in their finest uniforms with swords and sashes, while the ladies of Vicksburg dressed in their prettiest dresses. They said even some fellers played music and everyone danced.

I never questioned why we were still playing soldier if the Yankees were defeated and gone. When I was on duty walking that hill, it gave me time to think of my Lucinda. It shouldn't be long before they let us go home. I wished I had learned to write so I could send a letter to let her know I'd be coming back soon. Well, it wouldn't have mattered anyhow. There was no one at home who could read.

The next day, we were roused out of sleep to form ranks. I was so happy. *This must be it... we were going home. I just knew it!* They would tell us the war was over. Hoorah for President Davis!

Our sergeant said he didn't believe it was over; Naw sir. He put an end to my joy real quick. He growled, "Keep digging and working on them pits, boys. It ain't even started yet. They'll be back... just wait and see."

Well, shuckings! It seemed like a feller couldn't get a break around here.

We continued working on our position for some unknown reason. While we worked we waited for word to come to us from headquarters that the war was over. I wished they would hurry up. I wanted to go home.

During this time of respite, something very strange happened. A soldier from the 3rd Mississippi Regiment passed by our rifle pit one day and heard my last name. He stopped and looked in my direction. He walked over and squatted next to me in the trench. "Say, boy... is your last name Hillman?"

Trying to be friendly to a fellow soldier wearing gray, I stopped digging and smiled back up at him and replied, "Yessum, name is Riley... Riley Hillman. Hey... y'all looking for me?"

The soldier shook his head and stood. "Naw, I just heard the name and was wondering. Where you boys from? What unit is this?"

I said pointing towards the river. "I'm from way over that way in Slagle, on the Louisiana side of that there river, and this here unit is the 27th Louisiana Regiment, Company C."

He looked around, repeating to himself, "Twenty-seventh Louisiana, Company C."

"You got it, friend. Hey... why y'all wanna know that fer?"

"Oh, it's nut'en, nut'en at all. I have a friend who might be interested to know about y'all being over here... that's all."

"Hey... All righty then. We'll be right here, digging this here hole; right here. It doesn't look like we are going anywhere else soon." He gave me a smile and thanked me kindly for the information before he went on his way.

A few days later, still working in our rifle pit, I stood to stretch my back and get a drink of water. As I stood to wipe dirt and sweat out of my eyes, I saw that same Mississippi soldier with another feller in a gray suit talking to my sergeant.

I watched them for a moment. The new man in uniform looked familiar, but I knew I had never seen him before. As they spoke, this one feller, the one who looked familiar, looked straight at me and smiled.

Trying to be friendly to a fellow brother in gray, I smiled back before jumping into the pit. As his friend talked to my sergeant, he stood, just watching me. It made me a little uncomfortable; him watching me like that. Each time I looked his way he was staring and smiling.

Sergeant Cole saw the three of them talking and walked over to see what was going on. I couldn't hear what was said, but the sergeant looked surprised and glanced down in the pit at me. After a minute or so he called over to me. "Hillman... Get over here, boy."

Climbing out of the trench I replied, "Right away, Sergeant."

Everyone around me stopped digging. With my shirt in hand, I walked over to where the four men stood. Sergeant said, "Get yourself cleaned up, Riley. I'm giving you a four hour pass." On hearing that, the men in the trench looked around at each other, shocked.

Sergeant Cole gave the men an angry look, agitated the work on the trench had stopped. "I didn't say anything about anybody stopping work, ladies! Get your asses back to it. This has nothing to do with you people there. This is personal business here. I don't want to see your ugly faces staring up at me. All I want to see when I look into that pit is elbows and assholes... understand? Now get back to it!"

Grumbling curses under their breaths, the men in the trench went back to digging. I was surprised to get a four hour leave. I didn't ask for it, but getting out of work was always welcomed. I left the area and headed to my campsite to clean up. The two soldiers followed me.

I kept looking over my shoulder at the pair. They grinned and whispered to one another. When I reached a wagon with a water barrel on the back, I laid my shirt over the side rail.

I took a dipper hanging in the bucket and ladled water into a wash basin next to it. Taking my time I washed my face and hands in the clean water before empting the basin onto the ground.

Now wet and cooled off, I grabbed my shirt and dried my face and hands before pulling the somewhat wet garment back on. I ran my fingers through my wet hair, pushing it out of my face while turning towards the two soldiers who had followed me.

I didn't know what these two men wanted or why they were here. It looked very suspicious to me. My index finger slowly rubbed against my thumb. Eyeing the strangers, I said roughly, "Hey... what you boys want with me?"

They looked at each other and one laughed as he said, "Is that really you, Riley? My goodness, boy, you sho-nuff grown up now, ain't you, boy? I see Mama in those eyes of your and you've got Pa's chin too. Yes-sur, you sure do, boy!"

Shaking my head confused, I said, "I'm sorry... Hey! I don't know what y'all are talking about."

This soldier was about my height with the same color hair as mine, but thinning on top and showing some gray. His eyes were hazel, like mine. Holding his cap in his hands, he blushed and stepped toward me, speaking softly, "My apologies, Riley, forgive me. I'm..." He stopped and looked down at his cap before he continued. "My name is David... David Hillman." He looked up at me, favoring one eye and giving me a shy smile. "I'm your older brother. You probably don't remember me."

He was right. I didn't. I looked at him, confused. I didn't know what to say one way or the other, so I reached for one of the canteens in the back of the wagon and took a long swig while trying to figure out what he was talking about. I didn't know I had a brother, never crossed my mind. I couldn't remember much of nothing before the Moore family took me in. I had always looked at Mr. Moore as being a father to me, if I thought about it at all. And I didn't.

I looked at this man... this stranger standing in front of me with his cap in his hands. He looked like he was having a hard time talking. He said he was my brother and after studying his features I could see some resemblance but I didn't know him from Adam. As far as I knew, Mr. Moore was the only family I had.

I had to look way back into my memory. Back to when I was nine years old. Forgotten memories of a man and woman who I supposed were my parents and of a young man standing with them next to a loaded wagon as they talked with Mr. Moore before leaving without me.

The cool water lost its flavor in my mouth and I turned to the side and spit it out. I wiped my mouth on my sleeve as I stood there wondering what he wanted with me after all this time.

Still looking down at his cap in his hand, David said, "We didn't wanna leave you behind, Riley, but we had no choice at the time. It almost killed Mama to see you left there at that farm like that. She cried almost all the way to Alabama and then some too. Well... to Mississippi anyways. We never made it to Alabama. Anyways... It was a long time before she stopped crying over you, boy. Her and Pa both took it real hard leaving you behind. Pa... he did his fair share of crying too. They just had no choice."

Trying to be polite to this stranger before me, I asked, "So... how are they doing, now?"

"Old... they've both gotten old, Riley," he said, smiling at me, looking more comfortable.

I think we were both uncomfortable that day, standing by the wagon. I could plainly see we didn't have anything in common now... if we ever did. We might have been brothers with the same mama and papa, but now... now we were complete strangers. The only thing shared was the color of our uniforms.

We sat and talked a while longer. That is, he did most of the talking, and I politely listened. After he finished his say, we stood and shook hands. I watched the two walk away. David reached into his back pocket and took out a handkerchief and wiped his eyes. The other man put his arm around his friend's shoulder, trying to comfort him. David pulled his cap low over his eyes to hide his tears and looked back my way one last time and waved.

Both walked down the cemetery road toward town and their Mississippi units.

I didn't know what to think about David, the brother I never had. He was a complete stranger, someone I didn't know. If I had seen him on the streets of Vicksburg, I would have passed, never looking twice at him.

Standing there, watching them walk away, I sucked in a deep breath before slipping off my cap and shirt and heading back to my company and friends digging our rifle pit.

With all the work and hidden traps we set out, our sergeants still had us working every day; always working... always improving embattlements. No such thing as free time, now. When we were not digging or working on top of that hill, we were drilling.

We drilled in the trenches while our sergeants walked behind us, trying to break our concentration, yelling as we practiced loading and unloading guns. They'd tell us we were too slow at reloading, or one of them would come up behind and slap one of us on the back of the head and yell, "Bam! You're dead!" Yes, sir. We kept busy while we waited for the Yankees to come.

Chapter Six

A FEW MONTHS into the year, 1863, I had given up hope of word coming down that the war was over. Fortunately, not much went on in Vicksburg until April. Then Hell raised its ugly head.

It started on a clear spring day. A cool northerly breeze swept over the hill. The rifle pits were almost complete despite a tremendous amount of rain had fallen the past winter and the beginning months.

I had never seen so much rain and water in my life. The river on the other side of the town overflowed its banks, flooding the low lands for miles. Looking at the river from the bluffs, you could not see land on the other side of the Mississippi. It's what I would have thought an ocean would have looked like, if I had ever seen an ocean.

On this particular day, we were shoring-up the inside walls of our trench with lumber when we heard what we thought was thunder off to the east of our battle lines.

I stood straight, shading my eyes with my kepi and looked at the sky. Not a cloud in sight. Sergeant Perkins stood on top of our pit and stared into the distance. Each time it rumbled, sergeants up and down our lines stopped on top of their trenches, looking east. Listening and watching.

I walked over to stand next to Sergeant Perkins; both of us looking east. "Say, Sergeant, what's with the thunder? Hey… are we gonna get some rain?"

He shook his head not looking in my direction. "Nope. Not rain, Riley. That's not thunder, boy." He watched for a moment more and then turned his head toward the trench, but not his eyes, and loudly called out to the men nearby. "Let's hurry and get the work done, boys. I think we are gonna get busy here in a few days."

A few days? What was he talking about?

We didn't know what was going on to the east. It seemed the sergeants' disposition suddenly changed, like they were on a short fuse or something. It took nothing to set them off, and once they exploded, it was better if you were not close by.

It was puzzling to us working in the trenches. The sky was clear, and yet every now and then, we heard that faint booming far off in the distance. *Boom, boom... boom.*

We didn't know what was making that sound. It wasn't the weather, but it seemed the sergeants knew... but they weren't saying.

It turned out that Grant and his Union horde were on our side of the river, causing trouble. Someone said it was Greenville being hit, about forty miles away. That night our sergeants doubled the guard on our defenses. So I had company.

A few days later, stragglers began to come through our lines with all kinds of wild stories about the Yankees being as thick as fleas. They said they were heading our way.

Let'em come-- we were ready. We didn't care how many... we were ready. This past winter we had cleared the hills around our position of all trees and shrubs, making it clear to see for hundreds of yards in front of our trenches. We left nothing standing for the enemy to hide behind; a clear killing field. Our gun emplacements and rifle pits were all completed so we just waited.

We had even dug shallow pits into the slope of the hill they would have to climb, and placed sharpened sticks in them. The sticks wouldn't kill but they would hurt and make the rest leery of where they placed their feet.

A few weeks later, around the 18th of May, a civilian came out of nowhere on horseback. He rode up the slope in front of our lines, hard and fast on a worn-out horse covered with sweat and lather. Horse and rider leaped over our rifle pit, staggering as he landed on the other side and rode on by, yelling, "They're coming... they're coming!"

We were surprised by the horseman. We stood in the bottom of our trench, frozen with shovels in our hands. Unable to figure out what the heck was going on or what he was talking about.

Sergeant Cole came running to the rifle pit and yelled down to us, "Well… what are you ladies waiting for. Run and get your guns and get back here as fast as you can! Now, move your sweet little asses, ladies, we ain't got all day!"

Throwing down our picks and shovels, we scrambled out of that trench and ran to retrieve our rifles and cartridge belts. Our weapons were stacked neatly only twenty five yards away, but it felt like we had to run more than a mile to reach them.

Before we grabbed our weapons, we heard a popping noise of a handgun firing from our position behind the hill. We grabbed our rifles and ran back. It seemed like it took forever to get to our weapons and run back to Sergeant Cole waiting for us. I didn't think we'd ever make it in time.

Sergeant Cole had climbed on top of our rifle pit and stood with pistol in hand pointing at something down the hill. He calmly emptied his Griswold sidearm, reloaded and picked targets as he shot six more times.

We reached the entrance of our rifle pit and packed in before looking out the ports to the steep hillside. To our surprise, the Yankees were almost upon us. Just a few yards away, running up the hill as fast as their heathen legs could carry them. All breathing hard, climbing that slope.

Sergeant Cole was frantically trying to reload his Griswold. He stopped long enough to yell down at us, "FIRE YOUR WEAPONS, GODDAMN IT! SHOOT'EM!"

We had just enough time to raise our guns, stick them through the ports, and fire before they were upon us. We must've all fired at the once, because it sounded like one single shot when we unloaded into them.

We weren't prepared for the dust that threw up in front of our trench, blocking our view. Thank God it only obscured our vantage for a moment before it dissipated. We couldn't afford to not see out targets for long. Blinded, the enemy could advance closer than we wanted.

It was a good thing we had the new smokeless cartridges for our rifles, otherwise we would have been blinded a lot longer. They left very little smoke and we could shoot faster since all we had to do was put a shell in the chamber, cock it, aim, and fire.

When the dust cleared in front of our trench, no one was left standing. Every man in our trench had a look of amazement. This was our first time as a unit to fire at an actual foe. On the ground just beyond our position lay the twisted and mangled bodies of men in blue uniforms. Very few of them were moving.

Everyone in our trench was quiet, afraid to disturb the silence; nothing but hard breathing. We were all in shock at what we had just done. I don't think none of us had ever shot a man before. We stood looking around at one another, never thinking to reload our rifles.

Sergeant Cole, walking nervously back and forth on top of our trench, stopped and spread his arms out to his sides and called down to us, "Well... what are you ladies waiting for? Reload your goddamn guns! You know the routine, get to it, boys. They're not gonna wait for long. There's lots more where those came from. They'll be coming again, real soon now."

Glancing at the bottom of the hill where the tree line was, we saw birds take flight from the tops of the trees. Deer and other animals broke from the forest cover and ran in different directions to get away from the horde of blue uniforms pushing them out of their homes.

After a few more moments of silence, we heard shouts coming far off from the forest at the bottom of the hill. All of a sudden, Yankees poured from the tree line. They were not in such a hurry as the ones who came before. These men stayed within their lines as they walked up the hill, determination painted on their faces.

We reloaded our rifles and waited. Watching the Yankees come up that slope made us nervous. Some fellow soldiers were breathing hard and others praying out loud. I couldn't stop shaking, I was so scared. The last thing I wanted was to be here at this moment on this hillside right now. It seemed the closer they got, the louder my heart pounded in my ears, drowning out almost everything around me. And my mouth-- Jesus, it was so dry I couldn't spit; my mouth was like a wad of cotton.

I looked around at the other pale and frighten faces in our trench. Faces stained with sweat and dirt, glancing around at one another. I ain't never shot a man before, no, sir. And I wasn't so sure I had shot one this time, but mercy, there were so many out there coming up that hill. My hand shook nervously as I tried to wipe sweat out of my eyes.

I heard one man say, "My god, would y'all look at how many they are? Jesus... what are we gonna do?"

Sergeant Cole growled, "Quiet in the ranks! You do your duty and you just might live to tell your grandchildren how you whopped the Yankees this day single handedly."

We gave a nervous laugh, relaxing some of the tension. All this time, more and more of our boys were arriving at their positions up and down our lines. With our rifles reloaded, we waited; looking through our rifle ports, staring down that long slope in front of us. Waiting for the word from our sergeants to shoot and kill the enemy coming up that hill.

The cannons near our position burst into action, causing all of us to jump. The cannons near our trench belched thick, black smoke with a thunderous roar, the recoil lifting the wheels of the gun off the ground and backward as they fired. Soon dark smoke covered the top of our hill.

Sergeants along the line cussed and yelled as they called out orders. Sergeant Cole in a calm voice knelt on top of our trench and had us count off. Each man in our pit shouted out their numbers, all the way to the entrance of our ditch.

As soon as we finished, Sergeant Cole then said, "Odd number man, take two steps back. Y'all are gonna be loaders. You will make sure the man in front of you has a loaded rifle in his hands at all times. Is that clear?"

"Yes Sergeant!"

He then pointed at the last two men near the entrance to the pit. "You two there-- run to the supply wagons and get as many shells as y'all can carry now... hear? Now, hurry!"

The two men, eyes as big as saucers, handed their rifles to another man and took off running.

Sergeant Cole turned back to us and said calmly, "Steady men... steady. Just hold your position and wait for it. Let'em come to you. This was what y'all were trained for, so just wait. I'll tell you when to fire. If any of you men on the firing line gets hit, I want the man reloading his rifle to take his place. If they get too close, I'll call up everyone and all of you will have to shoot and reload for yourselves. Do I make myself clear?"

"YES SERGEANT!"

About that time, the two men returned, loaded down with

boxes of ammo. Soon afterwards the other three sergeants arrived from headquarters and positioned themselves behind us in our trench to make sure every man did his duty.

Funny, but by yelling something out loud like "yes, Sergeant" made me feel better. I felt the tension leave my body and left me feeling more at ease with myself. I felt calm and as I looked around me I could feel the tension in our rifle pit evaporate. A few of the fellows down the line from me chuckled as the anxiety left them. One man near me began to hum Dixie as he calmly looked out his port, watching the Yankees coming up that hill. Soon more and more men hummed along with him.

Sergeant Cole dropped into the pit to join the other sergeants. They walked behind us occasionally stopping and talking to the more nervous men--calling them by name, patting them on the back, and asking questions about their family back home. All sergeants made sure they knew each man in his unit. Not only their names, but the names of their wives and children and what they did before the war began.

Everything seemed calm and quiet in our trench and then the cannons opened up again. They fired, spewing smoke and thunder, over and over. Each time they discharged, I felt the heavy vibration through my body, making my thumb rub nervously against my index finger.

Sergeant Cole stopped behind me, looking at my hand. He reached over and moved me aside. "Let me take a look-see, Riley. Y'all doing okay there?" he asked, glancing at my hand as he moved closer to look out my rifle port.

I said nervously, "Hey... I wish I was someplace else, right now."

He smiled and said, "Me too, Riley; me too." He stuck his face in my gun port to see how close the Yankees were. Pulling back, he smiled and winked at me, patting me on the back, and called out, "Not yet, men... not yet. Let'em get a little closer. Let'em come to you."

I could now make out the faces of those Yankees in the front row coming up that hill toward us; that very hill in front of me. I turned to Sergeant Cole and said, "Sa-boy... I mean, Sergeant. They look close enough for me."

"Not yet Riley... not yet. Just wait," he said calmly. Now several lines of men in blue came up that hill.

My thumb itched as it rubbed my index finger, but I didn't have time for that, right now. I was busy. Oh, how I wished I could relax again. The closer they got, the more I felt the tension returning. Just waiting; watching those blue figures out there; directly in front of me.

They didn't look worried. They didn't look afraid. Some had bearded faces while others looked too young to be carrying a rifle or to be in the army, at all. I counted the buttons on their jackets. All of them dressed in blue uniforms, coming toward us. All of them, climbing that same steep hill, toward us. All of them, marching side by side in wavy lines, toward us.

It was a pretty sight to see, and yet it scared the living hell out of me. Everything, including the cannons, was muted against the thunder of blood pumping in my ears. It was so loud, I was afraid I might miss a command from the sergeant.

After a few moments, Sergeant Cole moved to another man and moved him out of his way to take another look. He nodded and smiled as he pulled his face out of the opening. Moving behind our line, he called out, "Get ready... don't shoot yet. I'll tell y'all when."

Then his commanding voice rang, echoed by the other sergeants. "All weapons in the ports!"

Rifles jutted through slotted openings. A few of the men down the line didn't wait, but fired. Nervous, I reckon. Their sergeants rushed over, cussing and calling them names for wasting shots. One sergeant took off his hat and slapped the back of a man's head. I smiled, glad it wasn't me.

As I laid my rifle level and took aim, I saw the surprise on the faces of the Yankees in the front row. I saw their eyebrows rise and mouths open as they saw our guns suddenly appear through the dirt wall in front of them. The realization struck home as they seemed to pause and look at their comrades.

Sergeant Cole tried to clear our minds of all worries as he drew our attention back to the business at hand. He calmly spoke in that same voice of his as he paced behind our line, "Steady, men. Steady... now, prime your weapons!"

As one, we pulled the hammers back on the rifles, hearing them click when locking into place, and laid our cheeks against the stock, looking down the long barrel. Picking our targets, we took careful aim as we waited for the command to fire.

Sergeant Cole stopped his pacing, and said evenly, "Steady, men... steady. Wait for it. Let'em be in a hurry... just wait. Steady your breathing... relax."

We waited, looking down the barrels of our rifles at the men approaching; getting closer and closer. The wait seemed to go on and on as we stood there, looking down that hill, waiting for the order to fire. It seemed the closer they got, the faster they moved. I sure wished the sergeant would give us the command to fire. "Steady... steady, men," he said again, just above the noise outside the rifle pit. Then..."Fire!"

A loud roar erupted, making our ears ring inside the closed trench. Then the cannons opened with canister fire, blasting everything in front, leaving nothing standing.

We exchanged our empty rifles as fast as we could for ones already loaded and shoved their long barrels into the port. We didn't wait for any command this time. We fired and handed back our empty rifles for another that was loaded. We fired as fast as we could get a rifle into the slot and shoot.

Suddenly the Yankees broke. With cannon smoke drifting heavy over the hillside, we stopped shooting. As soon as the air cleared, we saw the Yankees retreating down the hill, leaving their dead and wounded behind. No more straight lines, no more faces with determined looks. Now, it was a foot race to reach the safety of the trees.

We took our caps off and waved them in the air, screaming after them, giving our Rebel Yell. After a few minutes, reality set in as we quieted down and looked at what we had done. Bodies in blue uniforms scattered about on that hillside before us. Some were dead, but most were wounded.

Most of us had never seen a dead body before that day, or the horror of what the large caliber shells would do to the body. Some of the boys in our trench lost their stomachs and threw up. Others cried or prayed for those unfortunate souls lying on the ground out there.

Sergeant Cole, still pacing nervously behind us, said with a steady voice, "Good job boys... good job. I think they're finished for the time being. They won't be coming again for a while."

I tried to relax my tense body. I leaned against the wood planked wall and slid down to sit, my rubbery legs feeling too heavy and weak to hold me up. I raised my shaking left hand in front of my face; my index finger rubbing vigorously against its thumb, back and forth.

As I observed the others around me, I thought, *well the attack wasn't as bad as I thought it would be.* None of our boys got hit. I don't think any of those fellers out there even had a chance to shoot back.

I glanced at my shaking hand. I had just killed a man in cold blood, maybe more. *God forgive me for what I've done.* But instead of worrying about that, I was more worried about the other fellers seeing my hand shake. I was glad no one noticed how nervous and scared I really was. Jesus! I felt sick. I swallowed hard to get rid of the bitter bile rising in my throat. I was not going to throw up here in this trench. Not in front of the other men. I would be so embarrassed. That would only show my fellow soldiers how weak I was.

A few of the men hid their faces in their arms as they leaned against the pit wall and cried silently, their shoulders shrugging. I didn't know if they were crying for themselves, or the men they had killed on this day.

The Yankees down the hill called for a truce to retrieve their wounded and dead. Both sides blue and gray alike, left their defenses and helped remove the dead bodies and care for the wounded. No one wanted dead carcasses lying out in the open on the battlefield. We didn't mind helping clean the grounds in front of our lines. We sure didn't want to look at the dead or smell them. After clearing the field, the truce was over and our cannons opened up on their lines below us.

Chapter Seven

LATER THAT AFTERNOON our guns ceased firing. It became very quiet where we watched. Not even a bird made noise. Then the Yankee guns hidden in the forest down the hill began to return fire. We hunkered down at the bottom of our trench and waited for the bombardment to end.

Great explosions erupted around our position, shaking the ground and throwing us around like rag dolls inside our defenses. Blasts hurled large mounds of dirt into the air where it rained pebbles and clods of dirt on our heads, making it hard to breathe with all the dust it stirred.

The noise was deafening as we cringed together at the bottom of our pit. They forgot to tell us about this part when training. We tried to block the screeches by putting our hands over our ears.

Sometimes we screamed just to release the tension, which didn't seem to work too well. We even tried holding each other as we prayed with the shells exploding around us on that hill. No matter what we did, we couldn't block out the uproars or concussions from their shells. We suffered pure hell.

Our sergeants walked in the open as if it was a Sunday afternoon, showing there was nothing to fear. They would walk by and kneel down patting some of the men on the back making small talk and laughing as artillery exploded. They seemed oblivious to the cannonade attack.

When Sergeant Perkins came over to where I huddled with the others, I asked him, "How can y'all stand there and walk around with all them shells exploding around us here, Sergeant? Hey... ain't y'all the least bit scared?"

He slinked down close to my face so I could hear him. He smiled as he placed one hand on my shoulder. "Riley-- if God wants you, he'll find you, no matter where you are. When your time comes, there ain't nut'en going to save you. So, why worry about the things you can't control." He smiled, patted me on the back then walked off to talk to other men cowering in the bottom of our trench.

I watched him as he moved down the line, stopping now and then to talk to someone before moving on. I never forgot what he said to me that day. Those words had a lot of wisdom behind them. Yes, sir. And they've helped me many times when I was in trouble.

We spent the rest of that night and many more at our station on the line. I don't think I ever used my tent again during the siege. The first bombardment lasted all night and well into the next day.

Around ten o'clock the morning of the 19th of May, the shelling stopped. The silence was so deafening...

Sergeant Cole gave orders to clean up the rifle pit and make any repairs we could. "Get yourselves ready, boys, they'll be coming again soon."

From atop the hill, we heard drummers calling their troops together. The Yankees formed up at the base tree line, out of our small arms firing distance. Our cannons opened up with solid shots. Our artillery didn't do much damage to their lines. They mostly overshot, destroying tree tops.

Around two in the afternoon they charged our position, and this time, they weren't fooling around. The smoke from their guns hid them in a thick cloud of smoke as their lines moved back and forth climbing the hill.

They came fast, furious, and firing; stopping just long enough to reload while other soldiers passed them up the hill towards us. They went back and forth like that as they charged our position. They never let up once or gave us a break. They kept us busy shooting at those blue figures running at us.

Even with our good cover, many a good men on our side fell. More were wounded. I got a deep cut over my right eye, blood running down, blinding me. But I kept shooting and handing the empty rifle behind me and receiving a loaded one in return.

The more we fired, the more they came. Finally, with the invaders too close for comfort, our sergeant gave the order for the loaders to step forward to help. Now our firepower was increased, but we had to take time to reload, and that took away precious seconds from shooting.

Some Yankees made it to the top of the Stockade Redan to our right. Over there, there was a lot of hand to hand fighting. Men were screaming and cussing on both sides, fighting for their lives. I thought the Yankees were going to take the Redan and push us out of our position.

Suddenly, our boys got the upper hand and the Yankees once again ran home. Sherman's Division, 15th Corps left their colors behind. Nice flag it was. One of our boys from the 27th stood on top of the Redan wall and screamed the Rebel Yell while waving their Yankee flag over his head.

The soldier's uniform was ripped and smeared with blood, mud, and sweat. Dirt flew up around his feet from Yankee bullets below us. He planted the flag by his right foot in defiance and shouted, "Hey... Y'all come back now... heer!" and then he spit tobacco juice toward their line.

After a few more moments, the soldier climbed off the dirt wall. Our Colonel Leon Marks who heard about the captured flag rode up. The soldier snatched up the flag and trotted to the commander on his horse and presented the banner to him.

Colonel Marks was happy as could be. He shook the man's hand and patted him on the shoulder. Both men saluted and the colonel rode back and forth behind our lines waving the flag. Everyone on the battle line in their rifle pits and on the Redan stopped what they were doing and cheered. He was so proud of his regiment that day. He wanted everyone to see what his boys had done.

It was the first and only flag captured in the Vicksburg campaign by southern soldiers.

After the attack, we counted our dead and wounded. Fifty-eight of our men were killed and ninety-six wounded, where the Yankees lost about a thousand. The ground in front of our lines were littered with their dead and wounded as far as the eye could see. Another truce was called on both sides and the battlefield was once more cleared of the bodies.

As soon as the field was vacated, the truce was over and

the artillery on both sides commenced firing. We curled up once more in the bottom of our rifle pits and waited for the Yankees to stop their cannonade bombardment.

We were hit hard again on the 22nd of May. They came close, but still could not take our position. We fired down on them as fast as we could from our rifle pits. And like all of their attacks, we drove them back, leaving the slope of the hill once more littered with their dead and wounded.

After that day, we never saw a man charge the hill. They didn't need to. Grant let loose with all his artillery on our position and fired day and night, never stopping or giving rest. General Grant and his invaders just sat back and waited us out. By the end of May our unit was beat up. Craters covered our hillside. By mid-June, we were ordered out of the works a few men at a time for three days of rest while the assault continued.

I did a lot of thinking while held up in our trench during the bombardment. Mostly I thought of Lucinda and home, but the soldier who was my brother nagged at the back of my mind. While on my three days of rest, I took the opportunity to go to the Mississippi unit my brother belonged to.

I found his unit where bombs were falling in and amongst their lines. The whole place was in chaos and total confusion. Nobody knew who was in charge as their men waited at their posts for any attack that might come. I found one sergeant who was frantic, trying to hold the whole Mississippi unit together by himself.

Dodging the mortars coming from the Yankee position, I made my way to where he directed his men. I grabbed him by the sleeve of his jacket and asked, "Hey, Sergeant, can you tell me where I can find David Hillman?"

The sergeant first looked at his sleeve as though something was wrong with it. He pulled away and looked at me. "What?"

I repeated, "Can you tell me where I can find Company B?"

He shook his head and as if a light came on and he pointed. "Try over there."

I smiled and nodded. Dodging mortar shells, I found his company, what was left of it. I was told that David had been wounded and taken to a hospital. There were so many hospitals set up in Vicksburg; I didn't know which one he would have been taken to. After searching three in that general area, I found him.

The old, filthy barn smelled of death and rotten meat left in the summer heat too long. There was barely enough room to step around the wounded as volunteers went from one to the next giving what little help they could.

On the dirt ground of the makeshift hospital, he lay with a dirty blanket caked with blood spread over him. David had lost a leg and was burning up with fever. There were no medicines in the city and very few doctors were left alive.

He was delirious, rambling on, "Don't take my leg. Please, God... don't let them take my leg." He didn't seem to know the leg was already gone. He didn't know who I was or where he was. He kept falling in and out of consciousness as he lay mumbling over and over to himself. "Don't take my leg. Please, God don't let them take my leg."

With the putrid smell of blood, unwashed bodies, and gangrene mixed with horse manure in that closed barn, I was turning ill just being there.

The artillery barrage outside was still going on and I didn't want to get caught in this barn if one of those shells should hit. I felt trapped. It was hard to breathe with all the smell of rotting meat inside the barn. Gagging, I covered my mouth with a rag and left by a side door nearby as quickly as I could.

As soon as I stepped outside, I found myself standing at the edge of a large pit piled high with partial arms and legs cut off the injured soldiers. The discarded limbs were stacked almost as high as my waist, waiting to be burned.

My stomach gave a heave and bitter bile crested in my throat wanting to get out. With my hand over my mouth, I moved as fast as I could from the barn and its gory mess outside. I searched for a place where the air was not so strong with the smell of putrid flesh. Spotting wagons parked not too far away, I made my way to the nearest one and holding onto a wheel, I threw up everything I had in my stomach.

Pale and not so steady on my feet, I wiped my face on my shirt sleeve, and gripping the wooden wheel, I waited for everything to stop spinning. After steadying my stomach, I glanced over my shoulder at the bloody mess they called a hospital and hoped to God that I never would have to go to one of them.

Hell... I took better care of my animals than that. I looked once more at the hospital before heading back over to my side of the city where my unit was trying to rest. That was June 15th. We returned to our rifle pit on the ridge on the 17th.

It turned out to be a bad week for our regiment when we returned to our position on the line. Major Jess Cooper and Lieutenant Colonel McLaurin, both from our regiment, were killed that week. Also, Colonel Marks and Major Norwood were wounded and both died from their wounds on the 28th.

About that same time, our sergeants said we were cut off from outside help ever reaching us. No troops or supplies. We were on our own. We had to hold on as long as we could. To make matters worse, we were already short on rations. What we could catch or find ourselves, we could eat.

By the first of June, dogs and cats began to disappear. Soon after the last of the pets vanished from the beleaguered city, pigeons and all other sorts of animals and birds within the city also vanished.

Fat rats living off the dead and discarded body limbs ruled the land. They were everywhere. Fresh killed rats were strung up in the markets at a premium price for those who still had gold or Confederate currency.

The townspeople and the army protecting the city were now completely out of food. Everyone was starving. Many fights broke out trying to catch a fat rat that found its way near our trench. Hungry men were looking for anything to fill their bellies.

Once you overlooked the fact that they got fat by eating body parts and corps lying around... Well, once you overlooked that, then they weren't so bad. Cooked just right, they tasted almost like squirrel and I did love me some squirrel. Yes, sir, I surly did.

I learned quickly, in order to get the fat ones; you had to go where they fed. Charlie Company fared better than a lot of other soldiers in the city. Each day a few of us would sneak out and hunt rats or anything else we could find. We would trek to the hospitals nearby, and once you got past the sight and smell of the rotting flesh heaped in shallow pits, a man could knock four or five of those fat beasts in the head with a rifle butt and carry them back for supper.

The shelling never ceased or let up on its intensity from the 22nd of May until the morning of July 3rd. That day, we woke to the thunderous noise of silence. The quiet was so loud. One man near me jerked, sitting bolt upright in our hole. Scrambling to his feet, he went to his gun port and stuck his face against it. Standing there shaking, he then looked around at us and shouted, "Hey... what's... what's that noise I here? What's happening out there... are... are they coming again?"

I stood and snuck a peek through my gun slit at the empty hillside. I didn't see anything out of the ordinary... nothing... no soldiers, no flags flying... nothing at all.

My first thought was the Union navy had gotten tired of shelling us and maybe ran out of ammo and left. Or... maybe they were getting ready to attack again. A few of us strong enough grabbed our rifles and stood. I lifted my gun and stuck it through my gun port waiting, looking for a target. "Let'em come." I said to no one in particular. I was ready. Better than sitting around here in our trenches hiding from the shelling.

Slowly, men all along our lines started moving about, getting out of their trenches. Some held their weapons ready for an attack while others just looked around, empty-handed and confused.

No one knew what was going on, not even our leaders. Sergeant Perkins called our squad leaders together. After a short discussion, he and Sergeant Cole went to the command center to see what they could find out from headquarters.

The eerie silence remained over Vicksburg battlefield all morning. It was unnerving. I kept looking down the hill expecting an attack any moment. A runner from command passed through later that afternoon and told us General Pemberton surrendered the city. That was why the Yankees stopped shooting.

It had to be a lie. It had to be. Yes, we were physically weak, and yes, we were hungry but we could still shoot. We kept telling ourselves that General Pemberton wouldn't surrender the city right now. There was plenty of fight still left in us. If the Yankees would only attack us... we'd show 'em a thing or two, yes sir, we sure would.

Sergeant Cole and Sergeant Perkins came back from their meeting with our new commanders at headquarters. Both men were crying like a baby. Tears streamed down their faces with shame. They told us it was true. General Pemberton had indeed surrendered the city of Vicksburg.

We couldn't believe it. Men crowded around the sergeants asking questions, pulling at them to get their attention. I cried out in distress, "No! Say it ain't so, Sergeant... say it ain't so. We can still fight them Yankees. Let us attack them! We'll show-um."

Sergeant Perkins held up his hands, quieting us. "I know you could, boys. What's done is done. We have to respect his orders. He is our commander. Now listen up, we are to form ranks tomorrow and hand over our guns to the Yankees. I don't know if they will send us north to prison camps or parole us, we'll just have to wait and see."

Chapter Eight

GRANT'S GIFT TO the people of Washington would have been wonderful if it had not been over shadowed by the defeat of Lee at Gettysburg that very day. He gave the Yankee government all of the Mississippi River, effectively splitting the Confederacy in half; all on the Fourth of July, 1863.

The defeat at Vicksburg left a bitter taste in the mouths of the people living in that city. It took several years before the Fourth of July was ever celebrated again.

The morning of the 4th, all who could walk, formed ranks. In our worn-out, tattered uniforms that once looked so pretty, we marched out of the city with guns slung over our shoulders, barrels pointed down. We moved to where the Yankees waited for us.

We marched like we were on parade. Proudly we held our heads high because in our hearts we weren't defeated. We didn't surrender, General Pemberton did. We weren't ready to give up, not yet.

We came to a halt with the Union army around us. We stood with our chins lifted even as cat calls were thrown by some of the Yankee soldiers. As we stood in parade formation, Sherman's men, the ones from the 15th Corps, found out we were the ones who took their flag that day and wanted retribution.

An officer from Sherman's headquarters told them to shut their mouths and keep quiet in their ranks. There would not be any retribution for what we did. They were to honor the surrender of the Confederate defenders. They didn't like it one bit but they obeyed orders, and we didn't have any more trouble out of them.

As I stood in formation with the others of the 27th, I noticed General Pemberton standing in the shade of a tree talking with a Yankee dressed in a private's uniform, smoking cigars. I guess he was a private. The Yankee soldier didn't have any stripes or bars on his uniform. The soldier General Pemberton was talking to was dark complected, well fed with a full black beard and wore a slouch of a hat on his head.

The private looked very happy as he stood smiling and talking to General Pemberton. General Pemberton-- not so much. The general stood with his head bowed, smoking his cigar, listening and nodding his head every once in a while as the other man did most of the talking.

A soldier next to me nudged me and whispered, "Lookie there, Riley. That's old Grant himself talking to Pemberton. You see him over there?"

Several wagons were parked side by side near where we stood. When our turn came, we stacked our rifles into the back of one of those wagons. At the front of the wagon, a line of bluecoats exchanged their guns for ours. The guns we were issued at Camp Moore were much better than the ones the U.S. government had issued to their troops. They seemed real happy at getting them.

We formed into another line that led to a soldier sitting behind a table, taking down information about us. There were eight tables for our regiment with one of our officers standing behind in case they were needed.

When I got to the head of the line, the Yankee asked my name. I said, "My name is Riley Hillman, Private, Company C, 27th, Lou-sa-ana."

That little smartass soldier looked up at me like I was an idiot and said, "What did you say, I cannot understand a word you're saying, boy?"

I repeated it again, this time slowly, "Ri-ley Hill-man."

"Did you say Wiley? What kind of a name is that, boy?" he said irritated, interrupting me, shaking his head and acting cocky.

I tried to keep a civil tongue in my mouth. I repeated once more, "Ma name is Riley Hillman, Private, Company C, 27th Lou... see... ana reg... gee... ment, sur."

The man sitting behind the table looked up at me with a frown on his face, "Don't call me sir, boy, I'm not an officer. Now, can you spell your name for me?"

I shook my head, "Naw, sir, never went to school. Never had any need to read or write before." My thumb was working on my finger right about then. I was starting to get riled, but I held my temper.

The man looked down at his paper and said out loud as he wrote, "W...i...l...e...y, Riley. H...i...l...l...m...a...n Hillman. Private... Company C... 27th... Louisiana. Does that sound right to you?"

I looked down at him and the paper and said, "Yep... Sounds about right to me."

With a smirk on his face the soldier said, "Well... I am so glad you approve. Now move along, bub! Next!"

I moved over with the rest of our men standing around, waiting to see what would become of us. I thought for sure they would send us to prison where I would not be able to see Lucinda for a long, long time, or maybe a firing squad where they'd shoot us. Either way, it looked like I was not going home.

After a while, Sergeant Perkins gathered us around him. He asked us to kneel so everyone could see and hear him. Out of the hundred some-odd soldiers in our company that marched here to Vicksburg, less than half were able to march out of the city. The rest were all dead, wounded, or too sick to be where we were.

After he had everyone's attention he said, "Boys... It's like this. We are gonna move out to Enterprise, Mississippi here in a little bit and wait there for our parole. It don't look like they will be sending us to prison. Seems like their general, this General Grant, he don't like to keep prisoners. Thinks it's a waste of manpower. So we'll go on over to Enterprise and stay there for a spell unless... unless any of y'all want to try and cross the river and go home 'til you are called back up again."

Looking around he saw that most everybody's hand was up. "Well, that's fine, boys, but y'all going have to walk. There won't be no transportation available."

He looked around again and some of the hands had dropped. So he continued, "Now remember, the river out there is flooded and there ain't no bridges left standing for hundreds of miles."

All the hands went down except for mine and two others.

The sergeant looked at us. "You boys know what y'all doing?" We nodded. "Then you three are dismissed. Y'all can pick up your parole papers over there at that table and good luck to you, boys."

To another table where a soldier was sitting and writing, we moved and got in line. This line was shorter, hardly anyone in it. We got our parole papers and took off toward the city.

Chapter Nine

ONCE WE ARRIVED at the docks by the river, we looked across at all the water. There was water as far as the eye could see. No land on the other side. The flood waters went on and on, way past where the normal shoreline was supposed to be.

One man looking at all the water said softly, "Merciful heavens... would you look at that? I ain't never seen so much water in my life. Have any of y'all?"

I shook my head, and said more to myself than to anyone else standing there, "Uh-uh... no, sir."

He continued speaking, drawing my eyes from the water on the horizon to close by. "Look-a-here, at the way the current is moving. Y'all see how fast it's a moving there?"

Another man pointed to swirling water. "Look at all those whirlpools out there... y'all get caught in one of those, y'all ain't never gonna come back up. I'm a telling you... that thing will suck you right down to the bottom of that river in no time. I'm not so sure this was such a good idea now."

I looked at the other two men and said, "It don't matter to me, boys. Home is that-a-way and I mean to get there. You can stay here if you want but I'm a going."

We looked around at one another wondering if we had made the right choice. The river, the way it was now, could be the death of us all. The current ran swift with debris sweeping by. This was not going to be an easy task. We weren't in the best shape after being half starved as we were, especially for swimming a flooded river. I always thought of myself as a strong swimmer, but I didn't know about the other two.

I removed my ragged uniform, all the way down to my

long johns. As I worked on removing the rags, I thought back to the day when the uniform was issued to me. How pretty it looked and how proud I was to wear it. I even had a picture taken of me in it and had it sent to Lucinda.

We wrapped our clothing into a tight bundle and then tied it loosely around our necks with the piece of rope we used to replace our belts that had worn out. The old pieces of our belts had gone into the cooking pots to give the water some taste in a stew we made one day. We ate the leather of our belts about three days before the surrender.

Standing on the dock, we took one last look at one another. Slowly, one at a time, we lowered into the river, quickly feeling the tug of the swift current trying to take us as we held onto the dock.

Taking our time, we pushed away to let the river take control of our bodies. The current sent us moving quickly downstream along the banks. I was surprised at how cold the water felt for early July, and yet so very refreshing against my already hot and tired body.

We slowly made our way out farther toward the deeper and swifter water. Moving carefully, we looked for any kind of debris danger that could come our way from upstream.

The farther we went, the stronger and colder the current became; racing at an even faster pace. With the undertow dragging at our bodies, it was hard to keep our heads above water.

One of the men was caught off guard by the strength of the current and turned back, swimming for the nearby shore. The last I saw of him was when he climbed onto the bank on the same side of the river. We quickly lost sight of him as the other man and I let the river carry us.

I called over to my traveling companion, "Hey... keep calm... don't fight the river. Let it do the work for you."

He hollered back, "Thanks, I will. What's your name, soldier?"

I swallowed some water, fighting to keep my head up. "Riley. What's yours?"

I never got a reply. A large log collided with the man taking him under and away. I never saw him come back up, and now there was only me. I tried to keep composed and take my time to not tire myself out. I debated whether to go on or not. I decided to stay the course.

The current started dragging me toward a large whirlpool that drifted into the lane of the river I was in. If I was caught in one that size, it would suck me to the bottom, and I would have a heck of a time fighting my way up to the surface again. There were several whirlpools of all sizes. Some I could see, others I couldn't until I felt the pull on my body trying to drown me.

At the same time, I had to also watch for trees and other large floating trash in the river, giving them a wide berth when they came near. Some logs were so large they were hard to avoid while others lay just under the surface of the water. If I got caught by those branches, they could drag me below the surface like the other man who was with me; never to come back up again.

I rode the current for a long time. I kept working my way to the other side where the water was calm. At last, a sure watery death released me from its grip.

The swollen river slowed to resemble a swamp filled with standing forests. I no longer had to worry about the current or the whirlpools. Now, it was snakes and gators. Either was as bad as the river itself.

Fighting the water exhausted me. I was so tired and weak, yet I had to tread water to keep afloat for there was still no land. I grabbed a branch of a rooted tree to rest for a moment. As I held in place on the branch, I felt with my feet to see if I could touch bottom.

I rested a while longer, until I could go on again. I let go and swam for a few minutes before exhaustion grabbed at me again and I had to find another tree to hold onto.

At this point I was not feeling well. My stomach was starting to act up. I drank some bad water in the river and was starting to get sick. As I rested, holding onto a limb of the tree, I began to think that maybe this was not such a good idea after all. I had heard of people getting lost in the swamps and never being seen again. I didn't want to be one of them.

Falling from higher in the tree, a large, black, water moccasin landed next to my hand holding the branch. I let go quickly and sank below the surface, swallowing more bad water. I clawed my way back to air, splashing and gasping. I quickly searched for the snake but couldn't find him. I guess it had moved on.

Breathing a little easier, I decided that another tree farther along the way would suit me better. The day was getting late and I kept working my way west toward the setting sun.

Late that afternoon, I felt the muddy bottom with my foot. I could stand with my chin just above the water line. I still could not see any land but I knew there had to be eventually. The water couldn't last forever.

The sun sank well below the tree line and the night crickets in the trees began to sing around me. I was now worrying. At night I could lose my direction and travel in circles and get lost if I couldn't see the stars through the leafy canopy. Like I said before, a person could disappear in these bogs of the Mississippi River and not be seen again. This was man-eating critter territory. I was in a world of horse dung if I didn't find land soon.

Just before dark, my body began to shake with fever and it was hard to concentrate. All I wanted was to lie down and sleep, stop the world from spinning, but I forced myself to go a little farther. Once on dry land, I would be safe and rest. I didn't care if it was an island or not, just someplace dry. The shaking was becoming uncontrollable.

At last I spotted land and headed for it. I forced myself to focus on a faint shining pinpoint in the distance. Sloshing through the water and mud as fast as I could, I slipped and fell twice. I think.

I wasn't sure if that was a light ahead of me or something else. For all I knew, I could've been traveling in circles following a damn bug with a glowing butt.

My strength was definitely failing. The water I drank from the river was indeed making me sick... very sick. The swamp was spinning. I hoped I could make it to the dry ground before I fell unconscious. If I pass out in the water or near it, I would be gator bait for sure. I had to stay awake.

The last time I slipped and fell in the water, I lost sight of the light. It didn't matter. I made it upon dry land and trudged along until I was away from the swampy infestation.

Once out of danger of gators, I stopped to get my bearing. Holding onto a tree to keep me upright, I looked around. There...

far off in the gloom of the evening, I spotted the light again. Someone had to be there. Maybe I could get help if I could stay awake long enough. I hoped it wasn't a Yankee patrol. I headed for the light and what I hoped was safety.

I made my way through the thicket towards the light that guided me onward. I came upon an old shack made of planked lumber with a fireplace and chimney of baked mud. As I stepped upon the porch, I heard the lever action of a rifle cock, and a not so friendly voice say, "What's y'all want here, boy? Ain't nut'en left around here for you Yankees to steal; ya'll done got it all."

I froze. Dizzy, I raised my hands to let whoever it was see I had no weapons. Irritated that he called me a Yankee, I swore at him, "Sir, I ain't no damn Yankee. I am a soldier of the south, a Louisiana man."

The voice in the dark said, "Step into the light of that there doorway, boy, and let me take a look-see for myself."

I stepped into the light and slowly turned to show him I was unarmed. He said, "Where's your gray uniform, soldier boy?"

I pointed to the pouch hanging around my neck and said, "It's right here... that is, what's left of it."

The voice in the darkness said, "Well, I guess you might be what you say you are. You alone, boy?"

Nodding, I answered, "Yessum, just me and the snakes following me around."

He gave a laugh as I heard the rifle cocking mechanism release, letting the hammer on his rifle slowly down with his thumb. He came from the other side of the shack, taking a better look at me, "Yeah... you must be a Louisiana boy if-a-you'd been playing in the dark out there with all those snakes and ain't screaming and crying like a little girl. Come on inside there, boy, and dry yourself off by the fire. I wanna hear how you found me out here."

He stepped upon the porch, stomping his boot to knock the dust and dirt off and led the way into his little cabin. Just inside the doorway he sat the rifle down, leaning it against the wall. He continued farther into the room before turning to watch me. I stepped inside and walked to the fireplace.

The old man gave a little laugh and brought into view a handgun which he had hidden behind his back. I looked at the pistol, wondering if he was going to shoot me. He saw the look on my face and smiled as he looked down at the handgun and patted it with the other hand.

Looking back at me he said, "Sorry about that, son. No offense, I just wanted to make sure you weren't no scalawag or something like that sort. I figured if you were, that rifle leaning by the door would have been mighty tempting; Yes sir, mighty tempting."

I half turned and looked at the rifle. He continued, "It wouldn't have mattered because that rifle ain't loaded like my gun here is."

Standing by the fireplace trying to get warm I looked around the inside of the little cabin. The place was tidy and neat, like its owner. He was clean shaven and stood about five foot six--a half head shorter than me. He wore an old slouch hat that had seen better days, cocked at an angle over his left eye, covering white hair. The old man did not have one tooth in his mouth but the look he gave me, told me he didn't put up with any shenanigans either.

Standing in front of the fireplace, the room started to spin and my stomach began to heave. I tried to grab hold of something, anything, but my legs gave out and everything around me went black.

Suddenly I was back in the trenches at Vicksburg; fighting again. I looked out the small slit in front of me on the wall of my trench. The one I used for shooting. Down the hill from where I stood, I saw Lucinda walking slowly up that hill towards me. She could see me because she smiled and waved.

Behind her, farther down the hill, a mob of Yankee soldiers ran toward her. I tried to yell to her and warn her to get to safety but I couldn't get sound out of my mouth.

The Yankees kept coming, and I tried to shoot them before they reached her. I tried as hard as I could to protect her. I saw one Yankee stop and raise his rifle. I struggled to reload my gun as I watched him aim his weapon at her.

Frantic, I couldn't get the shell to slide into the chamber. My fingers would not cooperate. I looked around for help, but everyone in the trench was dead. The sergeants and all my comrades were laying on the floor of the rifle pit; all dead.

Smoke burned my eyes, and I couldn't focus on things around me. Terrified I could not save her, I looked out my port again. She was there and I tried to warn her again, but it was too late. I saw the smoke from the rifle and I screamed.

The old man laid his hands on my chest to hold me down. He said, "Shhhhhh... Easy, boy, you drank too much of that old river out there. You've been a very sick man, but I think the worse is past. You feelin' better there boy?"

Confused and breathing hard, I shook my head. I didn't know where I was. I asked, trying to sit up, "How did I get here and how long was I out?"

The old man smiled. "You came out of the river, sick as a dog. You've been here three days now, mostly tossing and turning with fever, sweating out that poison in your body."

The smell of gumbo hit me and my stomach screamed loudly. Embarrassed I said, "Excuse me. I ain't had nothin' to eat since I was paroled."

"Paroled?" he said surprised, raising one eyebrow, looking hard at me. "Son, did you just get out of prison?"

"Oh... naw sir. I ain't never gotten into trouble with the law. I was paroled there at Vicksburg. General Pemberton, he surrendered the city to the Yankees."

Excited, he said, "Wait a minute... Pemberton's army is on the other side of the river and so is Vicksburg. What... uh, how did you get over here on the Louisiana side of the river?"

"I swam. I didn't stop to think there was that much water in that river. Me and another man started out together. He didn't make it, though," I said remembering back to when that log caught and dragged him under.

Raising one eyebrow and looking at me in a strange way as if he didn't believe me. "You... you swam that river out there?" He pointed toward the Mississippi River. "That very river out there?"

"Yes-um, I did and I can tell you right now, I was very tired."

"I'll say!" he exclaimed, giving a little laugh. Excited he continued, "That's something, boy. I ain't never heard of nobody doing that when the water was this high. But, boy, didn't you know it was flooded. This year has been one of the worst flooding the river has ever seen."

I shrugged my shoulders. "I just knew I wasn't going to stay on the other side of the river with my family being on this side." I was determined to get home to my loved ones. I needed to know how they were doing. I needed to know if the baby she had carried was all right.

He studied my face in the light of the fireplace. After a few moments of silence, the old man sat down a bowl and wet rag he was using on my forehead and trudged to an old trunk and brought out a patched quilt. He motioned with the quilt. "Here son... take this. You can use it tonight to sleep with. I'm gonna take my bed back from you, that is, now that you are better."

A little unsteady, I slowly got to my feet and took the old quilt from him. I looked down and saw I was naked. My stomach gave a rumble and growl again as I covered my body with the old soft, warm quilt. I moved closer to the fire as the old man took my long johns laid out near the fireplace and handed them to me.

"Here, son," he said, shoving the garments into my hand. "So, Pemberton surrendered... and you! You swam the Mississippi out there all alone, huh?" It was more a statement than question. Giving me a toothless smile, he nodded.

Not waiting for a reply, he went to a cupboard near a small table with one chair. He took out the only two bowls there, along with a couple of spoons, before shuffling back over to where I stood by the fireplace.

I quickly got into my long johns and took the bowl and spoon he shoved into my hands. Giving me his toothless smile, he nodded toward the gumbo over the fire.

I spooned out a full bowl of the stew and surprised the old man by handing it to him. I guess he was shocked I had given him the bigger portion because he knew I was so very hungry. Pleased, he handed me the other bowl without a word.

I filled my bowl with what was left in the pot and sat cross legged on the floor near the fireplace. Before I could begin to eat I heard him mumbling. At first I thought he was speaking to me, so I turned to him, listening carefully.

The old man sat at his small table with his head bowed over his bowl. I could hear him as he spoke softly. "Thank you, Father, for the gift we are about to receive and for another day on this earth and oh... thank you for your gift of sending someone to visit me. I think I am about ready to see my family and friends soon, whenever y'all see fit for me to come home, that is. In your loving son's name, I pray... amen."

I watched and waited until he was finished and after him I repeated "amen."

He looked over the edge of the table at me, grinned and nodded approvingly before diving into the stew. Not another word was spoken until both bowls were empty.

When we finished, I gathered the dishes and cooking pot. The old man watched as I cleaned up and put everything away.

I asked if I could borrow some soap. He nodded and pointed to a washtub near one of the walls. I filled the tub with clean water from the well in back and set it near the fireplace.

I carefully unrolled my old uniform and sat my parole papers aside to dry. I couldn't tell if they were still good or not. It looked like some of the ink had run but since I couldn't read, it didn't matter. I washed out as much of the blood and dirt as I could from my uniform and laid it in front of the fireplace to dry. Looking at my clothes laid out there, I figured the pants would be the only part salvageable. My jacket was too badly gone to save.

Next I emptied the dirty water and refilled the tub. As I washed, we talked. That is, he asked questions--personal questions about me. Questions like, where did I live before the war. Was I married and if so, how many children did I have. When I was done, so were his questions. With the wet clothes laid close to the hearth to dry, I banked the fire in the fireplace and got ready to sleep.

The old man yawned. Said it was time to settle down for the night. He shuffled to his bed, turned down the covers, undressed, and crawled in and covered himself. I wrapped in the old quilt he had given me and made myself as comfortable as I could on the cabin floor.

As sleep brought Lucinda to my dreams, the old man across the room bolted up in his bed, coughing and gasping for air. Torn from my sleep I rushed over to see if he needed help. Before I got to him, he waved me off with his free hand and leaned over the side of the mattress. He hacked up blood into a piece of cloth in his hand. Placing the rag back on a small ledge next to his bed he got the coughing under control and cleared his throat several times before I heard the soft snoring coming from his corner of the cabin.

Chapter Ten

I FELT A nudge of a boot against my foot. I cracked open one eye and saw the old man standing over me, fully dressed. "Time to rise and shine, son. Get up... we're burning daylight." He walked over to a small shelf on the wall and picked up a large spoon and a bottle. He carefully set the cork on the wooden ledge and poured fluid onto his spoon.

Head tilted back, he raised the spoon up to his lips and let the liquid concoction slide to the back of his throat. He then hacked loudly and sucked air into his old lungs as he winced.

"Is that your medicine?" I asked.

Carefully, he replaced the spoon and the bottle back on the shelf. Turning to face me, he said, "Sort of... It was a gift from a young man who likes to play around making medicine. He's very good at it. It's something he was working on before the war. His name was George... George Tichenor, ever hear of him?"

I thought for a moment and nothing came to mind so I shook my head.

Surprised, he looked confused, he inquired again, "You sure? Cause he's in your army. He's a young man about your age-- cavalry, I think."

I thought for a moment more before shaking my head again, "No... don't sound familiar, but hey-- I was in the infantry, not the cavalry. Did he serve in a Louisiana unit?"

He looked down at the floor for a moment, rubbing his chin, thinking, before he lifted his head and looked back up at me, giving me a sly smile, "No... come to think of it. I believe he was in a Tennessee unit. Sorry, I just thought you might have come across him. Anyway... he gave me a case of this medicine he was working on. Said it would help my *condition*."

He turned back to the wall and picked up the bottle again, looking at it as he continued to talk, more to himself than to me. "Too bad it's my last bottle." He patted the bottle gently before placing it next to the spoon. Then turning back to me, he gave me a wink and a smile. "Come on, son, I've got something to show you outside."

Just before we left his cabin, I stopped him at the doorway by putting my hand on his chest. He looked down at my hand and then gave me a funny look that more or less said *don't touch me, boy*.

I took my hand off his chest, holding both up in front of me. "I'm sorry. I only wanted to know what's wrong with you. You don't seem to be well."

His old eyes soften as he smiled warmly. "Oh... it's nothing for you to worry about, son; nothin' at all. Come on, let's go outside. I've got someone special for you to meet."

Confused, I let him lead to the end of the cabin porch before carefully stepping off onto the ground, never looking back to see if I was following or not. He walked a small, well-worn path under a dense canopy of tree limbs with Spanish moss hanging overhead. About a hundred yards from the cabin we came upon a small clearing.

Hidden within a ring of trees were a small corral and a three sided shed. A young Spanish mustang mare, about fourteen hands high, light reddish brown with four black stocking feet and mane waited for him.

The mare looked to be about four years old and very edgy. By the way she acted I could tell I was a stranger to her, someone she was not used to being around. She kept stomping the ground, shaking her head, and sniffing the air. Nervous tension ran down her neck and shoulder as she stood facing us.

The old man walked up to the fence. Coaxing her, he said, "Come here, Sally, come here, girl. I got somebody here I want you to meet."

He turned to me, smiling with a twinkle in his eyes. "She's a little shy right now, you being a stranger and all." Placing his arms on the fence rail and resting his chin on his arms, he watched with loving eyes as the mustang danced around nervously. Turning his head toward me, he continued, "She'll cozy up to you once she gets more used to you."

He called to the mare again, reaching into his pocket. He brought a piece of carrot out. Prompting me, he put the veggie into my hand and motioned for me to give it to her. "She loves carrots."

I moved closer to the old man and called to the young mare. Hearing her name, she raised her head, shaking her mane, sniffing the air. She smelled the carrot and me. I held out my hand showing the treat. She stood about ten feet from me, watching my every move. Her nostrils flared.

I tried to coax her to come. She was not having anything to do with me. She stood her ground, stubbornly, looking at me and the carrot. Not moving from where she stood, she shook her head, snorting and pawing the ground with one foot.

She swung her body around and took off at a trot, strutting around inside the corral. She ran the enclosure along the fence line, tossing her head up and down as she went. She passed so close to me, I had to step back from the fence. I was afraid she was going to slam into me and the rail where I stood.

The mustang then trotted back to the center of the corral and stopped at the very same place she was before. She stood, facing me once more, shaking her mane. Defiant, she snorted and raised her head and whinnied loudly, shaking her head before once more looking at me, sniffing the air for the carrot.

I came back up to the fence, stuck out my hand again and waited. Standing next to me, the old man seemed to be enjoying himself. He smiled, watching the scene play out around him. Waiting to see which of us broke first. Would the mustang come over and take the treat from my hand, or would I give up on making friends with the mare?

We stood defiant, Sally watching me and me watching Sally under the shade of the trees overhead. My arm began to ache, sweat beaded on my forehead. The mustang lowered her head and took a few steps closer. She stopped once more just out of reach of my hand and shook her head in frustration. With her ears laid flat against her head she sniffed the air and took a step back.

I stood my ground and watched as more nervous tension ran up and down her. I didn't move my hand, but kept it steady, watching her the whole time, refusing to give up.

She wanted the carrot, but was not ready to take it from my hand. Then she eased forward a couple of steps closer, stretching her neck as she came forward. Keeping just out of reach, she stopped again. Nervous, she swished her tail back and forth, still uneasy, still unsure of the stranger holding the treat out to her.

Then she eased up to the fence and took the carrot out of my hand and chewed noisily as if she had known me all my life. The old man swore quietly to himself. "Well I'll be..." Then more loudly as he reached out with one hand to stroke the side of the horse's head. "I knew it. I just knew you two would get along just nicely."

I smiled as I rubbed her above her nose, letting her get to know my smell. She remained calm as I petted her but she continued to swish her tail back and forth, giving a nervous snort every now and then.

After a few minutes the old man pushed Sally away so she could leave us. He took me into the shed and showed me where he kept his saddle, bridle, and the horse's blanket. I wondered why he was showing me all this, but never asked. Guess he never got too much company in these parts.

Next, we went inside the corral. The mare nuzzled up to the old man nudging him, looking for a hand out. Seeing the he had no treats for her she turned to me looking for attention. I scratched her neck and rubbed her.

We remained in the corral with the horse for half a day. He had me work with her, saddling and riding inside the corral to see the way she handled herself. Then he showed me how to walk her after a workout and how to cool her temperature before giving her a rubdown and food and water.

I wanted to ask the old man why he was training me. He didn't expect me to be his wagon driver, did he? But when I got ready to ask him I saw the old man was tired. His face was ashen and he had begun to cough up blood again. I worried about him, but he kept smiling and telling me he was all right.

When we got back to the cabin, I sat him in his chair at the small table to rest, while I fixed something to eat. Later that afternoon, I borrowed a mirror and scissors to clean up my hair and beard.

When I looked into the small hand glass, I was shocked. I didn't know the unkempt stranger who stared back at me. The reflection in the mirror was of an older man with long shaggy brown hair and a straggly beard looking back at me. He didn't look anything like the man who had been plowing his garden a few years ago. I couldn't get over how old looking I had gotten in such a short time.

As I stared at my image I thought of home, my wife and the child I had not seen yet. I wondered how they were getting along without me. I wondered what she was thinking this moment. What would Lucinda say if she saw me this way? I had to get home, as soon as I could. I made up my mind that tomorrow I would start my journey back.

After I cleaned up, cutting my hair and trimming my beard, I looked and felt a lot better. I stared in that small mirror. I had gotten thinner. Now, with the beard cut short, I also showed a few scars on my face, scars that would remain with me for the rest of my life; a little something to remind me of Vicksburg.

We talked a while longer about my wife and my child. I said that I should leave soon to get to them. He nodded in agreement and said, "I know, son, but could you stay one or two more days? It won't be long now."

Not knowing what *wouldn't be long*, I said, "All right." It was the least I could do for everything he had done for me.

His coughing got worse. The next day I helped him get dressed. I was seriously worried about him. He remained in the shack while I took care of Sally. When I came back to the cabin, I found him lying on the floor; blood covered the front of his old shirt. I cleaned him up and laid him on his bed.

I knelt beside him. His eyes fluttered and finally opened, trying to center on me. He grasped my hand as if trying to hold on to something, anything. Focusing on my face, he took his other hand and patted me on the cheek. I thought he was delirious for he said, "Thank you, Gabriel. I have been waiting for you to come and take me home. Thank you for letting me have this time to finish my business here before I join my family and friends."

I took his hand in mine and held it. I said gently to him, "My name is not Gabriel... it's Riley... you remember, don't you?"

The old man gripped my hand tightly, smiling up at me and said, "I know, I know. You were sent to see me off. I want you to take care of Sally for me and there are a few things in that old trunk over there I saved for you too. Thank you, my friend, for being here for me. If you would, try to remember me from time to time."

I didn't know what to say to the old man. I didn't even know his name. My eyes were watering. I wiped them on my shirt sleeve and asked, "What... what is your name, old man? What do they call you?"

His voice was so weak and got weaker the more he spoke. "My name... *cough* is Charlie..." I couldn't make out the last name as his voice faded to nothing. I laid my ear to his chest and I couldn't hear anything. There was nothing. He was dead. I covered his face with part of his bed coverings and said a small prayer to send him on his way.

With the death of Charlie, there was nothing keeping me here. "Home... to Lucinda and our baby," I whispered out loud. I gathered small items I'd need for my trip back home. Charlie didn't need those things anymore so I helped myself.

I picked up his rifle next to the door and examined it. It was a Henry, lever action repeater rifle. Admiring the rifle in my hands, I said out loud, "Boy... if we had these at Vicksburg, we could've done a lot more damage to the Yankees than we did." I placed the rifle back by the cabin door, so I wouldn't forget it in the morning.

After I had collected what I could use, I remembered what he had said about the trunk. Now curious, I knelt in front of the old case and lifted the lid. Looking inside, I was surprised at what I found. On top was a new, wide-brim hat. I tried in on and found it a little too big for my head. I looked at the old man lying on his bed and thought, *why would he buy a hat too big for himself?*

I found an old catalog next to his bed and tore out a few pages. Folding the pages into thin strips I tucked them under the sweatband inside the hat. I tried it on again. This time it fit snugly. After wearing the forage cap I was issued so long ago, this new hat felt stiff and bulky with its large brim. It felt different, and I liked it.

Smiling to myself at my good fortune, I knelt to see what

other treasures the old man left for me to find. Under where the hat had rested was a new shirt, pants and leather belt; all too large for the old man, but looked to fit me fine.

Under the clothing, I found his revolver tucked inside a holster and a box of cartridges next to the gun belt. I turned my head looking at the old man and said softly in awe, "Who were you, Charlie. How did y'all know I would be coming this way and needing all these things? How did you know?"

I examined the hand gun. It was a six-shot Griswold which was becoming a very popular handgun and this one looked almost new. I took out everything else I could use from the trunk and eased the lid back down. I exchanged my old uniform for the new clothing. My once beautiful gray uniform was now just rags. A belt was needed to hold the pants up, but other than that, it all fit well.

I next tried the gun belt with the holster on my right side. It felt heavy on my waist and too high on my hip for me to get the Griswold out if I needed it in a hurry, so I tried it lower. It felt ridiculous, hanging low on my hip like that. Then I switched it to sit high up on the front of my left hip, angled towards my right hand so I could reach for it easily. That was it. Now it was easy to get to and out of the way.

There was plenty of daylight left outside and I had a long way to go. So I put everything I needed into a large handkerchief and tied it in a knot, rolled up my blanket and put on my new hat. I looked around the old shack one more time before I walked back to Charlie to thank him again.

I took my hat off and held it in my hand. Lowering my head, I said a silent prayer for the old man again. Looking the last time at the body of the man who saved my life, I bent down, patting him on the shoulder and said out loud, "I won't forget you, Charlie, I won't. Take care on your journey home. Maybe I will see you again on the other side."

I dug a grave next to the porch to bury Charlie. I wrapped him in his old quilt along with his bible and gently laid him at the bottom of the grave. By the time I had finished covering him the sun was below the tree line in the west. I left the shovel as a marker and walked back inside. It was too late in the day to travel. I would leave tomorrow early.

The next morning I got dressed and put the new hat on,

pulling it down on my head. When grabbing my bedroll and the tied handkerchief, I spotted a coal oil lamp nearby. This gave me an idea.

The old cabin where Charlie had lived had seen its better days. If left abandoned, the small house looked to me as if it would not last too many more seasons. I didn't think anyone was ever going to use this place to live in again so I decided to burn it to the ground instead of leaving it and let it fall on its own.

I put the bedroll and handkerchief back on the table and picked up the lamp and shook it. It was almost full. I poured the liquid onto the bed and around the room and then tossed the empty lamp into the corner.

Next to where I had found the lamp, lay four matches. I flicked my thumbnail across the head and it blazed to life. I watched to make sure it caught before I tossed it towards the bed. The flame flew through the air and landed on its mark. As soon as the match touched the oil, fire swooshed alive. The flames spread over the bed and raced across the floor. I grabbed my things and headed for the door.

I ducked outside and walked down the path toward Sally. I left the shack behind me with smoke pouring out the doorway.

Chapter Eleven

I GOT SALLY saddled and ready to ride. I walked her out of the corral for the last time. Holding onto the reins in one hand, I grabbed the saddle with my other hand and lifted myself onto her back. I turned back in the direction of the burning cabin.

Flames along with a large plume of black smoke rose high into the sky back where the cabin was located. I steered Sally away from her home, her corral, and headed west. I moved her deeper into the woods, looking for a road or trail of some kind to travel.

Not too long after leaving Charlie's place, I came across an animal trail that led to a dirt road running north and south. I faced Sally south and nudged her forward for a few steps before pulling back on her reins. I stopped and studied the road ahead of me, wondering what was down that way. Was it the right way to go home or would I run into a Yankee patrol that would try to detain me? I needed to head west.

Then I thought *what if I come across some of our soldiers.* They may try to persuade me to go with them. I had already had enough of this war. All I wanted was to go home and be left alone.

Then I thought *if I do come across a rebel unit they just might take me for a deserter.* If that happens, I might never see Lucinda or home again. I will have to be careful who I talk to on my way home. I'll have to avoid as many towns as I can, since people will wonder why an able bodied man is riding through their town instead of out fighting Yankees.

As I sat in the middle of the road on my horse thinking; I had no idea where I was going to find Slagle and home from my present location. The only thing I was sure of was that I was on the correct side of the river. I was on Louisiana soil and I had to find someone and take a chance on asking directions.

I pointed Sally north on the road and nudged her forward. I would find my way home. It might take some doing but I will.

After several days of travel on many roads, some only wide grass paths, to avoid both Yankee and Confederate patrols; I made it to Slagle and to my home. Unfortunately, when I arrived at my homestead, no one was there. The farm looked to have been deserted for quite a while. Weeds had taken over the plowed ground I left a few years earlier.

I figured Lucinda and the child might be staying at the Moore's place. I pointed my horse in the direction of his farm and got Sally moving.

As I rode up to the Moore's, I didn't see anyone around. Nothing but a few chickens scratching and clucking around the yard. I stood in the saddle and called out in front of the house. "Ayeee! anybody home?"

No answer. I waited a few minutes and then the old man came around the corner of the house carrying a double barrel shotgun--pointed at me. Surprised when he saw me his face lit up. He slung the shotgun under his arm. "Well, I'll be. Riley. What are you doing here? I thought you were off to the war, son?"

I dismounted Sally and walked over to shake his hand. "I was. I'm back from Vicksburg. I came home for a spell."

The old man laughing with tears in his eyes, "Sure glad to see you, boy. Not many men have come back yet. Maybe later they will. I know I'll be glad when my two boys come back. Yes, sir-ree. You know they went to Virginia to serve under General Lee, didn't you?

"Anyway... welcome home son... welcome home. Come on, let's go over and sit a spell on the porch and talk. The girls will be so glad to see you again too. They're outback working our little vegetable garden. I'll get'em to fix coffee and something to eat."

We walked up to the porch and the old man called out to his girls to come here and say hello. Both girls came running around the corner to see who their pappy was hollering about.

I could see in the girls faces they were hoping it was their brothers who had returned. But after seeing me, they were still glad and made me feel real good inside to see old friends. The old man and I sat on the front porch while the girls ran off to the outdoor kitchen that sat away from the main house.

I looked around to see if Lucinda was about. I didn't see her or Mr. Moore's wife so I figured they were somewhere about and would join us later.

After living on what I hunted since I left Charlie's place, I ate my fill of the collard greens and cornbread. When I finished, I pushed the plate away. "Whoa... That was mighty good, Mr. Moore. Thank y'all very much." Then looking around, I asked, "Hey, where's your wife. I haven't seen her since I got here?"

At my question, his face seemed to change. Looking at his half eaten lunch for a moment, he lifted his sad eyes back up to me. "I forgot you have been away so long. My wife... she died about three months after you left to go off to war. Lucinda and her little girl had been living with us the whole time since you were gone. That is, until just about a month ago."

Trying to hide the joy of hearing I had a daughter, I leaned forward touching Mr. Moore on his knee. "I'm sorry to hear about your wife, Mr. Moore. I truly am. Where is Lucinda now if she is not here?"

He reached over and patted me on my arm and said, "I'm sorry, son. I keep forgetting you've been away. A Yankee patrol came by and found her here with us. They said that all Injuns had to be moved to the Injun Reservation up in Oklahoma. Her being an Injun and all, Lucinda would have to go with them. I tried to stop'em, but I couldn't. She told me to tell you that she would make her way to where Texas, Oklahoma, and Arkansas joined together there. She said she would wait for you to get her there."

I shook my head, not knowing where she was talking about. He motioned for me to follow him into the yard. We walked over to a bald spot in the grass and he knelt, taking out his pocket knife. He opened a blade and began to draw in the dirt. He cut a cross and pointed at one corner with the blade.

"We'll call this part Oklahoma." He then pointed under the line. "This here is Texas." Looking to see if I was following him, he continued across the line next. "Arkansas is over here and this here is Louisiana."

He stuck his knife blade in the sand where all the lines came together and looked back up at me and asked, "Now do you see? You understand now?"

Maybe I couldn't read or write, but I understood pictures. Smiling at him, I nodded. I now knew where Lucinda was.

I looked back at Mr. Moore wanting more information. "So, Lucinda had a little girl, huh?"

Guiding me back to the porch he said, "Yep."

"Uh... what does she look like? I mean who did she favor-- her mother or me?"

The old man scratched his beard, looking at me sideways. "Riley, I don't rightly know. Babies all look the same to me. I mean, I couldn't tell you if she looked like you or her mother. I'm sorry Riley, but I'm the wrong person to ask those questions about. You'll just have to judge that when you find her. One thing for sure, she certainly has a pair of lungs on her. Yes sir, she sure does."

I gave a little laugh of pride at hearing that. I was now getting antsy to go to Oklahoma and find my wife and child. I needed to go as soon as I could. I told the old man I would leave in the morning. The sooner I got my family back, the better I would feel.

Chapter Twelve

IT WAS WHAT they called *the dog days of summer* here in Louisiana. The nights were just as bad as the days, which is to say it made sleeping indoors uncomfortable. Leaves on the trees around the farm hung dry and limp, not yet beginning to change colors.

That night I was restless, trying to sleep in their home. I could not close my eyes, thinking of my wife all alone and so far away in the Indian Territory. As soon as light began to show in the sky, I decided to get up and quietly get dressed.

I thought maybe I could sneak out early and not disturb anybody in the house. Let them sleep in a while longer. I found Mr. Moore had hooked up his freight wagon to my horse and his mule and it was parked out front of the house, waiting for me.

Both girls were up, also. They were busy in the cook house outside preparing coffee, biscuits, and eggs. After having a cup of coffee and eating our breakfast, Mr. Moore and I walked toward the yard.

The hot August air was heavy and stagnant; even this early in the morning. Hot... sticky and not a breeze anywhere— it was typical for late summer.

Mr. Moore and I talked as we headed to the wagon. I thanked him again for his hospitality and for the use of his wagon and mule. I told him I would bring them back as soon as I could.

Sally and Mr. Moore's mule stood together, hitched to the wagon. The mule stood patiently waiting as though nothing was going on. To him, it didn't matter one way or the other. It was just another day. But Sally, she didn't like the harness business going on; naw sir, not one bit. She stood next to the docile mule, and a nervous twitch ran up her neck as she shook her head, stamping one foot impatiently and chewing on her bit.

As I walked over I noticed a bag of grain and a bale of hay in the bed of the wagon. Mr. Moore suggested I take off my gun belt and tuck it under the seat with my rifle.

He said, "A man wearing a gun nowadays seems to always find trouble about. Nobody is going to pay any attention to an unarmed man driving a freight wagon on the road. You should fit in nicely out there; except for the fact most of the men your age are all off fighting the war. You... you just be careful out there, son... watch your back."

I nodded. "I will. Hey... don't worry about me. Hopefully, I'll be back in a few weeks or so."

I took off the gun belt with the revolver in its holster. I rolled it into a tight bundle and tucked it under the seat next to my rifle. As I placed it, I noticed a warm handkerchief that smelled of fresh baked cornbread tied up in a nice package.

I turned and shook the old man's hand then climbed upon the wagon and made myself comfortable on the bench seat. I looked toward the porch where Mr. Moore had joined his two daughters and waved. Taking the reins off the brake handle, I pushed the lever forward, releasing the hold.

I flicked the reins and Sally jumped nervously, snorting her dislike for the harness. The mule turned his head toward Sally and gave an ear splitting bray before moving forward, pulling the wagon. Sally shook her head, annoyed but after being forced along with the mule doing most of the pulling, she quickly fell in step with the beast and settled down to do her part.

It was a lovely, hot August day in Louisiana. A strong breeze blew from the southwest and not a cloud in the sky. As I rode along, I took it easy to save the mule and the horse from wearing out. It was slow going, but I knew I could go a lot farther if I didn't exhaust the animals too quickly.

Mr. Moore had made a trip or two over the years up to Shreveport. He said the traveling was good as long as I stayed on the main roads and didn't take any side trips along the way. He didn't like the forest there, it made him nervous. He said the woods were haunted. Me, I was not scared. I had been frightened enough at Vicksburg. If there were ghosts in those woods it was of the Indians that use to live there. Lucinda had told me to get rid of any Indian ghost, make peace with them and they should leave me alone.

Late that afternoon I found the road to Manny and headed north. Soon the trees of the Kisatchie forest closed in around the road, blocking most of the light.

The forest got its name from the Kichai Indians of the Caddoan Confederacy. This was their home when I was a boy. The government moved most of them. The ones left behind soon died or became civilized themselves.

This part of the woods looked to be impenetrable on either side of the road. It was dark and forbidding and made me feel uneasy. I moved my weapons closer in case I needed them. I heard strange noises coming from the forest. The sound of my wagon echoed off the trees, making it sound as if there was another road just beyond the tree line, with another wagon traveling along with me; Mr. Moore's ghosts.

As closed in as the forest was, I could still see the road ahead through the gloom. Thick timber of large yellow pines reached up to the heavens, their limbs lifting to the sky. High above me the sound of woodpeckers resonated as they worked drilled holes in the trees around me. Every now and then I could hear the cry of a hawk or an owl somewhere in the gloom.

I was glad it didn't look like rain. Sometimes when it rained, the roads dissolved into mud. With too much rain, the mud became a loose swamp of soupy mire, sinking wagons all the way to the axel making it impossible to move. I'll tell you right now, it can be difficult getting the wheels of the wagon, not to mention the animals themselves, out of that kind of mess, with or without help. I was hoping this wasn't one of those journeys.

As evening deepened, I spotted a clearing where I could pull over and stop for the night. A small creek meandered its way close by giving me and the animal's fresh running water. I pulled the wagon to the side of the road and unhitched my horse and the mule and led them to get their fill of water at the stream.

After letting the horse and mule drink, I gave them straw and oats to eat. Then I rubbed them down for the night and tied their front legs together loosely so they would not wonder off during the night.

With the animals taken care of, I built a small fire and fixed myself something to eat. Then I banked the fire and laid my bedroll out in the back of the wagon. Making myself as comfortable as I could, I lay there with my hands behind my neck and looked at the canvas ceiling of the wagon until I drifted off to sleep. I slept with my weapons within reach if I needed them.

Just before daylight Sally snorted and woke me up. I climbed out of the back of the wagon and yawned and stretched. I stood for a moment trying to wake up as I scratched and looked around for the coffee pot.

After spotting the container where I left it the night before, I proceeded to make a fresh pot. While the coffee was cooking, I put the horse's and mule's harnesses on and hitched them to the wagon. As I finished getting the wagon ready for travel, the coffee was beginning to boil over the fire.

I sat the hot pot on the wagon bench and reached under the seat to retrieve a shovel. Spreading dirt over the fire, I smothered it then placed my hand on the dead charcoals to make sure the mound was not hot. I didn't want to start any forest fire. As dry as it had been this month, a fire could easily get out of control.

Satisfied that the fire was cold, I loaded onto the wagon, sitting next to the steaming pot of coffee and made myself comfortable. I took a moment to pour myself a cup of brew before leading the animals onto the road again.

Without spilling too much coffee from my cup, I intended to have a few cups before the coffee got too cold. It seemed the mule and my horse had other ideas; both of them conspiring against me this morning. Every time I tried to take a swallow, they would find a rut or a hole in the road and aim the wheels of the wagon towards it. I ended up cussing and spilling more coffee on me than I got to drink.

Chapter Thirteen

AROUND NOON, TROUBLE dropped by. I was stopped by three riders who came up quickly on me out of the woods. These three boys introduced themselves as part of the *Home Guard*. The title of *Home Guard* seemed to be a name for someone who had finagled out of not leaving to fight the Yankees.

They would bravely thump their chest and tell you, if it came down to it, they were the last line of defense for the South. *Hurrah for Dixie.* After all, someone had to stay behind to protect the farms, women, and children from thieves and robbers. Unfortunately, most of the ones who did stay behind were the thieves and robbers like these gentlemen before me.

These *gentlemen* wore the Confederate gray kepi and carried old pistols and tarnished sabers. By the looks of the weapons, I would've been more worried they might explode in my hands if I had to use any of them.

The three heroes that blocked my way looked like they would have been more comfortable walking behind their animals instead of riding them. All three looked to be in their late teens; none older than twenty and none old enough to shave. These three were your typical yellow-belly bullies who always seemed to be in trouble and it was never their fault.

I pulled back on the reins, stopping my wagon. The leader of this so called cavalry unit of the Home Guard raised his hand to stop me. "Hey there... where y'all heading there, mister?" He eyed my horse and mule with interest.

I sized up the three youngsters and answered with a civil tongue, "Hey... I'm heading to Shreveport up ahead there. Is this the right road?" I could see antagonize these boys would only delay me further. If I wanted to proceed without trouble, I needed to play along a while.

The young man in the middle, who was clearly the leader of this band of defenders, moved his mule closer to where I sat on the wagon. Studying my wagon with interest, the boy was feeling brave and sure of his authority.

He reached up with his gun hand and lifted his kepi higher on his head, "Hey... I'll ask the questions here, and yeah this is the road to Shreveport, but ya still got a fair ways to go. What's yo business there in Shreveport, boy? Don't y'all know it's full of Yankee soldiers?"

I noticed as he talked, the other two boys walked their mules to the opposite side of my wagon. One rider rode to the back of the wagon and looked inside to see if there was anything he could confiscate. There was nothing there but straw and a bag of feed for the animals. The third rider busied himself looking at my horse.

The leader sat on his mule, eyeing Sally also. While they were busy admiring my horse I eased my foot down and scooted my bedroll over my guns with the toe of my boot to hide them.

The movement caught the eye of their leader and he looked back at me. I smiled at the young man and told him the truth. "Hey... I'm gonna pick up my family and bring them back home with me. Why?"

Giving me a hard look, he said irritated, "You still asking questions; boy? I told y'all, I'll be the one asking questions here, not you; ya hear?" His eyes were beginning to grow larger and his voice louder. He wasn't use to someone challenging his authority. He was used to threatening the very young or the very old.

The leader of this small patrol of the Home Guard was obviously quite uncomfortable sitting in front of me without the other two youngsters behind him backing him up. They were still busy snooping around my wagon.

The leader took a closer look at me and I could almost see the wheels turning slowly behind his dull eyes. He took his cap off and scratched his head and asked, "Hey... you look pretty fit there, feller. How come you're not off fighting them Yankees?"

The question got the attention of the other two boys. They

had not thought much about me being the same age of the men off fighting the war. Both young men stopped what they were doing and looked at me, surprised. Forgetting the wagon and its contents, they now saw me in a different light. Both boys eased their mules behind their friend and leader where they felt safer.

I cocked my head to one side looking at the leader and gave him a cold look as I leaned forward, reaching down below my seat. The smile faded from my face as my fingers wrapped around the butt of my pistol. "Who said I wasn't in the army?" I said. "As a matter of fact, I am in the army. I just happen to be home on parole."

The leader of this group was not completely stupid. He did know the right questions to ask, he just didn't have the courage needed to finish what he started. I knew who I was dealing with.

I had come up against his kind several times in the army. He was nothing more than just a bully... a braggart; always trying to lord over any and everyone around him... and yet afraid of his own shadow. Brave up to a certain point, and only a point, before slithering away like the snake he was.

The boys behind their leader worriedly looked at each other. Their eyes got as big as saucers as they edged their mules back a bit. He turned in his saddle to watch the other two pull away from him.

I removed my hat with my left hand and placed it on my lap. With my right hand, I brought my pistol up and hid it under my hat.

He motioned for his two compadres to move closer to support him. They reluctantly obeyed, neither wanting to be called a coward later. The two boys sitting on their mules behind their leader were very nervous. They could not keep their hands off their guns and jerked with every sudden noise, their faces almost as pale as death.

The young boss man, now with his reinforcements behind him again, got up enough courage to ask, "Hey... you got your parole papers wit'cha, mister?" All of them sat stiffly on their mounts ready if trouble erupted. Their hands rested on the old guns hanging on their hips waiting on their commander to say the word. As long as they remained in their holsters, I was fine.

I said, "Papers? Why, yes, I've got my papers, I keep them

right here in my hat so's not to lose them."

I narrowed my eyes, wanting to watch their hands yet trying to stare them down. The two behind the leader were absolutely terrified, their faces drained of color. They knew I was not the easy prey they had hoped for. Unarmed, I could have whipped all three of them together if it came to a fistfight. But as frightened as they seemed to be, they might be bullied into drawing their pistols and start shooting at anything that moved. I had to be careful.

To ease the tension, I asked, "Y'all want to see 'em? I've got'em right here."

Relieved to have something to do rather than try to stare me down, he said, "Yeah... sure... I'll take a look at 'em." He looked around at his two followers to make sure they had not drifted away again.

Watching him look away at his comrades, I tucked my pistol; barrel first, into my boot. Keeping it someplace safe where I could get to it.

I took my hat and flipped it over quickly. The sudden motion caught their attention; all eyes zeroed in on my hat and the quick movement. I took out the pages of the catalog I was using to size my hat. I picked one page that had no pictures drawn on it and handed it over to the leader.

The leader of the Home Guard took the paper and looked at one side and then flipped it over to look at the other side. He glanced up at me and I smiled. With a serious look of authority, he handed it back to me. "It looks all right to me. I just wanted to make sure you were who you said. Can't be too careful these days. We could've had ourselves a Yankee spy here for all I know'd."

I took the paper back and rolled it back up and tucked it under my hatband again and said, "No, you can't be too careful these days."

Looking more relieved and once again in charge of the situation, he backed his mule a few paces waved me on. "Move along, mister. You're free to go."

I put my hat back on, smiled and tipped the brim, "See you, boys." Then I flicked the reins and headed on down the road, not looking back. I left the three sitting on their mules next to the road, watching me move away.

I figured that none of those boys could read or write. I was afraid if I showed them my real parole papers, they might have wanted to keep them. Then I might have gotten into real trouble later on, if I needed them.

Chapter Fourteen

CLOSER TO NATCHITOCHES, I saw Yankees everywhere. One cavalry patrol passed me just outside of town. Every soldier in that patrol took a hard look at me, sizing me up. I tried not to look nervous and kept the wagon moving slowly as to not draw attention. Sure made me edgy, with all these Yankees looking at me the way they did.

As I rode through the small town with the river running alongside the main street, my thumb on my left hand began to rub slowly against my index finger. I kept my head down, hidden under the brim of my hat and took my time as I traveled through. I forced myself to go slowly.

Mr. Moore was right. Since I didn't show any weapons and I looked like I had business being there, none of the Yankees bothered to stop me or look my way other than that one patrol outside of town.

I didn't stop in Natchitoches, but kept on moving until I left the town behind. When I did stop, it was well after dark. I made camp under low hanging trees near the waters of the Cain River.

I did my chores around the camp about the same order as I did every night. First, rubbing the animals down and then feeding them before I fed myself. Before I bedded down for the night, I decided to set out traps and see what I could catch during the night. Fresh meat would be good in the morning before leaving and moving on down the road.

To my surprise, the next morning I awoke with a thick blanket of fog around me. As I was walked over to check on the mule and my horse something caught my attention. On the river almost completely hidden in the fog sat a dark monster. A Union naval gunboat had parked next to my campsite.

Sally was nervous with the big boat making strange noises so close to her. She pawed at the dirt and sniffed the air. She didn't know what to think of the monster out on the water. I didn't know what to think.

Looking through the mist I saw the Union flag flying from its mast at the rear of the boat. I slowly eased over to get the two animals so I could sneak away before they knew I was there.

I slowly walked my team to my wagon. After I had them hitched, I eased closer to the front of the wagon and reached underneath the seat and retrieved my Henry rifle. I took a look at the gun and thought to myself, *what the hell am I going to do with a rifle against a steel monster like that.* I shook my head and returned the gun under the seat; bad idea bringing the Henry out.

As soon as I had replaced the weapon, a door on the shore side of the boat opened with a loud screech and a bang. A young man walked out on deck with a bucket and rope. As soon as he saw me he waved like I was an old friend come to see him. I smiled uncomfortable and waved back.

He called over as friendly as could be, "How are you today, sir?"

Not knowing what else to do I raised one hand and called back, clearing my throat. "Hey… doing fine." My thumb began to work along my left index finger nervously. *Well, they've seen me now.*

Another man stepped out of the door, looking around to see who he was talking to. He looked like an officer. He spotted me and called out to me, demanding, "Hey… you there! You a Reb?"

Looking around me for a place I could run and hide, I called back. "Naw, sir, Just a farmer," I lied; working my thumb against my finger.

Scrutinizing me, he asked again, "You sure? Move over here away from that wagon so I can take a look at you, boy."

I gave him my best smile, nervous as I was. I slid from the wagon, leaving my guns stowed under the seat and moved down to the river bank. "Yessum… pretty sure."

He motioned me to the shoreline. The man with the

bucket didn't know if he should move or not. He stood, bucket in his hand, until the officer said something to him. I couldn't hear what he said, but the young man jerked a quick salute and ran back inside.

He pointed to a wooden ramp connecting the boat to land. I nodded, meaning I saw it and I moved toward the plank. He walked the deck, keeping pace with me to the plank. He stopped and studied me before joining me on the river bank.

He looked me over like someone would a good horse or animal at an auction. He walked completely around me, looking up and down. Then he stood back, rubbing his chin, and said more to himself than me, "Well, you sure don't look like a Rebel, son. Have you had breakfast yet?"

Totally surprised by what he said, I stood silent not knowing what to say. Was he asking to eat with me? I had not eaten, and I didn't know if I wanted to with these people. I didn't have enough food to feed many of them, if that was what he meant.

The man put his hand on my shoulder and led me toward the plank. That gunboat looked awfully intimidating up close like that. Was he going to make me get on that iron thing he came out of? Hell, if I got on it, they might not let me off.

He asked again, "Sir, have you eaten today?"

I shook my head. "Naw, sir, I haven't."

He waved for me to follow him up the wooden plank that bridged the boat to the land. I stopped at the edge, leery of the flimsy board and what might be waiting for me beyond this point. He turned, seeing I had stopped and waved for me to follow. "Come on over, son. There's plenty for you to eat."

I ran my hand through my hair to untangle the mess and reluctantly made my way across the plank. The board sagged, which worried me as I walked. I did make it to the other side without it giving out on me.

Once onboard, the metal flooring felt strange. My footsteps gave an odd sound as I walked across the deck. The officer motioned me to follow him through an open doorway. With my left thumb working my index finger, I gave him a nervous smile and nodded. Ducking so I would not hit it on the low overhead threshold, I reluctantly walked into the darkness beyond.

It was dark, stuffy, hot, and noisy. There was also an overwhelming smell of body odor and some kind of machine oil. I didn't like it one bit. I really wanted out of there and tried to turn and leave.

The officer grabbed my arm, stopping me.

He laughed and slapped me on the back. I was already missing the fresh air and open space outside. He said, "I know... It's a wee bit cramped in here at first. You'll get used to it."

Wee bit? He had to be joshing. It was more like *a lot* cramped and I wondered what he meant by 'me getting used to it.' How long were they gonna keep me here? I found it hard to breathe closed in the way it was. Nervously, I looked around in the darkness. Every loud bang or noise made me jump and want to run as far away as I could.

As my eyes adjusted to the gloom, I saw men moving around. Steam spewed from overhead pipes snaked everywhere. A few lanterns hung from the ceiling gave some light to the darkness, but not much.

The officer came up behind me and slapped me on my back making me jump. "I know... you feel trapped, right?"

I nodded as he passed me, now leading the way. I followed as close as I could, afraid I would get lost. He led through another set of doors into a well lit room where chairs sat around a long table. The smell of coffee and eggs struck me like a sack of grain and my stomach screamed. I looked around the large, bright room. I felt like this was more to my liking, but I still felt trapped.

Four men seated at the table, smoking cigars, looked curiously at me when we walked in. They smiled then looked to the officer, wondering where I came from. The man I was following leaned over and whispered to the men. They smiled and nodded in understanding and then went back talking amongst themselves.

My stomach growled once more announcing my entrance. They had just poured coffee and was about to serve breakfast. My guide motioned for me to sit at the head of the table. As soon as I was seated, he called to a colored steward standing nearby, "Michel... one more for breakfast."

The steward snapped to attention and said, "Yes, sir," then rushed off. He came back shortly and set a plate and hot steaming coffee in front of me. "How do you want your eggs cooked, sir?"

I looked at the Negro like he was speaking a strange language. He repeated, "Sir, how do you want your eggs cooked?"

I snuck a peek to see how everyone else's eggs were cooked. No one else had any eggs yet. I had no idea you could fix them any way but one. I had always eaten eggs the same way my whole life. Finally, I looked up at the steward, smiled and lifted both my hands in an '*I don't know*' gesture. "Surprise me."

He gave me a strange smile, as if I'd thrown him a challenge. He nodded and left the room. One of the officers leaned toward me. "Michel was a chef in his own restaurant back in New York before the war. The man's an excellent cook in his own right. We are so lucky to have him."

Since I had no idea what a *chef* was or did, I nodded in agreement. I watched as a plate of biscuits made its way around the table.

Picking two hot biscuits from the plate and holding one in each hand, I looked at the doorway as several more dishes of food arrived along with another enormous pot of steaming coffee.

I tried to look unimpressed by all the fixings on the table before me, but my stomach gave me away. With everyone silent, my stomach gave a loud scream making everyone at the table stare at me. My mouth was watering so badly, I had to keep swallowing to keep it from running down my face like an invalid. So much food. I thought back to Vicksburg and what we had to eat on those last days there. Lordy... the things we ate to stay alive. None of these men looked like they had missed any meals.

I still held onto the two biscuits. There was a plate in front of me but I was afraid if I put them down they would disappear. The colored sailor who they called Mickey, Michael, Michel or something walked into the room and took my plate away. My eyes followed him and my plate as both disappeared into the next room. I was glad I didn't put my biscuits on that plate. I would have never seen them again.

So I sat and waited with the two biscuits in my hands. I didn't take a bite out of either as hungry as I was. I didn't want to be rude and begin eating before the rest of the men at the table. I would wait until the others got their food.

The sailor serving the hot coffee walked by with the large

pot and asked if I wanted more coffee. I shook my head and he put the pot on the table and picked up a creamer, motioning again. I placed my hand with the biscuit over my coffee and said, "No, thanks... this is fine." He gave me a funny look and smiled at the other men at the table and left me alone. He worked his way around the table serving the others.

Michel came into the room and placed a colorful plate with a blue picture of their boat printed in the center in front of me. He then turned without a word and disappeared through the door again. I followed him with my eyes; still holding onto my buns.

Tired of holding them, I sat my biscuits on the plate and picked up the coffee and took a sip. Coffee was good. I picked up one of the biscuits on my plate and took a nibble. My eyebrows rose in surprise. It was very good. I don't think I had ever tasted one better.

About the time I finished one biscuit, Michel came into the room, carrying a small skillet. The handle of the skillet was wrapped in a dishtowel and I heard grease sizzling. He slid something onto my plate. It looked like eggs, and yet it didn't. I sat my biscuit next to the strange concoction.

I picked up a fork and poked it. I didn't know what to think of that thing on my plate. I had never seen eggs cooked like that before. I looked up and found Michel and everyone else at the table watching me in silence. It was quiet in the room, only the pulsation of the engine making noise. I was beginning to feel uncomfortable with everyone staring at me.

Then I began to get very nervous thinking of the stories I heard at Vicksburg from other soldiers who had experiences with the Yankees. Some talked about their cruelty to us southerners. My left thumb slowly began to rub against my finger, making me more nervous than ever.

My imagination ran wild. Had they brought me onboard to poison me, torture me, or just to watch me die? Was I their entertainment for the day... to watch me choke and suffer while they laughed in front of me?

The men at the table sat quietly watching me as I sat there with the plate of eggs. One of the officers said, "He makes the best omelet you will ever have in two lifetimes. I promise you. Go on. Try it. It is made with eggs, onion, mushrooms, and tomatoes. I think you will like it."

I gave him an unsure smile and looked at the object on my plate as if it was a snake. I glanced around the room at all those men sitting around the table looking at me; prodding me on. Watching and waiting. My thumb moved faster and faster against my index finger next to my plate.

I tried to smile, to show I was not scared. Sweat beaded on my eyebrow. My appetite vanished and my mouth went dry as I cut off a piece of the egg. With almost trembling fingers I lifted my fork with the egg attached and sniffed it. Smelled like eggs.

It seemed everyone in the room leaned forward at the same time, anticipating my first bite. Reluctantly, with regret all over my face, I closed my eyes and slowly placed the fork into my mouth, expecting it to be bitter or however poison tasted.

The flavor of the food slammed against my taste buds making my mouth to salivate and my stomach rejoice. *This... this was good, I mean really good.*

I opened my eyes and looked at everyone staring back at me smiling, waiting for me to give my praise. I slowly chewed my food and realized I was not dying after all. I swallowed.

Several of the men around the table started talking at once. One fellow half stood, leaning towards me and asked, "Well? What did you think?"

I looked at Michel who had moved away from the table but was still watching me, waiting to see if I approved of the dish. I slowly nodded and gave a small smile and simply said, "It's good... very good. I ain't never ate anything like that before- - never."

This seemed to please everyone for they all slapped the table with their forks, smiling. Some laughed out loud and everyone began to pass around the other dishes and started eating.

After we had finished, cigars were passed around. Everyone smoked and made small talk until a knock came at the door. A seaman came in, saluted and gave his morning report to the man sitting at the opposite end of the table from me. When the sailor was finished, he saluted again and left.

The man at the foot of the table leaned back in his chair and let out a long stream of smoke through his mouth. Then sitting forward, looking at his cigar he asked me, "Do you own any slaves, sir?"

After a good meal I was served along with the coffee and cigar, I was starting to take a liking to my new friends around the table until the subject of slavery came up. The room suddenly quieted and all eyes turned toward me; my left hand holding the cigar over an empty saucer froze.

What kind of question was that to ask a man? With everyone sitting at the table; looking and waiting for me to answer. "Naw sir... I ain't never had any use for slaves. If I can't do the work myself, then it don't get done."

He took his cigar out of his mouth with his right hand and jabbed it towards me; slapping the table top with his other hand. "Exactly! Smart man there. I agree." He jabbed the cigar back into his mouth and leaned back, observing me, looking down his cigar at me. "Do you know of many people living near you who do own slaves?"

I was starting to dislike the man at the end of the table. I didn't like the questions he was asking or the way he asked them. My thumb on my right hand slowly began to move against its index finger again. To keep it still, I squeezed my thumb against my finger. I said, "No. No, I don't. I'm just a poor farmer with a small tract of land. I grow just enough to take care of myself." I didn't mention anything about my wife or child. I didn't think it was any of his business, anyway.

Puzzled, he leaned forward in his chair, taking another drag of his cigar and letting out the smoke. "Really? I thought most everyone down here in the South owned slaves."

I looked him in the eye and said, "Well... you thought wrong, mister. Very few people around these parts have slaves."

Fingering the ashes off his cigar onto a small plate, he smiled as he looked at his other officers. "Well then, sir, what the devil are you people fighting this war for in the first place... if not for the slaves?"

With my thumb rubbing hard against my finger I leaned back in my chair and shrugged. "I don't know. Could be because you are down here."

He gave me the strangest look. Everyone at the table froze and everything got eerily quiet except for the noise from the engines' boilers. All of a sudden, he slapped the tabletop again. This time hard enough to bounce the small plate he was using as an ashtrays, spilling its contents and knocking over his coffee mug on the table and began to laugh loudly. After a few uncomfortable seconds the other officers at the table joined in. Everyone was laughing but me. I didn't see anything funny in what I had said.

After they were finished laughing, he stood, wiping his eyes. He thanked me for coming and entertaining them. I thanked him for the meal and cigar. The same officer, who invited me in, showed me the way out of the belly of that monster I had been trapped in.

I stepped into the light of summer, blinking my eyes to adjust and smelled the fresh air. I missed that, being inside the metal monster. The morning fog had lifted and the sky was clear. I headed for the board that led to land as fast as I could without looking like I was running for my life. Then Michel stepped out of door and called for me to stop.

I froze and turned, wondering if they were going to keep me from leaving. He gave me a shy smile and walked over to where I stood. He handed me a large cloth bag. I took it and looked inside. It was full of all kinds of food stuff and on top was a tight roll of a dozen cigars. I closed the bag and smiled back at him.

"Thank yee, sir... Thank yee very much. I will put this to good use." I tipped my hat to him. He smiled again, turned and disappeared into the belly of that beast.

Once I was back on dry land, I finished hitching my team to the wagon and left out of there leaving the river and Yankee gunboat behind. I turned my wagon north toward Shreveport.

Chapter Fifteen

THE HEAVILY FORESTED land I had been traveling through thinned to open farmland with patches of cypress swamps dotted here and there. After living most of my life in the wooded lands of central Louisiana, I wasn't use to the spaciousness. I felt kinda exposed... naked.

The farms in this part of the state had not been worked in a while. I figured all the able bodied men who lived in this part were off fighting the Yankees. As I slowly rode along the dusty road, I saw pastures and fields overgrown with shrubs, brambles, and tall weeds. There will be hard work ahead of them when they come back to their homes. That is if they come back and if they are still whole men. At Vicksburg I had seen my share of empty sleeves and pants legs where arms and legs should have been.

The road I had been traveling joined up with another; a better road that aimed a more northwesterly direction. It still followed the Cane River on its left and I figured it would eventually join back up with the Red. This new road had more traffic than any of the others.

Until now, I thought I was the only person traveling these roads. Some of the wagons moving in my direction looked similar to mine. That made it so much easier to blend in with the others. Now I no longer stood out alone.

I traveled the next seventy miles in two days, all the way to a small settlement across the river from Shreveport. When I got to the town on the east side of the river, I had to cross a bridge to get to the larger town. The river was crowded with all kinds of paddle wheel boats and Yankee gunboats parked along the shoreline on both sides of the river.

The town itself was infested with Yankee soldiers, sailors, and twenty-four hours a day saloons. The streets were packed of troops moving in and out. I wasn't about to stop anywhere within the city limits. I would push all the way through in order to get to the other side and find the road that would lead me north toward the Oklahoma territory.

I pulled my hat low on my head and kept my eyes on Sally's swishing tail as I moved my wagon along the streets of town. The less anyone noticed me, the better.

Nervous, I searched with my eyes for any signs of trouble. Drunken soldiers and sailors stumbled everywhere. I cut my eyes to the wooden sidewalk where soldiers staggered in a boozed stupor terrorizing the good citizens that crossed their path.

I noticed there were no women on the street where the drunken Yankee soldiers were causing trouble. Only a few old men and disabled veterans dressed in gray uniforms clustered in small pockets, watching the Yankees overrun their town with hatred in their eyes. All the veterans were missing either an arm or a leg. I felt the inquisitive eyes of those in gray as they stopped what they were doing and stared at me as I rode by.

A horde of young men in blue crowded the street ahead of me, laughing and talking loudly, and making wagons stop and wait for them get out of the way before proceeding down the street.

One drunken Yankee walked along side my wagon, following me down the street. "Say, Johnny Reb! Where are you going, *boy?*" The word *boy* was slurred in an unfriendly way. I ignored him and kept my wagon moving. Irritated, my thumb began to rub against my finger in aggravation. I would've loved to have gotten down and taught this Yankee some southern manners, but I didn't want to draw attention to myself.

The man was insistent. He kept following, calling out insults to get my goat. "Why are you not out fighting like all the rest of your people... *boy?*" He was really starting to irritate me-- badly. My thumb began working hard against my finger and the back of my neck was hot from aggravation, but I said nothing; naw sir, not a word.

The wagon in front of me stopped, causing me to halt. Waiting, I was trapped with this fool. He put one hand on the front wheel next to me and called up more forcefully, "Hey! I'm talking to you. You too good to fight for your slaves... *boy*, or are you some kind of coward. Yeah-- I bet that's it. You're a no good, low down coward, aren't you, boy?"

That was it. That was all I could take. Yankee or not, nobody called me a coward, not with what I lived through at Vicksburg. I took my reins and tied them to the brake lever and turned my head toward him, giving him a *'don't fuck with me'* look. The same look I use to get from my Sergeants when they didn't want to be bothered or I said something they thought was dumb. The Yankee stared into my eyes and hatred spread over his face.

A voice from the sidewalk hollered, "Hey, Yankee boy. Why don't y'all crawl back into that hole y'all crawled out of and keep your fucking mouth shut, Billy Yank?" It was one of the confederate soldiers leaning on a crutch with an empty pants leg hanging where his leg should have been.

The drunken Yankee snapped his head around, glaring red faced at the man. He moved from my wagon and stomped to where the cripple stood. He grabbed the gray uniform and kicked the crutch out from underneath the empty leg and pushed the rebel soldier onto the ground.

I rose off my seat then a friendly face appeared in front of me. He smiled. "Don't bother yourself there, son. You go on about your business. We've got this."

The friendly face in an old gray uniform hobbled to the sidewalk where a group of four gray jackets, each with an empty sleeve were pounding the drunken Yankee senseless with their good fists. When he got to the fight, he balanced himself on his good leg, and using his crutch as a club, connected to the back of the blue coat's head with a loud crack. The crutch broke, parts flying in different directions. And just like that, the fight was over.

The Yankee lay motionless on the ground, his face in the dust and arms stretched out on both sides. The small group of crippled veterans stood smiling and laughing as they helped each other dust off their old uniforms. Then as quick as a rabbit, the small group disappeared down the street, whistling Dixie. Two of the veterans hooked their good arm around the man who broke his crutch and helped him vanish from sight.

I shook my head and laughed. I guess even a debilitated southerner can whip a Yankee if he wanted. I grabbed my reins off of the brake lever and flicked them. My wagon continued on down the street. I had no other problem getting out of Shreveport. No one else tried to stop me or ask me any questions.

Chapter Sixteen

TWO DAYS LATER I arrived where the Red River turned west. I followed it for another day, looking for a good spot to cross. I found a place that squeezed down to a wide, shallow stream. The blood color of the river clued me in on why it was called Red River. It wasn't that color in Shreveport or anywhere south of that.

I found a sandy patch of land that would hold the wagon, and I proceeded to cross the river into the Indian Territory. I reached down and brought the Henry rifle out from beneath the seat and stood it upright against my leg. I didn't know what to expect from the people here once I crossed. My pistol I kept in its holster right next to me on the wooden bench.

The trees around me were beginning to change colors to red, yellow, and brown. The wind was gentle out of the northwest instead of the southwest. There were no roads in this part of the country, so I had to dodge shrubs and trees, making my own way, looking for a hill or high place.

I found a bald hill not too far from the river and took the wagon up the incline. I stopped at the top and stood, looking around to see what I could see. I spotted a plume of smoke, maybe five miles to the east.

I hoped the people there were the friendly sort. I wasn't looking for trouble and prayed trouble would not find me. I turned the wagon in that direction and flicked the reins. Maybe I would get lucky and find someone who might know the whereabouts of my wife and daughter.

Late that afternoon, as the sun was sinking below the tree line, I came upon a small settlement of wood and mud huts.

The Indians living there stopped what they were doing and stared at me like I was a ghost or some kind of spirit. Maybe it was because I was white and I didn't belong in their neck of the woods.

Whatever the reason, I tried to ask where I could find my wife and child. The folks acted as if I wasn't there and walked off, ignoring me. The ones who acknowledged me only spoke Indian, which I didn't understand.

Frustrated, I moved on, leaving the small hamlet behind. Maneuvering through the trees where there were no roads was not easy with the wagon. Many times I had to backtrack to find a way around. Darkness was closing in, and I needed to find a place to camp. I figured I would have to stay up all night and keep watch. I didn't know if they still took scalps and I didn't want to find out.

As I was looking for a place to stop, I came across an old cabin set in a small clearing. I pulled my wagon to a stop in front. Sitting in an old chair on the porch was an ancient Indian, hair like snow, wearing a frock coat and an old top hat with a feather tucked into the hatband. He raised one arm in a salute and said something in his language. I could see he was unarmed, so I left my weapons alone.

I didn't think he spoke my language, but I figured I would give it a try anyway. I took my hat off and asked as friendly as I could, "Sir, do you know of any Indian women who came into this territory in the last year or so with a baby girl?"

The old man, eyes shining brightly, got up and walked to the edge of the porch. Holding onto one of the post, he gave me a toothless smile and said, "You looking for a young Cherokee woman of us humans, carrying a white girl child?"

Surprised and relieved, I said, "Yes, sir, I am. I need to find her. She is my wife and her name is Lucinda."

Still looking up at me with old watery eyes, he studied my face. He stepped off the porch and came closer to the wagon, placing both hands on the front wheel. "Are you the one she calls Riley?"

Surprised, I about fell out of my seat. "Yes, I am. Do you know where I can find her, old man?"

He gave me a sly smile. "You got tobacco, Riley?"

Smiling back, I nodded. "Yes'em I do, old man."

I reached underneath my seat and retrieved my bag of supplies hidden there. I took two cigars out and gave the old man one. With a big smile on his face he motioned for me to hurry and give him a light. I picked a match from my pocket and raked it across the side of the wagon wheel.

My hands cupping the flame he leaned in, sucking on the roll. He got his end lit and moved back. Taking a deep draw of smoke into his lungs, he smiled and closed his eyes. A look of pure joy enlightened his wrinkled face as he slowly let the smoke drift out of his mouth, savoring the aroma. "Best thing you white men stole from us; even better than corn."

With the remainder of the flame from the match, I quickly lit my cigar. I ignored his remark as we stood and smoked a few more minutes. Then I asked him again. "All right, you've had your cigar. Now, where can I find my wife, Lucinda?"

He gave me shy smile. He reminded me of a horse trader with an old nag for sale--dodging my question. "This cigar sure would go good with whiskey or cup of coffee. Got any coffee or whiskey to go with this cigar, Riley? It sure would taste good right about now."

I grunted. "Since when did Injuns take up drinking coffee or whiskey?"

He gave me a hurt look as though I had cut him to the quick. "We gave you white people everything we had. We gave you our food, and taught you how to grow corn and tobacco. You would've thought that'd been enough. But no-- You come back and take our lands. Now, we have nothing left to give you white people; nothing.

"We have vices too, you know. I like a little nip of whiskey now and then, and I also like coffee and besides," he gave me that shy smile again, "your wife said you might come this way and if you did, you would give me some tobacco and maybe coffee. So, Riley, I will ask you again, do you have coffee?"

I didn't know how much he would try to get out of me before he told me where I could find Lucinda so I gave him my best intimidating look. It didn't deter him a bit. He held his ground, smoking his cigar and looking at me with those all-knowing eyes.

Finally, tired of waiting, I threw my hands up in defeat, "Okay-- all right. You win." Then pointing my cigar at him, I said. "Ya know-- you sir, are an Injun thief."

I reached under the wagon's seat and retrieved the sack I got from the Yankee gunboat. With my back to him, I heard him say, "I know, but as you white men say, it takes one to know one."

I turned around with the sack in my hand, mad for having to pay for the information of the whereabouts of my family. Realization hit me of what this old man had, which was next to nothing. If the roles had been reversed, I figured I would have tried to get as much out of him, myself. Looking at him and knowing he had me over a barrel, I began to laugh. After a moment, he joined in and we stood next to the wagon, laughing.

The old man rubbed his eyes now and then as he led the way to his small cabin. On the porch, I dusted off my boots and followed him inside. He fetched the coffeepot and filled it with water. I wrapped the dark beans in my handkerchief and looked around for something to pound with. The old man grabbed a club and took the wrapped beans. He placed it on the one table and proceeded to beat the bundle, crushing the beans. After a moment he dumped the contents of the handkerchief into the pot and sat it on the fire.

When the coffee started to boil, the timeworn Indian removed the pot and sat it on the table to cool. Spying a couple of tin cups on a narrow shelf, he walked over to retrieve them. I took the cups and blew away any dust or cobwebs inside. As I poured the black liquid, I explained I didn't have any liquor. "Lucinda doesn't like when I drink, so I don't very often."

The old Indian nodded in understanding.

We took our coffee and went out on the front porch where it was not so stuffy. He sat back in his chair and introduced himself as Salali; just Salali, no last name.

"She is not far from here. Tomorrow we will travel there together. We should rest and get an early start. I am not in the mood to travel tonight, and a white man traveling alone on Indian land is asking for trouble. It is not safe. We will stay here tonight. Tomorrow will be better, you will see, Riley."

Seeing that I wasn't getting him to show me where my wife and child was, I said, "That'll be fine, tomorrow then. By the way, what kind of name is Salali?"

Looking straight ahead into the woods beyond his cabin,

he blew on his coffee and replied stone faced, "Squirrel... It means squirrel."

I couldn't help but smile over my coffee cup. "Squirrel." I repeated softly to myself.

Daring me to make fun of his name, he said, "I think you got it."

Trying hard to not smile or burst out laughing at the translation of his name, I blew on my own coffee "Yup, I got it."

After dark, the crickets began their songs, filling the night air with their racket. The old man got up and walked inside his cabin leaving me on the porch. A couple of minutes later, he came back carrying four feathers and walked over to my tethered mule and horse. I watched as he tied two feathers to the mule behind his ears on his mane and then moved to my horse.

Curious, I called over to him, "Hey... what ya doing over there, old man? What are the feathers far?"

Turning and looking around at the trees and bushes that bordered his yard, he said calmly, "I would like these animals to be here when we get ready to leave in the morning. Horses without feathers belong to no one... but horses that have feathers do. Right now, there are probably six pairs of eyes watching us, wondering why a white man is here."

My left thumb automatically began to work my index finger as I looked nervously around at the brush and trees. I suddenly felt naked without my Griswold on my hip. The Henry and handgun were both lying at the bottom of the front seat wagon well. If there were Indians out there, I would not make it to the wagon in time.

Seeing my nervousness, Salali gave a short laugh. "My people are a curious breed. They wonder about many things. As long as they see you are with me, you will be fine, Riley. Do not worry, white man. I will protect you." He picked up my rifle and handgun and walked back to the cabin.

That last statement broke the spell, and I began to laugh uneasily looking around. I patted the old Indian on his back as he walked past into the cabin. To think this old Indian believed he would protect me if there were any trouble.

He too was laughing as we entered the cabin. I passed through the threshold last, but stopped and took one more look around; wondering what was beyond the clearing.

The old man, seeing me, came back to the door and stuck his head out. Satisfied everything was as it should be, he nodded, shut the door and barred it. He turned back to me and winked. "We will be just fine. There will not be any trouble this night."

We stayed up a spell, sitting and talking by the fireplace until the old man went to bed. I made myself comfortable in one corner. Propping myself up in a sitting position, my blanket draped over my shoulders, I laid the Henry and my handgun nearby.

I don't know why, but I felt I would not need them this night. I felt like I believe the old man and everything was going to be all right. Tomorrow, I would see my wife and baby girl. Tomorrow would be a new beginning.

Chapter Seventeen

LOST IN MY dreams, I suddenly jerked awake, quickly reaching for the Henry rifle; another nightmare. I hated dreaming about Vicksburg. I wiped the night sweat from my face and looked around, trying to remember where I was. Based on the light coming through the cabin windows, morning had come.

Along with the light, old Salali was up and stirring a pot of stew over the fire. The smell coming from that pot was terrible, like something had died... weeks ago. Last night's supper was not to my likings, either, and it looked like breakfast would be the same. The man could not cook. I don't know how he lived so long.

Standing next to the fireplace with his wooden spoon in hand, he turned his head toward me. "If I was a young buck and wanted to make a name for myself, I would be wearing your hair on my belt right about now." He gave me a toothless smile.

I yawned, stretched and rubbed the sleep from my eyes as I muttered back, "If you were a young buck, I would have shot you when I drove up last night."

Softly speaking the old man slowly shook his head side to side, leaning over his pot of stew. "Huh! You would have never seen me coming."

I stood and said softly to myself as I walked over to the fire to warm my hands, "You're probably right."

After eating awful tasting stew, which, by the way, he seemed to enjoy, we walked outside and found the team where we left them the night before. They had not disappeared as I had feared.

I hitched the animals to the wagon, and laid my rifle butt

into the well under the seat, resting the barrel against the brake lever where it would be handy. I buckled my Griswold snug to my hip and climbed onto the wagon.

Salali climbed aboard and sat next to me on the bench. I looked at him calmly staring in front of us with that ridiculous looking hat he had on yesterday perched atop his skull. Shaking my head I turned my attention to the animals, giving a flick of the reins.

Salali, without turning his head, said, "What... you don't like my hat?"

I glanced at it one more time. "It looks ridiculous."

Giving me a hurt look, he said, "I'll have you to know one of your great white fathers in Washington gave me this hat. He said it made me look so civilized I should always wear it."

Now watching the trail ahead, I said, "If it was Washington, then it wasn't one of my great white fathers."

Still looking straight ahead of us he nodded his old head, "Oh, yes... I forgot. You are one of the gray coats. You white men all look alike to me; blue coat, gray coat-- all the same to me."

I gave him a sideways look, studying his face. He was right. If I looked closely enough I would find that the southern government was screwing the Indians as much as the Union government. Nothing changed... nothing will. The men in power, in either government, will do whatever it took to keep the power in their grubby little hands and line their pockets with gold. It's like what my friend Tatum told me, "I have never met a poor politician."

I could see that someday, even this last reservation would be taken from the Indians, and somewhere in the government, someone would come out wealthy for their efforts.

The rest of the morning we spoke very little, keeping our thoughts to ourselves. A little after the sun was directly overhead, we came upon a clearing where a log structure stood. This, Salali told me, was the trading post.

I guided the wagon towards the front of the lone log building with a sign hanging above its door. I had no idea what the sign said and neither did Salali. The trading post had a sod roof and a large mud fireplace at one end of the building. The place looked to be fairly clean from the outside. A few Indians came out of the store as we made our way over, giving us questionable looks.

Salali pointed to the trading post door and said, "This is the place, Riley. We will find your Lucinda here."

I pulled the wagon to the front and stopped. My heart pounded and my thumb rubbed my finger raw. It had been so long since I last saw her. I hoped she didn't think I'd changed that much over the last year or so. There was so much going through my mind as I started to climb down.

Salali stopped me by touching my shoulder. "Let me go in and see if she is here."

Eager to see Lucinda again I shrugged his hand off of my shoulder and continued to dismount the wagon.

Salali stopped me again by grabbing my shoulder harder. "Riley, I'll go. You wait here."

I looked back at him smiling and said, "I'll go with you."

Salali bark at me, "No, this is Indian business, not white man's business. You stay here and guard the animals."

Hurt and angry, I kept my mouth tightly closed and nodded. We got down and Salali went inside. I waited by the wagon watching the door he entered, expecting my wife to come running out anytime now and into my arms.

A few minutes later, he reappeared alone but with a smile on his face. My heart jumped and caught in my throat. I moved forward to meet him, but he held up a hand stopping me.

When he got close, he looked around him to make sure no one was listening or watching. Speaking in a low voice, he said, "She is not here at the moment, she went to get water and should be back in a few minutes. We will wait for her here."

I was tired of waiting, I looked around asking, "Where's the well?"

Salali looked first towards the trading post and then motioned with his head. "Around back. But she..."

I didn't wait for him to finish. I took off toward the back of the trading post.

Salali caught up to me before I had gone too far. "If you will wait, she will be back in a moment. The owner of the trading post does not like when other white men come here unless they have silver or gold."

I didn't stop to talk. "Tired of waiting. I've waited long enough."

107

As I turned the corner, I froze. Salali, still trying to keep up with my long strides, ran into my back. A woman with a light colored top, dark skirt, and braided black hair stood with her back to me, pulling on a rope, drawing up water.

I lost my voice as I stared at the woman at the well. My legs rooted into the ground. I couldn't move. Trying to control my emotions, my eyes filled with tears. I wiped them away, trying to clear my vision.

As soon as the bucket reached the top, she grabbed it. Sloshing water over the side, she sat it on a ledge. I remained frozen where I stood, Salali now standing by my side, both of us watching her.

Chapter Eighteen

AS I WATCHED her standing by the well with the child at her feet, breath caught in my throat. I tried to call out but no sound came out of my mouth. I tried to move but my legs would not obey. Unable to move, unable to speak, I just stood there, waiting for her to finish with the bucket and turn. When she did, she froze also, dropping the bucket and spilling the water.

Her hand went to her mouth, her eyes large with surprise as she stared back at me. Finding my voice, I called to her hoarsely, "Lucinda."

Her eyes filled with tears as she shook her head unable to believe I was there. I ripped my feet from their roots and walking stiffly, I lumbered to her. Grabbing her possessively to me, I hugged her tightly to my body, lifting her up off the ground, spinning her around and around. I held her body hungrily against mine not wanting to let her go, savoring the feel of her body pressing hard against mine once more. I forgot all about the infant sitting in the mud next to the empty bucket screaming for her mother.

I eased her to the ground to get a better look at her, still holding her by the waist. Ignoring the child at her feet, she slowly reached up and tenderly traced the scar on my cheek with her finger. I took her hand in mine and placed it to my mouth, kissing it lovingly. She was laughing and crying at the same time.

The noise at my feet finally got my attention and I looked at the infant girl sitting in the mud, screaming her frustration to the world. I couldn't tell if she was upset that she was in the mud or frightened of the stranger towering over her.

I stood there stupid and tongue tied once again, studying the small face, wondering if this was the child I'd been hearing about since I returned. I didn't know what I was expecting. She was so small, sitting there on the ground with her outstretched arms reaching toward her mother.

In answer to the question on my face, Lucinda nodded. "Yes, this is your daughter, Rachel. She was born last April, two months after you left. A few months after that, the blue coats came and said I had to live on the reservation with the others of my kind."

I was about to say how sorry I was that I had left her in such a fix, when from behind me, a man called out, "Hey, you worthless squaw, where's that water I sent you to fetch. I don't pay you to sit around and jibber-jabber with everybody who comes by."

I didn't have time to turn and see who was doing the talking before Lucinda placed her hand over my heart to get my attention. I looked down at the fingers that touched me and then gazed into those eyes. Oh, how I loved and missed those dark beauties. She slowly shook her head, not wanting me to get involved.

From around the side of me, she called out to him, "Sorry, Mr. Atkins, I'll bring it right away."

Angrily, he snapped back, "Well, get your lazy ass moving, woman. I ain't got all day."

My body burned with rage. Nobody was going to talk to my wife as if she were trash to be thrown away. Nobody! My face red with angry, I started to turn once more to confront this sorry excuse for a human. Lucinda grabbed the front of my shirt forcing me to look at her. She pleaded with her eyes to not start any trouble with this man.

I gave in once more, but I told myself, one more word from Mr. Atkins's sorry mouth and we were going to have problems. I stood with my back to the man, trying for Lucinda's sake not to get involved.

Then the man from the trading post took notice of me. He could tell I was not an Indian but yet had no knowledge of who I was. For if he did, he would have kept his pie hole shut. "Hey, mister, you're not an Injun? What are you doing here? You come looking for a squaw? I'll give you a good price on that one there.

You'll have to take the kid, too. I'd hate to break up a pair."

My fists clinched, knuckles turning white. I closed my eyes holding down the rage boiling inside me. I'd heard enough. I couldn't let this insult go. Mr. Atkins was going to pay dearly for his disrespect to my wife.

I slowly shook my head and mouthed the word "sorry" to my wife as I looked down at her. She understood, for she took a step back to give me room to confront the man behind me.

As I turned, I pulled my Griswold from its holster. Cocking the hammer while I pulled the gun from my left side, I extended my right arm looking down the barrel of my pistol at the man.

Salali, surprised by my action, took his hat off and moved far out of the way.

The man seeing my revolver drawn and pointed at him froze. His mouth dropped open, stunned, as his eyebrows rose looking at me from the other end of the barrel. Words failed him as I walked, arm extended, to him and placed the end of the revolver between his eyes.

I smelled urine and glanced at the wet stain that appeared on the front of the man's pants.

It's funny how a certain word or smell can bring up remembrances. My mind flooded with memories of Vicksburg. Memories of men fighting on both sides like rabid animals. In an instant I was reliving the explosions, the bullets flying, men screaming and dying all around me. Desperate men, both blue and gray, fighting when they reached the top of our hill and we left our trenches to engage them using whatever we could lay our hands on to kill the other.

I remembered using a rock to bash an enemy soldier's brains on the floor of our gun pit. Another memory was of a soldier, wild and out of his mind, picking up a stick and stabbing his dead enemy in the face over and over again. It looked like a bloody piece of raw meat. Many a brave man pissed their pants those days during the siege. The smell brought all those horrible images flooding into my head.

When I came to my senses, I was standing over the shaking Mr. Atkins who had crumbled onto his knees. Tears streamed down his cheeks. My face was wet with cold sweat, and I had been biting down so hard on my teeth, I tasted blood.

I'd been holding my breath the whole time standing over this fool who insulted my wife. With my pistol pressed hard against his forehead, I gasped for air, trying to get my breathing under control. I realized that I had almost murdered this idiot for no reason other than he offended someone I loved.

I tasted bile in the back of my throat, and thought I was going to throw-up. I felt so sick to my stomach. My mind had been in a fog, reliving Vicksburg. Now, back in control, I relaxed my shaking hand and lowered my gun. The barrel of the Griswold left a perfect indentation of a red circle on Mr. Atkins's forehead.

I narrowed my eyes and looked down at the quivering, sobbing fool kneeling at my feet. He cowered on the ground with his arms folded over his head, weeping uncontrollably, trying to hide his humiliation.

Shamed that I had almost shot an unarmed man over the way he had talked to my wife unsettled me. The hand holding the gun shook. I slowly lowered my weapon and growled at him, "Hey... you almost bought yourself a plot of ground in Hell there. You can count yourself very lucky because I came awfully close to sending your worthless ass there. If I was you, I'd start watching what I say around ladies."

The man said nothing, just whimpered. I took my Griswold and eased the hammer down and slipped the revolver into its holster. Salali breathed a sigh of relief. "I think Mr. Atkins, here, needs to apologize to Mrs. Hillman there."

The man slowly lifted his head and glared at Salali with hatred. The old Indian stood his ground like a rock, his old eyes steady. The owner of the trading post could see his days of lording over these people had come to an end after letting them see him humiliated this way. "I'll be damned if I'll say that to a damn Injun."

I pulled my revolver out again, cocking the hammer back before it left its holster. I said loudly to him between clenched teeth, "Then prepare to meet your maker... shit head."

The man ducked, holding his arms out towards me, whining, "No, no, please. I'm sorry, mister. Don't, I'm sorry."

I said, "Don't tell me. Tell her, you fool." I pointed with my other arm to my wife.

Lucinda stood by the well watching the goings on, holding

Rachel protectively in her arms. She tried to get my attention to stop me. Calling to me, "Riley... Don't do this. He's not worth it. Don't lower yourself to his ways, please."

Mr. Atkins, cowering at my feet, glanced at her and mumbled under his breath, "I'm sorry."

Exasperated by dealing with this fool, I looked up to the heavens and said mocking him, "I'm sorry. I'm sorry? Is that the best you can do, you sorry piece of sh..."

"Riley!" she snapped, grabbing my attention. I wasn't use to her raising her voice to me that way. It took me by surprise. I turned facing her and she scolded me. "I have never heard such talk come from you before. Where did you learn such language?"

Almost in a whisper I said, "I'm sorry. I guess living with soldiers; you pick up some bad habits. You learn a lot by living with them day in and day out."

I turned back to the man still on his knees. I was tired of dealing with him. "Sir, if you know what's best for you, you had better beg this woman's forgiveness right this minute. I suggest you put your heart into it, too, because I'm finished talking to you. You either make your peace with her or you can make your peace with your god." I turned the Griswold toward his face and waited.

The man from the trading post leaned forward on his knees, reaching out to Lucinda. Tears ran freely down his face as he begged for her forgiveness. When it was done, Lucinda walked over carrying Rachel in her arms and said, looking down at him, "I forgive you, Mr. Atkins, I truly do."

I eased the hammer down on the Griswold again and said in a hushed voice, "That wasn't so hard, was it?" I put the pistol in its holster and motioned for Salali and Lucinda to go to the wagon. We were through here. I didn't want to stay any longer than needed.

I left the government man on his knees in the dirt behind the trading post and quickly fell in step next to her, watching the expression on her face as she kept her eyes straight ahead. She was still upset with me, so neither of us spoke until we reached the wagon.

When we arrived at the wagon, I took the baby, who was not happy leaving her mother's arms. She lifted her skirt to put one small foot on one of the spokes of the wheel. With one arm using the brake handle as a crutch she lifted onto the wagon and settled herself on the wooden bench.

Holding my daughter while she got settled, I reached up and handed Rachel to her. Lucinda handed her over to Salali next to her. I climbed aboard and took the reins in my hands. "Is there anywhere we need to stop first or anything we need to pick up before we head for home?"

Looking straight ahead, she said composed, "There is nothing I need here." That was all she said until we reached Salali's cabin.

The next morning, she was talking to me as though nothing had happen the day before. The incident from yesterday was now behind us, but not forgotten. She had gotten up early and was in heated conversation with Salali over a trade. We needed supplies for our journey home. Salali had the provisions we needed. She had found the bag containing my coffee and cigars. She knew he wanted these, and he knew she knew. It didn't matter to him; he wanted all of it, not just some.

I could tell she was getting the better part of the deal by the way the old Indian was dancing around the room, waving his arms and shouting. At one time, he called her a horse thief. She didn't say a word but slammed closed the bag, canceling the trade. Old Salali, exasperated that the trade was off then gave in to her every wish in order to get the tobacco and coffee she would allow him to have.

When the dust settled over the bartering, Salali had gotten his coffee and tobacco. She kept back a few cigars for me and enough coffee for us to drink on our way home.

Salali, on the other hand, gave up a small sack of flour, a slab of bacon, a few potatoes, corn, greens, two blankets and three cans of milk for the baby. I was surprised he traded so much for a few handfuls of coffee beans and a dozen cigars. Salali was still happy over the trade. To get her goat, he said smugly to me, "I was going to give you all those things for your trip, with or without the trade."

Lucinda on hearing him, said, "Me, too," which made old Salali and me laugh. Lucinda didn't see the humor in it. She never saw the humor in anything, she was always too serious. I seldom saw her smile and rarely did she laugh. She was just that way. I knew when she was happy though. She would sing some church song she'd learned some place or other. When I heard her humming or singing quietly to herself-- I knew she was happy.

Chapter Nineteen

WE SPENT ANOTHER night at Salali's before heading to Slagle and home. On our way back through Louisiana, we avoided both Shreveport and Natchitoches altogether.

We arrived in Slagle mid-September. Leaves on the trees were turning colors. The days were still warm, but the nights had been a bit cooler. It made it more comfortable to sleep at nights. Fall had definitely arrived here in Louisiana.

As we pulled up to our homestead, I looked at the overgrown garden across the road from where I worked the last time I was here. That was when the men from the army had come by and taken me with them. That was almost two years ago.

I thought to myself that I needed to start clearing as soon as I could so I could plow come spring. We were going to need a garden by then for sure. It was too late in the season to do any planting now and if we had a bad winter it wouldn't be good for us.

I sat on the wagon and thought long and hard as to what we were going to do. As I looked around at my place, one thing was for sure. We were not to stay here. We were going to need help to survive this winter.

I said to Lucinda, "Hey... you know, if we stay here, we might have a hard time of it. I mean look at this place; we don't have any farm animals left to speak of except for this here one mule and a horse. No garden-- nothing canned or put away to eat this winter. We're not ready to take on this place and make it ours again. Not yet. We don't even know what kind of winter we are gonna have, and then there's the child to think about; little

116

Rachel there. We've got to get some help. That's all there is to it."

Lucinda touched my arm. She wasn't a woman of many words, but when she spoke, I listened. She said simply, "Mr. Moore will help us. He's a good Christian man."

I had already figured that, so I looked at her and nodded. "Hey... my thoughts exactly; I know he'll let us work his place in order to feed us this winter. In the spring, we'll start fresh again. I can bring the mule over and have the ground cleared and ready to plant this spring."

I turned the wagon around and proceeded to the Moore's place. When we pulled up in front, he and his two daughters came out on the porch to welcome us back.

She handed him the child and he carried her to the porch to show the girls. I jumped from the wagon and ran around to the other side and helped Lucinda down. Both girls had made a big fuss over Rachel by the time we stepped onto the porch. The whole family was thrilled to see Lucinda and the young girl again, giving her hugs and a kisses and playing with the baby.

Overwhelmed with the attention, Lucinda almost smiled, but she quickly got her emotions under control before anyone could notice. I could see by the red tint her of cheeks; she was embarrassed by all the attention. And although she did not outwardly show it, I think she was happy to see all of them too.

Happy we got back safely, Mr. Moore motioned us to chairs. "Y'all come on over and sit a spell on the porch with us and have some coffee, y'all hear. Although, I must apologize, it's only chicory. We ain't seen any real coffee around here in ages or at least over a year now. I've gotten kinda partial drinking this here chicory brew. So, now we call it coffee. It's pretty good, once y'all get used to it."

The girls, happy to have company hurried off to get the coffee and readily returned with a tray of cups and a large pot of steaming coffee. I gently blew on the steaming fluids to cool it. It might not have been real coffee, but the chicory sure smelled good.

The old man started a slow rock in his chair. "So, now tell me, how was your trip, Riley? Did you find the place without much trouble?"

I nodded. "Yessum... Not much trouble." Sitting back in my chair with my cup of hot coffee in my hand, I told my story.

The old man sat awestruck, with Rachel on his lap, as I told him about the river monster anchored on the Cane River.

Then I told him about Natchitoches and Shreveport, and how a handful of disabled Confederate veterans took care of a troublemaker. He seemed to get a kick out of that because he had me to tell him that part again.

When we were finished with our coffee, I explained how our homestead had fallen into disrepair and was now overgrown with weeds and brush from months of neglect. I asked if he might help us by letting us work for him until next spring or until we could get a garden started and our house repaired well enough to live in.

He smiled and reached over and patted me on the knee. "Son, I'd like nothing better than to have extra help around this place. It's starting to be a bit too much for me to work, with both my boys fighting in Virginia."

"Well, all right then. Now that is settled, is my room in the barn still available?"

"That's not necessary, son," he said shaking his head. "I would rather you and your wife there, take the boys room. That way you two would have room for the baby to sleep nearby. And besides..." he smiled, sitting back in his rocker, winking at me. "I think the girls there will love helping y'all with that little one there."

Smiling at Mr. Moore, I reached over and patted the old man on the knee. "Thank you, sir, thank you very much. We are so in your debt."

Starting his rocking again he gave me a nod and a smile. "Ah, it's nothing, son... nothing at all. I'm glad to have help around this place."

Chapter Twenty

OVER THE NEXT few months, Lucinda and I worked for the Moore family around their home. When we were not working at their place, we would take the wagon to our own little farm and work there.

There was a lot of work that needed to be attended to at our place in order to get it livable again. The house needed a good cleaning and repairs inside. The field across the lane needed brush removed then the fences needed mending, also.

By the end of October, we were as much ready for the change in the weather as we would be. Now each morning started off with frost on the ground. It was cold nights and warm days. Work at the Moore's farm had pretty much come to a standstill. The leaks had been patched on the roof of the barn and the house.

The corn and hay from his fields had been harvested and tucked inside the barn for the animals. Firewood had been cut and stacked neatly near the house. Yep, most everything was done and waiting for winter to settle in. Unless it was an unusually harsh winter, we would be comfortable and well fed.

Around the second week of January 1864, bad news arrived. A rider from the army came by. I was in the barn feeding the animals when I heard screams. I grabbed my Henry rifle sitting by the door and rushed into the snow, cocking the rifle as I left the barn. I didn't know what kind of trouble I was running into, but I was ready.

I saw the rider leaving by the road. He wore a gray uniform, and tipped his hat to me as he passed, riding slow. He had such a sad look on his face.

Screams came from inside the house. My heart pounded in my chest, not knowing what was going on. As I approached the front porch, I came upon Mr. Moore sitting in his old rocking chair. Tears streamed down his face, shoulders pumping up and down.

Keyed up, still not knowing what had happened, I shouted at him, "Hey... what's going on here? What's happened?"

The old man said nothing, his body shuddering, crying uncontrollably. His mouth moved as though he was trying to speak but nothing came out except a wail of misery.

I quickly looked around searching for any sign of trouble and found none I could see. The door to the house opened and I spun back around with my rifle bringing it up to my shoulder. Lucinda walked out onto the porch and looked at me. She didn't seem to be in trouble so I lowered my rifle and calmed some. "What's happened, Lucinda? Is everyone in the house all right?"

She dabbed under her eyes with a dishcloth as she walked to the edge of the porch where I stood. "It's the boys, Riley..." she said starting to cry again. "His two boys... they're both dead."

I was stunned. I couldn't believe it. I didn't know what to say. "How... where?"

"At a little town in Pennsylvania, six months ago," she said, as she got control of her crying.

I went over to Mr. Moore's chair and knelt beside him. He stopped his rocking when I gently touched his arm. He never looked up. Just sat there with his head down, holding a piece of paper in one hand.

Speaking softly I said, "I am so sorry for the loss of your boys. They will be greatly missed by the ones they left behind. Be proud they gave their lives for their country and their family. I, too, will miss them... very much"

The old man, nodded without speaking. He reached over with his free hand and patted mine and began to slowly rock again.

I stood back and looked at Lucinda. She shook her head, meaning there was nothing I could do, so I trudged to the barn and went back to my chores. Lucinda would have to comfort him and the women inside. The South was losing too many of its sons in this useless war of theirs.

Mr. Moore aged that winter. His gait got slower and he

didn't stand as straight as he used to. The hair on his head seemed to be thinner and whiter than previous years. The life that was in his step, seemed to have left him.

Spring came and went and the war was almost forgotten here in Slagle. I did double work, both at the Moore's place and my own. All the plowing and planting had been taken care of. I rose well before the sun, and came back way after it set, dead tired. All that was left was to wait for God to produce the sunshine, heat, and rain.

One afternoon Lucinda and I returned to the Moore's farm from a visit to our place. I needed a piece of chain to fix my plow and I didn't have any extra there at my place so we left early. It was only mid-afternoon, plenty of daylight left.

Mr. Moore was sitting on his porch, fanning himself and drinking a cup of coffee as we pulled up. He called for us, sit for a spell and have coffee with him. The girls, sitting with him, went back inside and came back shortly with a couple of cups of the chicory coffee that we now drank and loved.

While I was waiting for my coffee to cool, Mr. Moore cleared his throat and became serious, eyeing me over his cup. He took a loud sip of his coffee and said to me. "Riley, son-- are you in any kind of trouble you haven't told me about?"

Cocking my head to one side, I thought for a moment as I took a careful sip of my own coffee. "Naw, sir, I don't believe so. Not that I'm aware of anyhow. Why?"

"Oh, I guess it's nothing, I was just curious... that's all... just curious. There was a rider dressed as a soldier that came through here earlier today. He said he was a looking for you and wanted to know if I knew you and if I did, where would he be able to find you."

Catching my attention, I said, "Oh?"

"Yeah, I told him you were not here at the moment, but I did expect to see you in the next few hours or so. He said he would come back this way in a week or so and see if he could catch up with you then."

"Did he say who he was or what it was about?"

The old man scratched at his whiskers thinking for a moment and then said, "I can't remember his name now. Seems like my memory is not what it used to be. Sorry son."

Lucinda looked at me and asked, "I wonder why a soldier

is looking for you. You didn't desert the army, did ya?"

Hurt to think she would ask me that, I looked around at everyone sitting on the porch. Everyone was looking at me, waiting for my answer. I blew on my coffee and said quietly, "Oh, naw! I ain't in no trouble. At least none that I know of. Hey... I was paroled officially at Vicksburg and I have the papers here to prove it. I have them tucked away right here in my hatband."

I took my hat off and removed some papers from under the hatband to show them. "You see? They told me I could go home if I wanted to."

Satisfied with my answer, Mr. Moore smiled and sipped his coffee, nodding in approval. There was no other reason not to believe me.

Lucinda was not satisfied. She frowned as she held her cup on her lap, looking down at it, thinking. She was afraid they were going to take me away again and she would have to go back to the reservation. This war was destroying us here in the south and there was nothing we could do except ride the tide and hope we landed on our own two feet when it was all over with.

I reached over and patted her hand giving her a reassuring smile. "It will be all right. Hey... I ain't going no place." Giving me a slight smile, she took another sip of her coffee but she was not convinced.

From over my shoulder, I heard the sound of a horse coming down the road. Mr. Moore looked up sharply. He slowly stood and pointed with his cane. "Speak of the devil."

I turned. A young rider dressed in a mud splattered old patched gray uniform with three chevrons on his sleeve rode up to the front of the house and stopped just short of the gate.

Still seated on his horse, he took his old slouch hat off and called over to Mr. Moore who had gotten up and walked to the edge of the porch. "Nice weather we're having, ain't it, sir?" He gave a youthful smile.

Mr. Moore smiled back at the young man and said, "Yep. Gonna get warm later on. Young man, you didn't wait long before coming back this way. Y'all get down off your horse and come on over here and have some of this here poor coffee of ours. It ain't much, but it beats doing without. Come on, boy, there's plenty." He turned to his daughters. "Bring another cup, we have a guest."

The soldier loosely tied his horse to the small fence next to the gate. While walking towards the house he beat his clothing with his hat, knocking off the dust and mud on his uniform.

Hat in hand, he reached the porch and stopped, politely waiting for another invitation before mounting the steps.

Smelling the strong chicory in the coffee brought a smile to his young bearded face, lighting up his blue eyes making them shine brighter. He pushed his hand through his curly blond hair, pushing it back out of his face. He accepted the coffee offered him with both hands; bowing as if it were a great award he was receiving.

The young soldier's eyes lit up when he noticed the young woman serving him his coffee. His cheeks flushed red on his tanned face. The young woman's face also turned a dark shade of crimson as she stared into his eyes.

The two stood motionless for an awkward moment until the girl's father, watching them nearby, cleared his throat. Embarrassed, she turned toward the noise and saw everyone was quietly watching the two of them. Her cheeks burned hot as she made a pitiful attempt at an excuse before rushing back into the house.

The young sergeant's gaze followed her movement until she disappeared behind the door. His eyes lingering long after she had vanished. After a moment a curtain at the window moved just enough to let someone inside the house to peek out. The young man smiled at the opening of the curtain and it snapped back closed.

The young soldier suddenly realized everyone around him was silent and staring at him with questionable looks. His cheek and neckline a bright crimson, he reluctantly abandoned his search for the young lady.

Uncomfortable under the scrutiny of the others on the porch, he quickly took a sip of his hot coffee, trying to think of something intelligent to say. Even the locust singing in the nearby trees, with the racket they made, seemed to be motionless, waiting for what the young man was going to say.

Frantic, to find the right words that could explain his action, the young sergeant took another sip of his hot coffee; his eyes darting left and right, thinking, thinking. He looked up at the sky, "Yep, it looks like it's going to be a nice day. Cool... no sign of rain."

Mr. Moore slowly began to rock his chair, wondering what was going on between this young cavalier and his daughter. His eyes now glued on the young man's face, the old man stopped his rocking once again and leaned forward in his chair. "Yes, it does at that."

The locust in the trees seemed satisfied with the response from the young man. They cranked their noisy songs back up to full volume.

Seeing everyone's eyes on him, he looked at the floorboards of the porch at his feet. I had been in awkward spots like this myself before, not knowing what to say or do. I, too, had a hard time talking to Lucinda when we first met. I broke the silence by speaking up, "Hey... Why don't y'all pull up a chair there and sit for a spell. I see by your uniform you're in the army. What unit y'all with, Sergeant?"

With visible relief the young sergeant cut his eyes from the porch to look at me. The expression was of thankfulness at being saved from an uncomfortable situation. Stepping upon the porch he grabbed a chair and pulled it over to the edge where he had been standing. He turned the chair around and straddled the back.

He looked at me with his easy smile that lit his face. "Currently, I am assigned to part of the old 27th that surrendered at Vicksburg. I presume you, sir, are Private Hillman... Private Wiley Hillman of that same regiment?"

Mr. Moore began to choke and laugh at the same time. In between the coughing and gasping he managed to ask the young sergeant, "Wiley... where did y'all get that name, son?"

Confused the sergeant took out a piece of paper from his breast pocket and looked it over before handing it over to me. "Isn't that your name there on the parole list?"

I looked at the paper and handed it back to him, "I wouldn't know, Sergeant. I never learned to read or write. My name is Riley and I was at Vicksburg when they surrendered."

Finding this very funny, the old man slapped his knee with his free hand and said, "Damn Yankees probably couldn't understand a word y'all was a saying when they asked your name."

Lucinda sitting across from him, rebuked the old man. "Mister Moore, please. I don't appreciate that kinda talk... I don't think is funny at all, sir."

"Uh... excuse me, ma'am. I forgot a lady and baby was present." Looking shyly at the others on the porch, he saw he was the only one who found it funny. He stopped laughing and muttered into his cup, "Well, I thought it was funny."

The sergeant turned his attention back to me, refolding the piece of paper, stuffing it into his jacket. "We'll get it straightened out later, Private Hillman. In the meantime, my name is Sergeant Kyle Cloud and I am here to officially inform you that your parole is up. Sir, your country is in need of your help again."

Chapter Twenty-One

OH LORDY... SURPRISED, I said, "I thought I was finished with the war?"

"Naw sir-- we won't be finished until all them Yankees are driven across our borders and they sue for peace. Until then, we all must do our duty."

Mr. Moore leaned forward in his chair. Eyeing the young man sitting across from him, he lifted one brow. "Son... just how old are you? You look awfully young to be a sergeant, boy." He motioned to the hardware on the young man's hip. "What I mean is, son, that gun on your hip looks to weigh more than y'all do. How long have you been in this here army of yor'en?"

The young man blushed, embarrassed by his youthful appearance. "I joined when I was sixteen. I lied about my age and they didn't seem to care. I will be nineteen next month. Sir, I have seen a lot in my time in the army. These stripes weren't given to me. I earned every one of them."

He turned his attention back to me. "I, too, was at Vicksburg. Afterwards I stayed at Enterprise until they allowed us to go home. I remember you and two other men attempting to swim that swollen river. I thought you three were the bravest men I had ever seen. I mean-- to try and swim that river--the way it was out there. Awfully brave, I thought. Did all three of you make it?"

Lucinda's eyes flashed as she grabbed my arm, "What river. What river is he talking about?"

I patted her hand, smiling. "Oh, that river over there by Vicksburg."

Persistent, she asked again, "Which river was that?"

I didn't really want to talk about my misadventures after leaving Vicksburg. Trying to wave her off the subject, I merely said, "It was the Mississippi."

Her eyebrow rose in wonder. "You swam the father of all rivers... and you lived to tell about it?"

I shrugged like it was nothing. I didn't want to tell her it almost killed me and was probably the stupidest thing I ever did.

She didn't say anything else about it. She just sat looking at me in a strange way, pride showing in her eyes.

I looked at the sergeant, shaking my head. "No, not all of us made it across. One turned back and the other was dragged down by a tree that floated by and hit him."

"Sorry to hear that. Well, I thought that was the bravest thing I had ever seen," he said. Then in a more official voice, he continued. "Private, I am here, sir, to inform you that your parole is up and you are to report to Rapides by the Red River where you and other soldiers will be building a new fort. It will be named Fort Randolph in honor of our new commander. You will report no later than September first of this year. Do you understand?"

"Fort Randolph?"

"Yes... it's gonna be built there on the river bank below the rapids near a little town called Alexandria. General Kirby Smith of the Trans-Mississippi Department of the army is the commanding general in charge of this whole area. He is having forts built along the river to defend our state from the third invasion of the Yankees. Fort Randolph will be the first of many."

I said, "Well, at least this time I'll have time to get my family settled in before I have to go."

The young man happily informed me, "Oh, you can take your family with you this time. You can settle your family there in Alexandria. That way you can live at home and go to the fort each day to work. When the fort is attacked your family will be far enough away that they should be safe."

I said, "Okay, but you see here, my wife is an Injun."

He looked first at Lucinda and then back at me. "Last time I checked, the Injuns in Oklahoma were fighting on our side. They hate them Yankees even more than we do. It might bother some of the people living near the fort, but I don't think it will matter much one way or the other if your wife is an Injun or not."

Turning his attention back to Mr. Moore, the young man stood and bowed. "Sir, I thank you for your hospitality of allowing me to join you for refreshments. My business here with Private Hillman is done, but before I take my leave, I would very much like to thank the young ladies who served me such a fine cup of coffee before I take my leave."

Impressed by the politeness of the young man, he said, "Son, I have enjoyed your visit very much." Turning his head towards the front door, he called into the house. "Susan! Mary! Y'all come on out here and say goodbye to our honored guest before he leaves."

Placing his right leg forward, he took his hat in hand and snapped his arm out to his side then folded at the elbow bringing the hat over his heart. He leaned forward into a deep bow towards Mr. Moore.

The old man smiled at the youth and nodded in reply. The door to the house opened and the two girls came out on the porch, wiping their hands on their aprons. The young man still bent in a bow, lifted his head and looked at the girls. He straightened his body and smiled.

Susan stepped forward first and curtsied. He deeply bowed again with his hat over his heart; he mumbled his thanks for the coffee.

Susan smiled. "Sir, you are quiet welcome. We have enjoyed your visit very much, sir."

Then Mary stepped forward, her face flushed, eyes large like an owl, opened wide. Enthralled with her beauty, the young man leaned closer to her. He stood before her for a moment, filling his eyes with her beauty. Mary stared up into the face of the young man.

Everyone sitting on the porch was now watching the two young people. Kyle reached out, took her hand, and slowly rubbed his thumb across the top of her fingers, ever so gently. In a soft voice, barely audible, almost in a whisper, "Thank you for the wonderful coffee. I would be so honored if maybe I could stop in again and have another cup of this wonderful coffee of yours... if I get out this way again."

Her mouth dry, holding her breath, she nodded and spoke

softly trying to keep her voice steady. "Sir, you are always welcome here... for coffee. I too hope you stop in again... soon."

Reluctantly, he let her hand go, but held onto her eyes. With their eyes locked, he turned his head slightly to the old man sitting watching them. "Sir, I want to thank you again for your hospitality. You are a most gracious host. I do intend to stop in now and then to see if Private Hillman here is putting his house in order to be ready to move in September." Then tearing his eyes away from Mary he looked at me. "Maybe we will ride together when the time comes."

He finally pulled away from Mary and turned his attention to Lucinda, bowing deeply. "Ma'am, we were not introduced properly, but I am glad to have made your acquaintance, too."

Embarrassed, I felt my face burning. "I'm sorry, I forgot all about introducing my wife to you, Sergeant."

"Kyle; call me Kyle. You can call me sergeant when we get to the site where the new fort will be built."

I nodded.

Sergeant Cloud waved for me to follow him. "Walk with me a moment, Riley."

I left the others on the porch as I walked him to his horse. He pulled his hat back onto his head before climbing onto his mount. I stood next to his horse, placing my hand on his saddle. "Hey... I'm sorry. I got caught up with being called up that I clean forgot to introduce to my wife."

The sergeant sat on his horse looking at the young lady still standing on the porch. Mary was watching the young cavalier as he smiled at her. Eyes remaining aimed at the porch, he said, "Hey... that's all right, Riley. It could've happen to anyone. I can call you Riley, can't I?"

"Hey... fine with me."

"Good. By the way, Riley, do you know if Mary there is promised to anyone? I mean... is she spoken for?"

I looked back where the two girls stood together watching us and shrugged, "I don't know, I've been away for a long time but I don't think so. I haven't seen any young men coming by here. Most everyone her age is off to the war except a very few."

His face lit up making him look even younger. He pulled back on his reins, moving his horse away from me. "Good." He took off his hat and held it out towards the young woman, giving her another nod. Touching his heels to the mare's sides, the horse took off at a run down the lane.

I walked toward the porch. As I closed the gate, I heard a rebel yell coming from down the road.

Mary, surprised by the young man's battle cry, put her hand over her heart. She quickly rushed to the front of the porch. Using one hand she hung onto one of the porch post, leaning out as far as she could, breathing hard and looking down the road in the direction he rode. "Merciful heavens, what was that?"

Everyone on the porch stood, looking down the lane. I walked back to the porch, speaking more to myself than anyone. "That, young lady, was a very happy young man blowing off steam." Then I began to hum Dixie. The young man reminded me of the few good days I had in the army.

Lucinda eyed me, looking for answers as to what we were going to do. I shrugged and said defensively, "I don't know. Hey... when the time comes, I'll have no choice in the matter. I'll have to go. At least this time, I can take y'all with me."

I turned to Mr. Moore and his two girls. "There is time before we have to go. I'll make sure everything that has to be taken care of in the fields and around the house is done before we leave."

He nodded as I walked toward the field and the chores that had to get finished before dark.

Chapter Twenty-Two

A WEEK HAD not passed before the young sergeant rode by again. I knew right away he wasn't here to see me, though he pretended it was the reason for his visit. He followed me around while I did my chores, asking me questions about Mr. Moore's daughter.

Tired of the questioning, I stopped working and told him, pointing towards the house, "Why don't you just go up to the house and ask her yourself?"

Horrified at the idea, he jerked his hat off his head and nervously wrung it in his hands, looking toward the house. "I can't do that! W-What would she think? What would I ask? What would I say?"

Exasperated and tired, I said, "Look, Sergeant--"

"Kyle," he interrupted.

I looked at him, wondering what he was talking about. Seeing I was confused, he repeated, "My name is Kyle... Kyle Cloud. You won't have to call me sergeant until we get to the river fort."

"Well, Kyle," I said, straightening up from working on my chores, "I don't have the time to stand around jawing with you all day. I've got a lot of work to do and little time left to do it."

His face brightened as he asked, "Could you use some help?"

"Huh?"

"Work-- I mean do you need help working around the place. I could do that."

"Don't you have some other place to be? Maybe, looking for more recruits or some'um like that."

Unfazed by my comment, he dismissed my efforts by waving his hand, "Naw. I'm finished with all that. I let all the men on my list know when to be in Rapides. You were the last on my list."

I said, "That's nice. Now lookee here, Kyle. If y'all don't mind, I'll see y'all in September, all right?"

Still ignoring me, he leaned against the corral fencing by the barn, watching the house. After a moment he turned his head to me and said, "I was a farmer once." He paused, still looking at me before continuing. "You know... before the war. I could give y'all a hand around this place; if you'd like. I'd just work for food and a place to sleep-- what-a-you think?"

"I think-- that is not up to me to decide. That would be Mr. Moore's job. It's his place, not mine."

"Oh," he said, turning his head back toward the house again. With his back turned to me he asked, "What-a-you think my chances are?"

"Why don't you quit pestering me and go to the house and see. Please!"

Nodding, he pulled his hat down on his head and pushed away from the corral, marching toward the house. "I believe I will."

With that determined look, he made a beeline to the porch where the old man sat and rocked. Once he arrived, the young man stopped short of the porch steps and took his hat off and the two of them talk for a minute. After a moment or so more, the old man sat up straight and called out for me. "Riley, come here, boy!"

I leaned my pitchfork against the wall of the barn and joined them. Kyle was grinning like a coyote that swallowed a chicken. Mr. Moore waved his arm in the direction of Kyle. "This young pup here wants a place to stay until y'all leave this fall. Can you use another hand around here, Riley?"

I looked from Mr. Moore to Kyle. "I suppose another hand around the place would make things a little easier. If you don't mind, that is? He can have my old room in the barn and I can get him working tomorrow, if that's all right with you, sir?"

Mr. Moore waved his hand dismissing us. "Yes, yes, yes. Take care of it for me, would you, son."

"Yaw sir." I motioned for Kyle to follow me. We walked

back to the barn and I took him inside and showed him my old room.

Looking around, he said, "Well, it sure beats trying to sleep in that leaky tent I was using. Now that my government work is finished for the time being and I ain't got nobody back home waiting for me. This..." he nodded his head looking around the small room. "This will suit me fine until we have to go to the fort."

The door to the small room opened and Mr. Moore's eldest daughter, Mary stepped through carrying bed sheets, pillow, and clean towel. As soon as she saw Kyle she stopped; frozen in place, clutching the linen in her hands. She stood just inside the doorway with her eyes fixed on Kyle, unable to move, holding her breath.

Kyle looked at the doorway where Mary stood. As soon as he spotted her he froze too, his face blushing red. Neither one spoke, neither one moved. I stood to the side and waited for someone to say or do something. Finally, I took the bedding from the young woman's hands and laid it on the bunk bed in the corner.

When I turned back, neither one had moved. I waved my hand in front of Kyle's face, getting his attention. "Hello-- Is anybody home?"

Breaking the trance between the two, Kyle looked at me embarrassed and said, "Very funny." He then looked back at the young woman. Reaching out he took her hand in his. "My name is Kyle... Kyle Cloud. What's your name?"

The young woman gasped as he touched her hand. She looked at her captured hand before losing herself in those eyes of his. With a voice just above a whisper, she exhaled breathlessly, "Mary."

Gazing into her eyes, Kyle slowly lifted her hand to his lips and kissed the small hand. "That is such a lovely name for such a lovely lady."

Mary quickly lifted the other hand up to her mouth and giggled, her face turning an even darker shade of red.

I rolled my eyes. I'd seen enough. "Mary, why don't you take your hands and go back to the house. You'll see him again at suppertime."

She gave me a look as if I had slapped her. She turned

back to Kyle, smiling, almost drooling as she recovered her hand. Blinking her eyes as though she had just woken from a sleep or trance she turned and reluctantly left the room.

Kyle followed her to the door of the barn before stopping and watched her go. His eyes following her every move until she went inside the house and out of sight. When she was not visible any longer, his eyes remained on the door where she disappeared. He whispered. "What a girl! What a girl."

I passed him at the doorway, heading back to work. "Yeah. Hey-- supper's at five. Familiarize yourself with the place today. Tomorrow we work."

He didn't say a word. Still watching the door to the house, he lifted a hand and gave me a small wave. I walked back to where I had left my pitchfork and went back to work.

That night while the family was having supper, Mr. Moore asked Kyle, "Son, tell us about yourself, where are you from?"

Kyle raked collard greens off onto his plate. "My family is from up around Winnsboro; northeast of here. My grand pappy is known as the only man from Louisiana who fought in the Revolution War."

"I didn't know anybody from around here fought in that war," Mr. Moore said.

"Yessum, he did. Him and Davy fought together in South Carolina, over there. They were real good friends. You heard of Davy Crockett, haven't you?"

"Son, everybody knows about Davy Crockett and that place in Texas."

"Did you know that him and a few of his friends came by my grand pappy's place before they left to go to Texas? They stopped in to shoot and kill themselves some coons to make hats. My cousin Daniel made a real impression on Davy by his shooting. When they left to go to Texas they asked Daniel if he would go. Shame none of them came back, real shame."

Mr. Moore said, "Yes, it is. Well, you are sure welcome to stay here until y'all leave to go to Rapides. Now, pass me them greens over here, boy."

Kyle surprised me. He turned out to be a hard working young man with a good head on his shoulders. By the end of August, most everything around the farm was picked, pickled, or put away for winter. The house, barn, stables, and corral were all in good repair. The fields were harvested and reseeded with winter hay. Even the garden out back had been picked cleaned except for what the August sun had burned up on its own.

Pickling and canning jars filled with fruits and vegetables lined the walls along the root cellar above the potato and corn bins stuffed full. All of it waiting for when needed later on. The loft in the barn was also piled high with hay and barley for the farm animals. What few thing left to do, Mr. Moore's daughters could handle on their own.

On the day we were to leave, I had the wagon packed with our things and parked out front while we said good-byes. Tears ran freely from all. No one had a dry eye. Rachel, now two and a half, didn't understand why all the adults were so sad. She clung to her mother's skirt and cried because everyone else was crying.

The old man tried hard to control his tears, but couldn't. He sat and rocked in his old chair. He was afraid it might be the last time we saw one another. Little did we know it was the last time we saw him alive. Mr. Moore died peacefully five month later, sitting in that same rocking chair of his on the front porch.

Before we left, Kyle took Mary's hand and walked over to where her father was rocking and knelt on one knee. He placed one hand on the old man's arm getting his attention. Looking up at him, Kyle said softly, "Sir, before we take our leave of you, I would like to ask permission to marry your daughter when I come back this way. I don't know when that will be or when this war will ever be over, but it has to end someday and when it does, I'd like to come back and take her for my wife. That is-- if that's all right with y'all."

Fighting back tears, the old man never said a word. He just nodded and tried to smile.

Kyle patted him on the arm and said, "Thank you, sir." He stood and took Mary's hand again, gave it a little squeeze. Both Kyle and Mary walked over to the other side of the wagon to say their good-byes in private while I helped Lucinda and my daughter get comfortable in the back of the wagon.

Kyle took off his hat and gently, at first, kissed her on the mouth before he pulled her tighter against him; smothering her with his kisses. After a moment she pushed herself away, gasping for air. She gave him a hungry look, licking her lips. She reached and grabbed the front of his jacket pulling him up against her and pushing him back against the wagon, pressing her lips and her body against his; devouring him.

After getting my family settled in the back of the wagon, I looked around the side to see if he was ready. It was plain he wasn't. I left them alone and walked back around to the front of the wagon on my side and climbed aboard. I sat for a moment, holding the reins in my hand, staring straight ahead, waiting for them to finish their good-byes.

One of the horses snorted. I thought to myself, *I guess he's tired of waiting too*. Finally, I took a deep breath and said sharply, "Sergeant Cloud... time to go, Sergeant."

Breathing hard, red faced and smiling like a jackrabbit in a carrot patch, he climbed aboard. He looked at me and said pointing down the road in front of him, "Well, let's go, Private. Let's go."

I flicked the reins and we moved out. Kyle turned and watched Mary as long as he could; leaving the Moore family standing in the lane waving to us.

Chapter Twenty-Three

A FEW DAYS later we pulled in front of the headquarters of the Trans-Mississippi Department of the Army on the south side of the river near a small settlement called Alexandria. There was no fort, no work site just a wooded hilly area overlooking the river a few miles south of the rapids. The land was in the process of being cleared by several hundred slaves.

Kyle and I went inside where an army aid told us where we could find housings for my family. He said as soon as we were settled in, I was to report back here to be assigned to a company.

As we were about to leave the office, the door to the command hut opened and a Confederate officer in a new gray uniform walked inside and stood in the doorway blocking our exit. Kyle and the quartermaster snapped to attention. I stood next to Kyle and looked at the new officer. He looked familiar but I couldn't place where I had seen him. I didn't think he was at Vicksburg. Maybe if I gave it a minute, it would come to me.

He looked directly at me and smiled. His smile said one thing, but his eyes said something else. He walked up to me. "Well, well, well, as I live and breathe. I know you. You like Indians, don't you?"

I didn't say a word, but stared at him. The memory of him seemed to be just out of my reach. Given time I know it would come to me.

The officer reached into the breast pocket of his coat and brought out a pair of spectacles and placed them on his face. My blood went cold as dread washed over me like a tide. I suddenly wished I had my revolver with me. The sergeant behind the desk

137

shouted at me. "Answer the lieutenant, Private!"

I snapped my head around and looked at the sergeant standing at attention behind the desk like he was crazy. I said, "Lieutenant?"

Kyle elbowed me in the ribs, trying to get me to stand at attention also.

Beaming with anticipation, the lieutenant spoke to the man standing behind the desk, "At ease, Sergeant." Looking me over from head to toe, he continued talking to the sergeant standing behind the desk. "Uh, Sergeant Wood, who or what is this here person standing in my office? I see no uniform on this *person*. Is this individual a general?"

The sergeant chuckled and said, "Naw, sir. That ain't no general, sir."

The lieutenant leaned forward and sniffed. "Hmm... he smells like one of those darkies out there working on the fort. Sergeant... see to it that he joins them tomorrow morning when he shows up for work detail."

The sergeant looked at me sideways, uncomfortable. "Yaw sir. I'll see to it, sir. What about his friend here? They both arrived together."

Lt. Atkins then took note of Kyle who had remained standing at attention the whole time. "Yes, and who might you be? I see you are wearing sergeant's stripes. Do you know this person?" he indicated me.

Kyle answered sharply, "Sir, I am Sergeant Kyle Cloud, assigned to Captain Randolph's staff, and yaw, sir; I do know Private Hillman here. We rode together to work on the fort and I assure you, sir, I can vouch for him. He is a good man."

The Lieutenant Atkins looked at his fingernails and replied in a bored manner, "First of all, Sergeant, there *is* no fort as of yet. Not until it is built. Secondly, you should be careful who you vouch for. Third, I'll be the judge of who is a good man around here. Is that clear, Sergeant?"

Kyle glanced at me and then looked back at the lieutenant. "Yaw sir, very clear."

"Then you are both dismissed, get out of my sight." He waved his hand as if shooing a fly.

Kyle and I hurried to the wagon. Seeing my tight lips and my stubborn face, Kyle shook his head. "Jesus, Riley, we just got here and you're already in trouble. Who the hell was that back there you pissed off?"

From inside the wagon, Lucinda called out angrily, "Kyle, you watch your mouth, young man!"

"Yessum, Mrs. Hillman, I'm sorry," he said, lowering his voice and blushing.

I flicked the reins and clicked my teeth. "Get up there, girl!" I called out, moving the wagon forward; heading back down the road towards Alexandria.

We rode a while in silence, me staring straight ahead, not wanting to talk. Kyle glanced at me every now and then, patiently waiting for any kind of answer or response from me.

A couple of miles down the road we found the tract housing, just this side of the settlement of Alexandria. The squatter town was owned or appropriated by the army for its married men. The single men lived in tents near where the fort was being built.

The smell of newly cut pine floated up and down the street where newly constructed one room houses stood. The units poorly built that they were, looked more like a shanty town thrown together at the last minute.

The streets were dusty for this time of year but when the spring rains came, there would be flooding in the houses built in the low places. We searched for an empty house on higher ground.

We passed by several families busy settling in as we made our way down the dirt path that served as a street. Both sides of the lane were lined with wooden planks or small post, laid out together to make a walkway leading from one house to the next.

I motioned to Kyle, pointing at a place ahead that looked promising. We would take a look and see if it was occupied or not. We pulled up and Kyle jumped down and knocked on the door. No one answered so he looked through the one window, sticking his face against the glass.

He smiled and turned to me and winked. I called to Lucinda in back of the wagon with Rachel, "We're home!" and climbed down.

The one room house was small. Smaller than the place we lived in back home, but it would do for now. I figured we could be a little cramped for the time being. What we were not used to was having our nearest neighbor a matter of a few feet away instead of a few miles.

After we finished unloading and moving everything inside Kyle and I left Lucinda and Rachel to unpack while we took the empty wagon to the depot for storage. We found the place with no trouble and parked the wagon alongside several others. After removing the harnesses from the two horses, we led them to a large corral next to the barn. Kyle and I leaned against the railing and watched the animals as they ran free with the other horses.

After a few minutes, Kyle looked at me. "Now, what was that business back there at the command post and who is this lieutenant tight-ass? Do y'all know him from somewhere? He sure seems to know y'all."

At first I said nothing. I didn't want to explain the meeting between Atkins and me at the trading post when I fetched Lucinda to bring home. Kyle was not part of the problem, and I wanted to keep it that way.

After a moment or two I said, not looking at him, "Oh... it's a long story, Kyle. The less you know, the better off y'all be. Just let it go for now. And Kyle," I looked at him, resting my cheek against my hands on the railing, "for the next few weeks, I'd keep your distance from me. At least at the fort, but remember this, at my house and under my roof, y'all are *always* welcome."

He didn't say a word-- just nodded. We watched the horses for a few more moment before walking back to the new house that Lucinda, Rachel, and I would be living in. Kyle ate supper with us before he walked back to the stable and retrieved his horse to ride back to the fort.

Chapter Twenty-Four

EARLY THE NEXT morning, about an hour before daybreak, I stepped outside our living quarters just in time to catch a ride on a freight wagon heading for the fort. I climbed on the back of the already half full wagon and made myself as comfortable as I could with the other men riding. I left my guns at home with Lucinda since I would not need them for a few weeks at least.

We moved slowly down the dark street stopping every few minutes to let someone else get on. The men riding in back made room as others climbed aboard. When the wagon hit a rut or a hole in the road, everyone in back jostled around bumping into each other. Remarks from the men caused the driver to curse over his shoulder at them in return.

As soon as the wagon stopped at the command post, I saw Lt. Atkins waiting with another man-- a very large man. As soon as he spotted me, he motioned to the huge mountain of a man who carried a bullwhip.

Compared to the other men standing around, he was a giant. The man had dark colored hair that hung down to his shoulders and a heavy beard stained with tobacco juice. He carried a whip coiled over one shoulder and around his big barrel of a chest. As soon as the weasel of a lieutenant pointed me out, he began making his way over.

The men closest to me took two or three steps backward and turned their bodies away, hoping the goliath was not looking for them. I glanced at the empty space suddenly formed around me.

My eyes moved along the empty ground to where the

mountain of a man big boots was planted like two large tree stumps. Once there, I lifted my gaze looking up and up until I had to lift the brim of my hat to see his face above me. *God, he is big!*

I again looked around at the men standing in a semicircle away from me. I heard the leather creak in his whip as he tighten his grip. I leered at the whip in his huge hands and then up at him.

I tried to swallow, but my mouth was too dry. Not knowing what else to do with my hands I let my left hand walk its fingers up my shirt to my chest and stopped. Once there my fingers fidgeted with the buttons on my shirt.

The glare he gave made everyone standing near to shuffle a few more steps away. Rubbing my finger against my thumb at that same button on my shirt, I tried again to swallow.

Speaking German and broken English, he growled in a deep voice, "Ja; you. You follow me now?"

He didn't wait for an answer but turned on his heels. Taking long strides raising dust clouds around his feet, he trudged through the dirt at a quick pace. I swallowed hard and took off after him. His pace was fast and I had to hurry to keep pace. He led me around the side of a small hill next to the river where the construction of the fort had already started.

Fascinated by the small clouds of dust lifting up around his boots as he walked, I did not see him stop until it was too late. I slammed into his backside and began to back pedal in a hurry to get away from him, tripping over my feet and falling to the ground.

He growled at me like an animal bearing his teeth and bent down to my face. Big muscles bulged on his neck and arms as he grabbed me by the front of my shirt. He lifted me off the ground as if I was a stick. "Watch your step, bub. You can get hurt like that, ja?"

Stuttering nervously, I said. "Ja; I mean, yaw sir."

Eyeing me to make sure I was paying good attention, he lifted the arm with the whip and pointed at the hillside where slaves were digging. He motioned with his hands for me to join them.

I looked at the half naked black bodies shoveling on the side of the hill and was shocked. I had never seen so many

Negroes this close in my life. There were hundreds of them, all stripped to the waist working fast and furious.

The big man sneered at me again, pointing at the working slaves. "Go. You dig with them. You eat with them and you drink their water. You go now."

I thought to myself, so *this was what that piece of shit had in mind for me.* I smiled back at the giant, nodding to let him know I understood. I glared at the giant and said, "I have no problem working here with them. Tell the good lieutenant I said thank you. I would rather be here with them than over there with him."

He smiled which looked like an animal showing its fangs. "We'll see about that."

I removed my shirt. After grabbing a shovel next to a work wagon, I schlepped to where some blacks were digging and began working. My pale white skin stuck out amongst the black flood of bodies that surrounded me. The blacks nearest me stopped and eyed me uncomfortably as if I was in the wrong place. I paid them no mind and kept digging.

I heard the whip crack behind me, causing even my body to jump, though I was not struck. An angry voice yelled at the men who had stopped working, "Get your lazy black asses back to work, you heathens! There's nothing for you lazy-ass people to look at here. Put your backs into those shovels, you've got a long day ahead of you." Then in his normal voice he added, "That means you too, white boy."

A few blacks nearest to me snickered nervously and quickly glanced around to see if the big man heard. I saw the tension in their bodies relax when they saw he was not going to use his whip on them for laughing.

I began to dig at my usual pace so as to not wear myself out too fast. I had a long dig ahead of me and I wanted to pace myself. I lifted my third shovel load of earth and I heard the whip crack, dirt flew next to my leg. I jumped and stood straight looking surprised.

The overseer growled, "Faster! Work faster unless you want to feel my whip."

I tried a quick swallow, my mouth dry as a bone and nodded at him. I started digging faster attempting to work at the same pace the slaves were. He nodded and moved down the way from me. Even though he stood down the line a ways, he was still watching me.

After a while one of the blacks worked his way over to me, digging as he went. The trousers he wore were dirty and patched. The pants came down as far as his knees and held up by a piece of rope tied around his waist. His hands and feet were heavily callused. His skin was almost black as coal, shiny from sweat that dripped, and his hair and beard looked like a bird's nest. I've seen curly hair before, but I ain't never seen anything like *that*.

The man spoke softly and quickly. "What you doing here with us black folk, master?"

I didn't look around or stop my work. "I ain't your master, so don't call me that."

The darkie said, "Yessum," and kept on digging. After a few more minutes working next to me, I could see curiosity burning deep inside him. To be truthful, I was curious, too.

Suddenly he stood and looked to the overseer. Calling out as though singing a song in a deep baritone voice he sang out, "*Water!*" Several men around him joined in, keeping pace with their shovels, singing loudly, "Huh! *Bring me some water... please...huh!*"

The big man cracked his whip and pointed to some young black boys hauling water around in buckets. "Over here with that water." The youngsters toting the water buckets rushed over, sloshing water as they went.

They ran over to the men and handed out dippers of water. I stopped and set my shovel down to get a drink of water too. I heard the whip snap loudly and everyone around me flinched. I looked at the overseer as did the others. The huge man grinned as he pointed at me with his whip shaking his head slowly side to side. "No! Not you, white boy. You get back to work. I'll tell you when you can drink."

Hot and sweaty, I tried to swallow but my tongue stuck to roof of my mouth. I looked longingly at the water bucket and the boys carrying them. The whip cracked again and the dust next to my feet jumped into the air. The boy nearest me dropped his bucket, spilling the water and froze. Everyone around me halted and turned toward the overseer, bowing their heads. The whole side of the hill became very quiet and still.

The big man growled at me. "If you don't want a taste of this," he shook the whip towards me, "Then I need to see only your elbows and your asses, nothing more." He then turned his attention to the youngster who dropped his bucket. "You, pick up your bucket and get fresh water and then get back to work."

The boy quickly grabbed the container and took off at a run. "Yes, sir, boss... right away, boss man."

I was astonished anyone would deprive a person of a drink of water. But he did. Hot and thirsty, I stood breathing hard, looking at him with hatred in my eyes as work around me went on.

Thinking back to Vicksburg, I remember going without food or water lots of times. I could go longer before I got too thirsty. At least at Vicksburg, we didn't work this hard in the heat of the day without food and water. There, we mostly stayed in our trenches, saving our strength, while sitting under a shade of canvas.

I turned my eyes from the overseer to look up at the sun. Shading my eyes with one hand I noted the sun was still not overhead. It was going to be a long day.

I heard the whip crack and my right cheek burned as though it was on fire. I reached up and touched my face. My fingers came away bloody. He gave me a low chuckle and said, "If I wanted too, I could flick a fly off your nose. Ja I could... if I wanted too. Now, boy, you get to work."

I obliged as fast as I could, but I thought to myself, *one of these days you gonna get what you and your friend deserve. Yes, sir, you just wait and see.*

The blacks were working at a faster pace than I was used to. I quickly got winded trying to keep up with them. After a while, I stopped again and looked at the overseer to see if he was watching me and he was. I wiped the sweat and blood off my face, smiled with my dry lips and got back to work digging once more but at a little slower pace.

I was glad it was September and not July or August. It can get brutal working in the sun in those two months. In Louisiana, not much went on in the heat of the day. It was almost as hot now as it was in August, but every once in a while a cool breeze would come off the river, and it felt so good.

After another hour of digging, the same young slave edged

over to where I was working. I guess curiosity had gotten the better of him. Looking around as he worked his shovel to make sure nobody was watching at the time, he asked, "Boss, you sho stirred up a hornet's nest with that man. What'd you do to him, boss?"

"I ain't your boss, friend, and I really don't have time to talk about it right now. I'm a little busy," I said between shovel loads of dirt, not looking at the man.

The man stopped his work and laid the shovel aside. He stood up straight and stretched his back, flexing his muscular arms and shoulders. I heard his back pop twice before he reached back down and picked up his shovel moved away. "Whatever you say; boss man."

With several hours of digging and trying to keep up with the slaves, the shovel began to feel like a plow. My arms were heavy with exhaustion, scooping the red clay on that side of the hill, and the sun was well past its zenith. Salt deposits were collecting on my body and around my mouth. I needed water, and I needed it now.

I paused for a moment and stretched my back; longing for water as I looked around and spotted the young black boy with his bucket. I watched him as he moved amongst the slaves on this side of the hill, giving them dipper after dipper of the sweet liquid. My lips, caked with salt, burned as I licked the chapped and cracking skin, tasting the twang.

With my breath rattling in my throat, I glanced over and spotted the overseer watching me with an evil grin on his ugly face. I was so close to the river. I smelled the water, and yet he would not let me get near it before feeling his whip across my back. He was baiting me to see how long I would last before I collapsed. The image of the giant wavered back and forth in the thick heat that rose from the ground between us like an evil mirage. I rubbed my eyes trying to get the sweat and salt out to clear my vision. Seeing I was not getting water, I went back to work before he decided to show off his talent at using his whip.

An hour later I had reached the end of my limits. Exhausted, the ground slowly started to revolve around me. I heard the overseer shout, "Break time... time to eat! Drop your shovels and move on down to the food wagon. Hurry, you ain't got all day."

I dropped to the ground on my knees, holding onto my shovel breathing hard. After a moment when I got my breath under control I got back up and stumbled to my shirt lying on the ground. Sweat running into my eyes and still breathing hard, I watched the slaves as they left the hillside, walking quickly toward the river to wash up before going to the food wagons that had pulled up next to the river.

I reached down to scoop up my shirt and the earth began to spin causing me lose my balance and fall to the ground. I sat up, shaking my head to clear my vision. I sat next to my shirt to rest for a moment while I waited for the earth to stop spinning. I held one hand up to shade my eyes from the sun to see what time it was. It looked like it was well after two in the afternoon. *I guess being a slave, you don't eat until last.*

I pulled my tired, aching body off the ground and trudged to where the slaves were heading. I hung my head as I walked. Looking up hurt my eyes and only made me dizzy. It felt better if I looked at the ground rather than through the heat waves wavering in the air.

I suddenly came upon the foreman standing between me and the retreating backs of the blacks. I lifted my dizzy gaze and squinted up at the big man, one eye closed, giving him a smile with my cracked lips. "Nice day today, ain't it?"

His big, ugly face turned into a smile as he placed the butt of his whip against my chest, holding me in place. "You kill me. You know that? That's so funny. Where are you off to, funny man?"

I nodded my head towards the backs of the slaves leaving the worksite, "Hey... I thought I would just follow them and maybe get a bite to eat."

He slowly shook his head from side to side, smiling, "Oh no, bub. You don't eat with them. Shame though, the rest of the whites have already eaten. Tsk, tsk, tsk. What a shame, I guess you missed the call. That is too bad, is it not? Just terrible... ah, such a shame."

Then his face seemed to brighten. "But look. I saved you a canteen of water and a nice piece of bread. Why don't you go rest yourself for a spell? Go... sit... enjoy yourself under the shade of that wagon over there and enjoy your bread and water."

I looked around; there was no shade in sight--only the

wagon where they kept the shovels. My hands shook as I accepted the canteen and the piece of bread. I was not going to drink from the canteen this close to him. I didn't trust him with his whip. I would wait until I was well out of range of both him and his whip.

I made my way to the wagon and found a small strip of shade underneath the wagon bed. I crawled under and sat cross-legged, bending my head down since there was not enough headroom to sit up straight.

I took my handkerchief out of my back pocket and with shaking hands poured a little water on it to dampen it. I took the rag and gently dabbed my cracked, blistered lips and face. Trying to soothe the flesh made it sting more.

As I sat there nursing my aches and taking small swallows of water, I saw a rider come by and hand the overseer a message. He nodded his head to the rider and watched as the messenger rode back in the direction of the command post.

He looked down at the paper and then over at me. With his usual scowl on his ugly face, he crumpled the note in his fist and marched toward me. I cringed, watching the dust clouds rise around his feet.

Nervous, my thumb automatically began to scrub against my index finger. I wondered to myself, *what the hell is wrong now?* I looked around to see if there was any place I could retreat to for safety. He didn't look happy.

I tried to ready myself for the trouble coming, watching his arm with the whip, ready to move if he let go of it. If I had to, I would keep the wagon between me and him as long as I could.

He stopped short of the wagon, glaring down at me he said, "You're needed at the command post, now. Get your shirt and get your ass over there, pronto."

And just like that, he turned and stomped off in another direction leaving me under the wagon. Relieved, I didn't realize that I had been holding my breath the whole time. As soon as he disappeared from sight I let the air gush out all at once.

Slowly and carefully, I crawled from underneath the wagon, still expecting some trick to get me to relax before he would rush back and grab me.

Out from under the wagon, I looked one more time around to make sure the giant was not coming back. Seeing no one, I put my shirt on and emptied the canteen over my head. I headed to the command post on the other side of the construction site as quickly as my unsteady legs would allow me to move. I looked back several times to make sure the giant with the bull whip was not following me. I wondered *what kind of trouble was I in now.*

Chapter Twenty-Five

As I TRUDGED to the command hut, I was hoping Lieutenant Atkins was not waiting with more punishment. I prayed he wasn't playing games with me again. He seemed to be going out of his way to get back at me for the trouble I gave him in Oklahoma.

I didn't like bullies. I didn't put up with them in the army training camp or at Vicksburg, and I didn't want to put up with them here. If I could just stay out of his way for a while maybe we could learn to get along and maybe both of us could do our duty. If not, one of us was going to get hurt before this was over with.

I made a mental note to look for him when it came time for the shooting to start. Not that I would harm or shoot the man myself. *Oh no, not me.* I wouldn't do a thing like that; naw sir. Well maybe. *Dang it... I just don't know -- probably not.*

Anyway, the fact of the matter was I wanted to know where he was when the shooting did start. I didn't want him watching my back or standing anywhere behind and I sure as hell didn't want to be accidentally shot in the back by any friendly fire. I wanted to concentrate on shooting at the Yankees in front of me, not worrying about anyone around me.

When I arrived at the command post, I stood just outside the doorway for a moment in order to pull myself together, fully expecting Lt. Atkins to be inside with more shit details for me to do. I took a deep breath to expel my nervousness and braced myself. My mind now clear, I banged on the door and an unfamiliar voice called, "Come!"

Caught off guard by the unknown person, I marched into

the room and snapped to attention at the one desk and saluted. "Private Riley Hillman, reporting as ordered, sir!"

A slightly balding officer wearing a uniform that looked to have seen better days sat behind the one desk in the room. He glanced up at me in passing for only a moment, returned my salute and said just above a whisper, "Private Hillman, where is your uniform, son?"

Eyes focusing on the wall above his head I answered with a crisp voice, "Sir, I ain't had a decent uniform since I left Vicksburg, sir. My old one fell apart just about the time we surrendered."

He cleared his throat. "I see. So, you were at Vicksburg with my old friend Colonel Marks. We lost two very important battles that week. Neither one, we could afford to lose, but I didn't call y'all here to discuss lost battles or lost friends."

I jumped in with my answer, "Naw sir!"

He pushed his chair back and stood. "I am Captain Randolph. This here fort we are building will carry my name. We will start on another fort in a week or so just up the river there from us, and together we will stop any Union warships that come within range of our guns."

I said a little softer, not knowing if he wanted an answer or not, "Yaw sir."

He then walked around the desk to a large map hanging on the wall. With his back to me, he continued, "Sergeant Cloud," he half turned and looked at me over his spectacles, "you know Sergeant Cloud, don't you, Private?"

"Yaw sir, I know him."

"Well, he informs me that you two are from around these here parts. Is that so, Private?"

"Yaw sir."

"Good. He also informs me you are not a learned man."

I looked confused not knowing what he was talking about. Seeing the expression on my face he continued, "He informed me you cannot read or write. Is that so, Private?"

"Oh... Yaw sir. I mean, naw sir. I can't read or write."

He nodded and turned to me. "He did say you two knew this part of the country like the back of your hand."

I nodded and said, "Yaw sir. That we do."

He smiled and said, "Good! Now, I want both of you men

here at my office first thing tomorrow morning. Bring your own horses and guns if you have them."

"Yaw sir, bright and early, sir."

"Good. Private Hillman, you are dismissed." Without another word he walked over to the big map on the wall, keeping his back to me.

Saluting his back, I stood and waited for him to return my salute. After a moment, not hearing the door close, he turned to see if I had left. Seeing I was still standing in his office, saluting, his face flushed as he gave me a quick salute and said, "That's all soldier."

I walked outside, closing the door behind me. A big smile crossed my cracked lips causing me to wince. I knew what Kyle had done. He had volunteered us for some job to get me away from the overseer and Lt. Atkins's grasp. Well, this was the best news I could've gotten because anything was better than what I had just gone through today.

I followed the dusty path leading away from the command post to catch transportation back to the house. As I walked, I spotted Kyle on his horse coming my way. I raised my hand, waving to get his attention. He saw me, smiled, and waved back with that youthful smile on his face.

He brought his horse over. "My god, Riley, you look like shit."

I reached up and patted the horse's neck and started rubbing it, holding the animal in place. "Thanks, I feel like shit, too."

He looked down at me and said more seriously, "Pretty rough on you today?"

"Pretty much so, but I'll live. Hey... thanks for getting me out of that little detail the good lieutenant put me on."

He smiled, giving me a feigned alarmed look. "Me? I didn't do anything. Captain Randolph was looking for someone who knew the woods around here and it sounded like a job for a slacker. So naturally, I thought of you. I figured it was easy so I volunteered you and me. That's all."

"Lucky me," I said, laughing.

Kyle got serious again. "Tomorrow, meet me here at sun up, mounted and armed. We are going to go see what the Yankees are up to, all right?"

I patted the horse one last time before gently pushing him away. "Will do. I'll be here."

"Good. See you in the morning," he said as he guided his horse back onto the trail.

I continued to the supply wagons and found one ready to leave. I asked the driver if he was going anywhere near the tract housing. He nodded and motioned for me to climb aboard. I thanked him and hopped on back, making myself as comfortable as I could.

Chapter Twenty-Six

AS SOON AS I walked inside the little house we were now living in, Lucinda looked at my cracked lips and the salt stains on my shirt and pants. She planted her feet defiantly in the middle of the room and threw her fist on her hips, demanding to know what had happen to me. I had told her about the lieutenant being the same man who ran the trading post in the Oklahoma territory.

Her face turned dark, her eyes blazed with fire when I explained what had happened today. She had warned me before to stay out of his way. "That man is up to no good, mark my words."

Now Lucinda was never a woman who spoke much. As long as I'd known her, her conversations were no longer than four or five words at a time, at most. But today I received the longest tongue lashing I have ever received from her. She was one upset Injun, ready for the warpath. This was one side of her I didn't see often but when she got like this, it was best if I stayed out of her way and steered her away from anything breakable.

"Merciful father in heaven, what has happen to you? Come over here and sit down and let me take a look."

I sat at the table facing her. I smiled up at her, "Aw... it ain't nut'en."

"How did you get like that?"

"Hey, I'm fine," I said, reaching for her skirt to try and draw her closer.

Ignoring my efforts she sputtered, "Jesus, Riley. Isn't there a river nearby where you could get water to ease those cracked lips? Goodness gracious, what happened over there?"

I grabbed her by the waist and pulled her to me. I was feeling frisky with all the attention she was giving me. She grabbed me by my hair and pulled my head back, making me look her in the face. "You tell me who is responsible for this."

"Well--"

"You just wait until I see that man."

"Now--"

"Mercy sakes alive, Riley, they sure have got my blood running hot."

I tried to talk two or three times and then just gave up sitting with my hands on her hips in front of me. I nodded at the appropriate places, listening to her rant, while trying every once and again to get a word in edgewise.

I waited 'til she finished, astonished at the length of her conversation. I had no idea she could get so mad and use those kinds of words. Why, she was almost cussing.

After she had blown off steam, I sat quietly and watched her move around the room grabbing a basin and towel. She walked over to the bucket of water in the corner of the room, and using the dipper, ladled water into the bowl.

When she came back to me, I said, "I am fine, Lucinda. Really I am. I just waited too long before I got to some water, that's all." I gave her an inquiring look and asked, "Woman, I've never heard you talk so much at one time. What's going on with you? How come y'all all fired up and on the warpath like this?"

She set the bowl of water on the table a little too hard, sloshing it onto the tabletop. She turned on me, her eyes flashing fire. She paused for a moment, letting her anger subside; picking her words carefully. "I hate it here! I hate this army life! I hate this war! I just wanna go home, Riley. I wanna go to our home and live there."

I let her finish her ranting before I said, "Okay, I understand ya hate it here but what can I do about it, huh?"

She sat across from me, looking at her hands in her lap. I noted whatever was bothering her, she was over it. She was forced to accept the fact we were staying here to the end. Like it or not.

I reached out and took her hand and rubbed my thumb along the top of her fingers. "This war can't last forever. It's a matter of time before the South wakes up and realizes they have lost the war. When it is over, we'll all have to come around and see things the way the Yankees want us to." Looking at her, I gave her my special smile. "But enough of this kind of talk. Y'all come over here and put yourself here on my lap and tell your Riley what kind of day you had."

She looked up at me sharply, her eyes shining dark. A wicked smile crossed her lovely lips. She took the wet rag she was using on my blistered lips and slapped at my hands reaching out for her. "I know what y'all want, you dirty old man, but nothing is going to happen until you take a bath."

"All right, but could you first put some of that salve you keep in the little jar on these poor old lips of mine?"

She touched my straggly beard and softly said, "Sure and maybe I'll trim your hair, too."

Laughing I said, "Just like an Injun, first thing they want to do is scalp the white man."

"You hush and bring water for your bath. I'll get the jar and the scissors."

I smiled as I watched her move toward the cupboard with a little extra swing in her hips. I noticed she had gotten a little thicker in the hips and her breasts seemed to have grown a little larger. It looked good on her; I liked it very much. I picked up the bucket in the corner. "You know, Lucinda, I don't know what it is, but you have really looked good lately. Ya look like you've put on a little weight too. It looks good."

With her back to me she said, "Being pregnant will do that for you."

The bucket fell out of my hands and dropped to the floor with a thud. Caught off guard I stood there dumbfounded with my mouth hanging open, trying to think of something intelligent to say; just anything. I never realized she was carrying a baby.

She turned quickly hearing the bucket hit the floor. She put one hand up to her mouth to cover the giggle; looking at the expression on my face. After what seemed like a long time, I finally found my voice and asked, "How long?"

She dropped her hand and gave me a sober look. "Late Spring or early summer."

"That is wonderful news. When it comes time, will y'all have anybody here to help you?"

She said, "Oh yes. Our neighbors will be there. I have already been invited to the women's prayer meeting on Wednesdays and Sundays although there is no preacher here in this community. Do you want to come?"

I shook my head and waved her off. I didn't care as much about religion as she did. I knew it made her life easier when she was with other people who liked to pray and sing church songs but I didn't care for it. It wasn't for me.

I had been alone all my life and I liked it that way. I didn't like crowds. I liked being around Lucinda because she made me feel complete. She was the only one I let into my heart. She was my anchor. She kept me from going wild and doing foolish things with my life. I loved her, and I needed her.

I smiled when she told me about the prayer meetings. "No thank you ma'am. You go. You enjoy that kind of thing more than I do. I'll stay here. But for now, I'll get water for that bath."

Chapter Twenty-Seven

EARLY NEXT MORNING, just as the light of dawn broke in the east, I met Kyle near the construction site of the new fort. A low fog had settled close to the ground overnight. As he rode up, I noticed he was not wearing his old faded uniform jacket. He was dressed as I was in civilian clothes. I also noticed along with his sidearm, he carried his shotgun tucked under his saddle.

Kyle told me once that he liked to wear his pistol on his right hip with the butt grip facing forward. He said he was not out to impress anyone on being a gunslinger. He knew he couldn't draw his gun in a hurry. It didn't matter because once he got it out of the holster, he proved to be a sure shot.

Me, I always carried my Griswold across the front of my left hip with the grip facing forward. I always joked with Kyle that I might not be as sure a shot but with quickness I could get my gun out and maybe put the fear of God in them and scare them some... maybe.

Kyle pulled his horse up to a stop a few paces away. "Morning, Riley."

I smiled back at the younger man, "Morning, Sergeant. Hey... looks to be a warm day after this fog lifts, doesn't it?"

Kyle looked at the sky, standing in the saddle and sniffing the air. "Yeah, it does." Then sitting, he reached into his saddlebag and brought out a box. "Here, I happen on these yesterday while getting supplies." He tossed me the small box the size of my hand.

I caught the small package and shook it. "Bullets? What size?"

"Forty-four's for your Henry there." He pointed to my rifle tucked under my saddle.

"How did you find'em? I only have a few shells left and I couldn't find anymore."

"Well, there's twenty in that box there and I won't tell you where I got'em, that ways ya won't have to tell any lies if anybody should ask, all right?" he said, winking at me.

"Hey... good enough." I leaned around and put the box of cartridges into my saddlebag.

We rode to the command post, tied our horses to the railing and then headed inside. The smile on my face disappeared as soon as I walked in. Lt. Atkins looked up from his cup of coffee.

My hand automatically reached over and touched the butt of my gun. The action was not missed by the lieutenant nor the captain who raised his eyebrow and growled, "Private, are ya gonna pull a gun on an officer of the Confederacy?"

My hand jerked away from the pistol, shocked at what I had almost done. Speaking to the captain, Lt. Atkins shook his finger at me. "Sir, I must protest! This man is already under arrest for insubordination and now he comes in here armed?"

Capt. Randolph stood from his desk and looked at us like we were two schoolyard bullies trying to determine which one was the meanest. He spoke to me first. "Private!"

I snapped to attention, his voice losing its edge he calmly said, "Private, we must maintain discipline here. Were you or were you not going to pull your weapon in this office?"

I took my eyes off of the lieutenant who had moved to stand next to the captain. In a clear crisp voice I said, "Oh, naw, sir. I was not."

"Good. You don't look like the type of person who would do a thing like that."

Speaking to the captain as though I wasn't in front of him, Lt. Atkins pointed again angrily at me. "You take the word of this... this non-ranking soldier over the word of a fellow officer and gentlemen?"

The lieutenant turned to another officer leaning back in a chair, drinking coffee, listening to all that was going on. "General Smith, sir... this is intolerable. This man," still pointing at me and shaking his finger, "This private, sir, is supposed to be under arrest for insubordination and threaten an officer as it is and yet here he stands before us now, free... and carrying weapons-- weapons sir!"

The general cleared his throat, leaned forward in his chair and sat his cup of coffee on the desk. The man looked at me first and then turned his attention to the lieutenant. "Young man, how long have you been an officer?"

Turning red in the face for being asked such a question by the general the lieutenant replied, "Uh, three months, sir, but I don't see..."

General Kirby Smith raised his hand to silence him. "I have known Captain Randolph here long before this war ever started. I trust his judgment of characters without a doubt. If he says this is the right man for this job, then that is all I need to know. You, sir, on the other hand, have not proven yourself to me as of yet, so until y'all do, I will reserve my judgment of this individual until he proves himself otherwise. Is that clear, sir?"

Turning his head and looking back at me, the lieutenant answered stiffly, "Yes, sir."

Capt. Randolph spoke softly to the general, "Sir, you said you wanted someone who knew the layout of the land and the backwoods of this part of Louisiana, and Sergeant Cloud says he is the best man for the job. Sergeant Cloud here has been very loyal and useful to me since we began planning these forts months ago. I trust his judgment explicitly, above all else in these matters, sir."

He turned to Lieutenant Atkins. "Sir... I don't dispute your words. I am unfamiliar with you. You have been with us only a few weeks. You are the junior officer in my command and when you prove yourself to me-- then I will have more faith in what y'all might have to say. Until that time, I don't know what disputes you two boys have with each other but both of you need to put it aside and concentrate on the job before y'all. When this war is over, you two can settle your differences the way y'all want to, but not right now... not on my watch. I have enough problems as it is without you fighting amongst yourselves. Do I make myself clear?"

Lt. Atkins gave me a hateful glare before turning to the captain. "I am at your service as always, sir."

Capt. Randolph turned to me and raised his hand

prompting me to answer his request. I looked at him and said evenly, "Hey... I can wait, sir." And then I added looking at the lieutenant, "until the war is over."

General Kirby Smith walked over to us and took our elbows to lead us to the map on the wall. As soon as he started to point at places on the map, I interrupted, shaking my head. "General, sir, I can't read a map. I can't even read, but if you show Sergeant Cloud here what you want, I will listen and together we will get the job done."

The general paused a moment studying my face. I could tell he was wondering maybe I might not be such a good choice for the job he needed me to do. He looked around at the other two men in the office. Lt. Atkins stood with his arms folded with a smirk of pleasure on his face at my ignorance. Captain Randolph didn't say a word but nodded for General Smith to continue.

General Smith turned back to me and motioned for me to stand closer to the map on the wall. "Private, think of this map as if it was a drawing made from above." He pointed to a small point on the map. "See here. This here small square, this is where the fort is out yonder that y'all are building right now. We are here, ya see?"

He looked at me to see if I understood. I nodded and he continued, "I want y'all to go up the river here on this side." He traced his finger along the wavy line. "Then work your way back on the other side, while y'all are looking for any signs of Yankees out there, all right? I want y'all to do a good job of it, too. Don't dilly-dally around, and don't leave any stones unturned, all right?"

Together we answered, "Yaw, sir."

"Good, then get out there and do a good job of it. I want you two out every day until y'all find the Yankees, and when ya do find them; then I want y'all to track them. Find out where they are and what they're up to. Report back to Captain Randolph." He turned to Capt. Randolph and said, "I'll be taking my leave of you, Chris. I will take my escort and join my army west of here."

Everyone snapped to attention and saluted the general. He returned the salute and motioned for Captain Randolph to walk out with him. Outside, both men joined a group of mounted riders. When the general climbed his horse he pulled his old hat over the nearly bald spot on the front of his head and looked down at Capt. Randolph and saluted.

He took a deep breath of fresh air, filling his lungs as he looked at the sky for a moment. Turning his attention back to his friend standing next to his horse, he said, "Well, Chris, you get these forts finished as fast as you can and maybe we can stop those Yankees from using the river. I'm taking my staff to Texas. Do the best you can with what you've got because the South ain't got much left to give. Good luck, my old friend." He reached down and took Capt. Randolph's hand and shook it.

Kyle and I stood next to the door and watch as General Kirby Smith and his staff rode off. I never saw him again. I heard that after the war ended, the United States government put a warrant out for his arrest. They wanted to charge him for treason. I also heard he was the last high ranking general of the Civil War to surrender his forces to the Yankees. He surrendered in Texas right before we did here at Fort Randolph and Fort Bulow in March of '65. I heard he escaped the Yankees and fled to Cuba.

As soon as General Smith and his staff were gone, Kyle and I mounted up. We gave Captain Randolph one last salute before we headed out toward the river. The fog had lifted with the rise of the sun. We stopped at the water's edge and let our horses drink.

Kyle looked at me and asked, "What's going on in your mind there, Riley? Except for back there with the lieutenant, you look different... happier. So, what's up?"

Watching my horse drink, I smiled. "Lucinda is with child."

"Whoa... you rascal, you! You don't say?"

I nodded, looking back at the lapping water at my horse's feet.

"Well, congratulations, boy," Kyle said taking off his hat and bowing. Looking down at his own horse drinking water he said, "You know, I sure hope this war ends soon. I'm ready to get married myself and start a family; Just as soon as I can. Yes sir, Riley, Mary's a mighty fine woman. She's gonna make a fine wife."

"Yep-- I'm ready to get back to my home too. But first let's get this war over with."

When the horses had their drink we moved across the river and onto the bank. We headed upstream to begin our search.

By mid-morning the heat returned and we shed our jackets, tying them on the saddles. We followed the river a ways to the rapids. Here the shore was low in places. Rocks and stumps stuck above the waterline here and there, usual for this time of the year. Rain had not fallen for weeks, and wouldn't for a few more. The trees along the river banks bloomed in their full autumn hues of brown, red, and yellow.

We stopped and looked around, listening to water run over the rocks for a few minutes. Our plan was to confuse the Yanks by giving the impression we were nothing more than two old friends hunting for food. We weren't in uniform and if we were caught... let's just say we would either be successful or the smartest dumb spies they would ever come across. And if we couldn't pull off this charade then we would hang for sure.

We camped out that night close to the river north of where the two forts were to be built. The next day we searched the woods around the river and made our way back to the fort just before dark with nothing to report. After reporting to the First Sergeant of our search I went home to Lucinda and Kyle went to his barracks where he slept while at the fort. This went on like this for several weeks with no signs of any Yankee forces. We liked it that way. With no Yankees, there was no trouble, just two good old boys out hunting. What a job.

One night around dusk we made camp close to the river, out in the open. While we were cooking a rabbit we caught, a large, black, steel monster of a boat, lying low in the water, eased by drifting down stream. Our stomachs felt queasy as we watched it drifted past us without making much noise.

On the deck of the ship stood a sailor, standing watch-- holding a rifle. He didn't look too friendly as he watched us. I was hoping to hell the doors on the side of that thing stayed shut.

Kyle's mouth gaped, fascinated at how big and ugly it looked. He'd never seen a river gun boat up close. As he watched it drift by, he said, "Golly, would you look at that, Riley."

"Uh-huh."

After it floated out of sight, he let the air out of his lungs that he had been holding. "How does that thing stay afloat like that? I mean, the damn thing is made of steel, ain't it? I would think it would sink to the bottom of the river, made the way it is."

I told him about the time I had been onboard one when traveling to Oklahoma to find Lucinda. Kyle looked at me with one brow lifted. "Uh-uh. No you didn't."

I smiled and said, "Yes I did." Then I got a stupid idea. One I thought was funny. I gave Kyle a sly look. "Hey... how would ya like to see the inside of one of those boats?"

He thought I was joshing him. Seeing I wasn't, he looked at me across the fire like I had grown horns on my head. "And how would we do that, pray tell? What we gonna do? Go over there, knock on the door, and ask if anyone is home? It does have doors; don't it?"

I nodded. "Yeah, it does. But hey-- those people are just like you and me. They ain't no different than us 'cept sometime I can't understand what they are talking about... but yeah, let's go and pay them a visit tomorrow and see what happens."

"You're joking, right? You are crazy, Riley. You know that?" he asked, not knowing whether to take me serious or not.

I glance at him over our small camp fire. I gave him my most serious expression. "Hey... do I look like I'm joking. I'm serious. Would a spy do something that dumb? Huh? Hell, no. Just let me do all the talking and don't look so military. Slouch a lot, act like I do."

"Well, if this works, it will make some story to tell Capt. Randolph when... I mean, if we get back to the fort." He gave a nervous chuckle, stirring the coals with a stick.

Chapter Twenty-Eight

THE NEXT MORNING we broke camp about daybreak, saddled our horses, and refilled our canteens from the river. I took the lead, walking my horse at an easy pace through the trees. After a few minutes of travel, a big deer ran across our path, surprising our horses. Kyle and I pulled up short. Another ran across our trail. I slowly reached for my Henry and Kyle reached for his shotgun.

We waited and listened. Both ready with our weapons. We heard something moving through the brush stepping on the dry leaves. We waited motionless. They had to come through here to get to the river. We would wait.

What seemed like an eternity, we sat quietly behind the cover of some brush nearby; waiting. After a while, three full grown does slowly stepped out of the brush into the open, sniffing the air. We slowly lifted our guns. I whispered to Kyle, "I'll take the one on the left."

As I spoke, all three deer froze and looked in our direction. We both shot at the same time. Two deer dropped like rocks while the third danced her way into the thicket. I looked up to heaven and whispered, "Thank you for making them stand still like that for me."

Kyle looked over at me. "Did ya say something?"

I shook my head no as I moved toward our horses. After securing the carcasses to our mounts, we continued through the forest on foot in search of the Yankee gunboat.

We found the river monster just north of the rapids where I figured it would be. The water would be too low for the heavy boat to go any farther. They would have to wait for the spring rains to come and fill the river.

About to come out of the woods into the open, we spotted the Yanks. A group of men waded in the shallow depths, eyes down as if searching for something under the water. I said to Kyle, "Ya ready for this?"

He swallowed hard with a worried look on his face. "Ready as I'll ever be, I guess."

"We'll leave our weapons in our saddlebags so as not to scare them. Armed men tend to make'em nervous."

He gave a chuckle and said, "I can understand that."

"Remember now... don't look military, all right?"

We rolled up our revolvers in their belts and placed them in our bags and walked into the open towards the boat. As soon as we broke cover, I lifted my arms and yelled to let them know someone was coming. "Ooowe! Ooowe!"

The three men in the water stood straight up and jerked their heads around toward us. One man yelled something to the ship. A side door of the vessel burst open and several Yankee sailors poured out and ran along the side of the boat; all carrying rifles. The sailors lined up behind the rail and leveled their rifles, aiming at us.

I shouted back, "Whoa! Don't shoot! Don't shoot... we ain't armed, we're friends! See... no guns."

The rifles remained aimed until the same man who was wading in the water called to the ship again, "Hold your fire!" He made his way out of the water, followed by the other two men and came to where we stood on the bank.

Nervous about the men on the deck of that metal monster rifles aimed at us, Kyle and I kept our hands high in the air. Both of us stood there grinning like Cheshire cats. I noticed the three men in the water were officers. When they got close enough, I said as friendly as I could, "Hey... what are y'all doing out there in the water? You'll catch your death, being that cold."

He gave us a scowl. "None of your damn business. What are you two boys doing out here?"

I smiled, holding my hands high in the sky and said, "Hey... my friend and me are out hunting and checking our traps we laid over yonder next to that there ugly boat of yours. When we came up, we saw y'all out here and wondered if y'all would do some trading."

Annoyed he said, "Was that you out there shooting a while ago?"

I nodded. "Uh-huh. Yep, that was us."

"Put your arms down, you look ridiculous. Both of you put your hands down."

We dropped our hands as he walked closer to our horses, getting a better look at our game slung over the saddles. One of the other men wading in the water walked came closer to me. "You look familiar. Have we met before? What is your name?"

I stood back and looked him over. He did kinda of look familiar to me. I said cautiously, "Riley... my name is Riley Hillman." I told him the truth because I didn't want to get caught in a lie later.

He scratched his chin as he studied the sky. I looked up too to see what he was looking at. I then looked at Kyle. Kyle was as stiff as a board and pale as a ghost, rubbing his right hand along the side of his pants leg nervously.

Recognition lit up his face as the officer suddenly snapped his fingers and looked again at me, smiling. "Now I remember you. You visited us once before, I believe it was last year while we were anchored just north of Natchitoches."

"Well, I'll be," I said, smiling and shaking his hand, pumping it up and down. Kyle looked at me like I'd grown a second head.

The Yankee officer turned to the other man inspecting our deer and said, "Sir, I know this man. He visited us aboard our vessel last year."

The man studying at the venison carcass turned his angry gaze to the man. "What was a civilian doing aboard this vessel?"

The face of the younger officer blushed. "We brought him onboard and fed him. We thought we would show these southerners that not all Yankees are war mongrels. I'm sorry; it won't happen again, Admiral."

"I should hope not. Civilians are not allowed aboard war vessels anywhere or any time. Is that clear?"

The officer with his face flushed snapped to attention and said, "Understood, sir."

"Good." Then turning back to me he said, "So, what do you want for one of these deer."

I looked down at my feet for a moment, scratching my

beard and then cocked one eye back up at him. "Oh... how's about a hundred rounds of 44 magnum shells, five pounds of coffee and three pounds of sugar and... oh, uh fifty cigars, too."

Kyle looked at me like I was crazy.

Admiral Porter laughed. "You're a crook, you know that? I'll tell you what. I might give you fifty cigars for the whole deer but certainly not the shells nor the sugar and coffee. We have a policy of not giving out ammunition to civilians."

I came back with, "Hey... now who's the thief here? Are y'all trying to rob me, General? I know you can give up coffee and sugar for a friend. We're all friends here, ain't we?" I said nodding, smiling and looking around at the other Yanks.

He narrowed his eyes, giving me a shrewd look, wondering if I was in fact a friend or a rebel spy. He said unsympathetically, "First of all, mister, I'm an admiral not a general. There are no generals in the Navy. Secondly, I think you are a horse thief and a swindler. Thirdly, we would like to be friends, so I will give you the coffee and the sugar--"

"And the cigars and shells, too?"

"Definitely not! No shells and that's final."

"Well, what if I told y'all that there were two rebel forts being built just south of here and will be completed and waiting for you boys when you come down there so they can sink your boat and block the river?"

Kyle grabbed my arm, turning as pale as a ghost. I shook him off. Turning to face him, I smiled and winked, letting him know I had this.

Admiral Porter looked at me surprised. "Where?"

I looked back down and scuffed the ground with the toe of my boot. "So... y'all don't know about the forts, do ya?" I cocked one eye up at him again, smiling I said, "So... what about them shells, Admiral?"

"If your information is good, I will give you your shells, too." He took the reins of my horse and led it to the bank of the river and handed it over to one of the sailors. Kyle and I watched as they unloaded the deer and one of the sailors jumped on Sally and took off riding her downstream past the rapids.

Kyle grabbed my arm again, jerking me towards him. "What the hell are ya doing, have ya lost your damn mind? Ya gonna get ya-self shot for this, Riley. They gonna stand ya up next to a wall and shoot ya to death. The Confederate government don't take kindly to soldiers giving out military information."

I waved him off and said quietly, "Relax Kyle, the forts ain't no secret. Everybody that lives along the river knows about them. If the Yankee navy don't know about them yet, they'd find out soon enough when they scout the area. Maybe they will think twice before charging down the river there and fighting their way past us."

Kyle shook his head giving me an angry look, "I still don't like it, Riley; naw, sir, not one bit, but I'll play along as long as y'all don't give out any more information, ya hear? I'm telling ya, we're gonna have to talk about this later one, boy."

I held up both of my hands, fending off the verbal attack, "All right, no more information."

The scout returned, riding fast and furious. The sailor was off the horse before it had come to a complete stop and ran over to the admiral next to the ship.

Breathing hard, the sailor saluted and gave his report. The admiral looked at where we waited and then resumed talking with the sailor. From where we sat on the riverbank, we couldn't hear what they were talking about, but I figured the rider found the forts just as I said. I just hoped he didn't look too closely.

The admiral talked a few minutes more before the sailor saluted and ran onboard the ship. Kyle and I saw the admiral studying us. From where we sat in the shade, we stood and got ready to talk.

The sailor who had taken my horse came back out of the ship and ran down the plank to where the admiral stood; carrying two sacks. We watched as he slung the four white cloth bags over my saddle. The admiral and one of the other officers remained near the boat, talking, while a third officer, the one I knew, led my horse up the bank to us.

"Here's your horse, along with what you wanted. The admiral was very generous," he said, handing over the horse's reins as soon as he reached us.

Taking rope, I asked him, gesturing with my chin towards the two men by the vessel. "Who's the other officer standing down there and why is an admiral out here anyway? I thought they all stayed behind desks somewhere safe."

He laughed. "Oh no-- not this one. He likes to be where the action is. The other officer is Lt. Col. Joseph Bailey. He's an engineer. He's looking for a way to build a dam so we can keep enough water in the river to shoot our boats past those rapids without damaging the hulls when the water is low like this."

I laughed, watching the two men wade around in the shallow part of the river. Pointing to the fast moving water just beyond the anchored ship, I asked, "Why not just wait until the river is higher before trying to pass the rapids?"

I could easily see he didn't want to give out any more information. Finished, he held out his hand. "Thank you for the information about the forts. I think we will be on the look-out for them when we get past these shallows."

I took his hand and shook it. "Those forts down yonder sure got a lot of awfully big guns they are gonna put upon them walls overlooking this here river. Awfully big ones, yaw, sir, they do." We actually only had two cannons. The others were logs cut and painted to look like siege guns. That was all the South had given us so far. We were promised more, but I had my reservation. The way the South was falling apart, I doubted they would ever arrive. I truly thought all we had at the fort was all we were getting.

When I mentioned the supposedly big guns at the forts, his eyes got a little larger and his face seemed to pale. It might have been my imagination but I thought I saw something when I mentioned the artillery. He mumbled softly, "Thanks. I'll inform the admiral, I'm sure he will want to know that little piece of information."

We parted ways. Kyle and I walked back into the woods, leading our horses while the Yankee officer made his way down to the river. As soon as we were far enough away, Kyle punched me in the arm. "Riley, whose side are you on, boy? What the hell were y'all thinking, giving them all that information?"

"Hey... settle down, Kyle. They'd be sending their own spies out sooner or later to check the area. I didn't tell 'em anything that they won't find out themselves. That is, except maybe the fort's guns. I did lie about that. Didn't I? That'll give 'em something to think about. Yes, sir-ree. Hey... once they see those Quaker-guns of ours, they'll think twice before they try to run past us on that river. We'll need to get back to the fort and report to the Captain about what they are fixing to build."

Kyle snickered. "Yeah, but after the first time they make a run by our forts they gonna see most of our guns are nothing but fakes. Then all holy hell will break out. We won't be able to defend those dirt piles, and the river will belong to them from Shreveport all the way to Baton Rouge." He wagged his head as we walked. "I'm telling you, Riley, this is gonna come back and bite us in the ass. You just watch and see."

Chapter Twenty-Nine

"YOU SAID WHAT?" screamed Captain Randolph jumping out of his chair and rushing around the other side of his desk to stand in front of us. I started to speak but he waved me off. With a shaking hand he pointed at me and his southern drawl seem to vanish from his speech as he continued, "Wait a minute... wait! You told Admiral Porter, the goddamn Yankee commander of the whole goddamn river navy that we were waiting for him down this goddamn river here with... wait, let me get this straight, with not one but two fully armed fortresses?"

Proudly, I nodded. "Yaw, sir, I did. Hey... it seemed like a good idea at the time."

"Good idea? Good idea, my ass! I ought to have you shot, Riley! All the crazy, knuckleheaded, things to go and do. Did your parents drop you on your head when you were a child?"

Confused, I didn't know what he meant by that. I tried to speak and defend myself but he kept cutting me off with his hand.

"Don't you say a word!" He jabbed his finger in my face. "Not a goddamn word! I don't want to hear any of your pathetic excuses! You hear me? I don't want to hear them, Private. I can't believe this... Jesus!" He threw his arms up, and stomped over to the map pinned to the wall. He took his finger and traced an imaginary line from where the forts were still being built to where the rapids were located on the map.

As he looked at the map, Kyle leaned over and hissed quietly at me making a funny face. "I told you that this was going to bite us in the--"

"And you, Sergeant," Capt. Randolph turned on Kyle, "you are supposed to be in charge of this reconnaissance patrol. Where were you all this time? What were you doing while Private Hillman here was giving out vital information to the enemy?"

He held up his hand stopping any attempt for Kyle to answer him. He continued chewing on him. "I don't want to hear any pathetic excuses from you either... none of you two heroes. There is no excuse for what you did out there... None! Why... I ought to take those sergeant stripes of yours and give them to someone who actually has a brain."

Captain Randolph stood next to the map on the wall and took a deep breath, his temper deflating. Letting the air out of his lungs slowly he looked at the floor. After a moment of debating what he would do, he lifted his head. This time he spoke in a more calm voice, almost like he was speaking to himself. "I see the intelligence is lacking in my command. Tharfore, we must work with what we have. So... my two know-it-all spies... how do we turn this, to our advantage?"

Kyle took a step forward. "Sir, if I may speak." The Captain motioned with his hand for him to continue. "Sir, I've been thinking... it will take weeks... maybe a month even, before they can build a dam there in the river. And after they do, it will probably take another week or more, unless we get a lot of rain, before the water rises high enough so that they can use it to get their gunboats across those rapids right there.

"So I figure we have a month to six weeks, depending on the weather, before they can use the river to their advantage. Now with the information we planted in their minds... maybe, just maybe they will move more cautiously now, fearing the defenses we said we have here. We can always send sharpshooters to harass them as they work on building their dam too."

Captain Randolph nodded. "Yes, I guess we could at that. But, son, have you seen any sharpshooters out there working on those forts? We don't have the luxury of having sharpshooters assigned to our command. I could send you two heroes back out there to harass them while they work. That might cause them to keep their heads down for a while. Well, with the way our two forts are positioned on the river they can't get a good look inside them to see we don't have real cannons on those walls."

Kyle smiled and said, "Naw, sir, they can't. From down there on the river these forts look mighty impressive up here on these river banks. Private Hillman and I can go out and take pot-shots every now and then at them Yankees. So they will have to keep their heads down and their minds off of their little dam while we're out and about, that is. Kinda keep them on their toes so to speak. Get them to wait and wonder when or where the next shot will come from. That should slow them down and keep them on edge. We'll make 'em keep looking over their shoulders every time they leave their boat to work on the dam."

The commander sat at his desk and leaned back in his chair. Now smiling for the first time since we first walked into his office, "General Banks of the Union army is busy west of here chasing my old friend Kirby who is heading for Texas. So he won't be able to send troops to help the gunboat take on the forts. The river navy will just have to take care of clearing the river themselves. I want you two renegades to ride out tomorrow and every day y'all can to keep an eye on the building of that dam out there. Now don't get caught, but keep them busy defending their boat and stop the work on that dam as much as you can." Turning to face me, he snapped, "Riley!"

Already at attention, I said, "Sir!"

He came around his desk to stand in front of me, his face only inches away. He spoke calmly. "Riley, do *not* go back down there and talk to those people again. Do I make myself clear?"

Nodding, I answered, "Yaw, sir, very clear, sir."

"Good," he said, patting me on the shoulder before heading back to the map. When he reached the wall, he half turned and said, "Sergeant Cloud, go and requisition extra ammo for your weapons. Get whatever y'all need to do the job. You two are dismissed. Now, get out of here and make sure y'all keep them busy. Delay them as long as y'all can." He turned back to his map, ignoring us and began tracing an imaginary line with his fingers on the wall map.

We saluted his back and left the little command hut, not waiting for him to return our salutes.

A week or so later, Kyle and I arrived at the command post to get our orders for that day. Work on the two forts had been progressing well over the last few weeks. The dirt walls rising high over the riverbanks were now beginning to look more and more like a real fort instead of mounds of dirt.

As we stood outside the command post, I watched as a large wooden crane lifted a massive tree trunk high above our heads onto one of the fort's walls. The crane was moving a huge tree trunk painted to look like a canon down onto one of the gun ports on top of the wall. Below the wall men were busy cutting and shaping another log to look like a siege gun barrel. From where we sat on our horses, they looked pretty impressive to me.

We received our orders and Kyle and I rode out, leaving the construction area of the fort behind. As we were leaving, we happen to see Lt. Atkins and his friend, the overseer, standing together talking near the main gate.

Ignoring them, we rode right by, not bothering to salute the lieutenant as we passed. Both men stopped and glared at us. After passing, I turned in my saddle and watched them for a moment longer to make sure there were no shenanigans going on behind our backs. Neither Lt. Atkins nor I smiled. We stared at one another with hatred in our eyes. I did not trust that man, and not about to ride away with my back turned to him.

After a moment of watching the two of them watching us, I turned back around in my saddle and rode on. Kyle and I made our way upstream to where the Yankees were working on their dam. From our hiding place in the woods overlooking the worksite, we watched about twenty sailors wade knee deep in the shallow waters. They trudged back and forth, moving from the shore to the rapids, carrying rocks and logs while others were hard at work digging with shovels, making some kind of wall. Sentries stood watch looking for any kind of trouble, should it come.

A small group of officers stood in a cluster close to where the dam was being built. One officer gave out orders to the men working. Every now and then, a sailor would run up to the officer and salute before running back to the warship with a message or a foreman directing the building of the dam.

We moved slowly forward, picking a good site to observe from. From our hidden place, we took our time and aimed. We fired several shots that hit the water and rocks around them, and a few hit the boat itself, but none of our shots hit any of the workers or officers. We weren't trying to kill anyone, just wanted to put the fear of God in them long enough to stop the work.

Our ammunition was smokeless so they had no idea where the shots came from. They kept looking around to see if they could tell which direction we were. If we had been using the older rifles, like the Yankees, they would have been able to see the smoke discharged.

When the shooting began, everyone in the water dropped what they were doing and ran; dancing their way back to their boat. The guards fired back where they thought we were, missing us. They gave cover fire until the last man disappeared safely inside the vessel.

We waited safely in the woods and watched until they decided to come outside again. We mostly hit the boat around the steel doorway. It was fun watching them flounder around on the boat. They never knew where the shots came from.

We stayed a while longer and took pot shots every time they tried to leave their boat. Later that afternoon, we had had enough fun for the day. We saw what we came to see and interrupted work on their goal. That was enough. Kyle and I decided to scout farther upstream to make sure the enemy was not massing and planning to outflank us.

Kyle and I rode out every day for the next few weeks to check on their progress and take a few shots just to keep their heads down and to stop work. We never rode up to the ship on our horses or placed ourselves where they could see us. We left our horses in a safe place in the woods far away, and made our way on foot to the riverbank.

Since we were out, we thought we might as well bring some fresh meat back for Lucinda to cook up. The fort looked forward to whatever we brought back, whether it was deer, hog, or turkey.

September turned to October then November. The winter rains had come to Louisiana. Not the flooding rains of spring, but a slow, bone-chilling drizzle that sank into your bones and dampen the spirit, aggravating everyone and making everything gloomy and downright miserable.

The work on the fort had slowed, so had the building of the dam. Kyle and I still rode out each morning to cause havoc and watch them scramble out of the water and run for their boat. But on this day something was different.

Kyle and I picked a good spot to hide and notice two

gunboats instead of one. We settled in a good place to watch. We rested and munched on cold biscuits as we waited for the workers to come out. After a while the door to the side of the ship opened and a head poked out for a few seconds.

Seeing no trouble, the man stepped onto the walkway that led forward and aft of the ship. We waited patiently. Kyle and I let them work in peace for about an hour, letting them think it was going to be safe to work today.

At the sound of the first shot the work crew looked in our direction. Dropping their tools, they ran toward the boat. By now Kyle and I had gotten pretty good at hitting what we were aiming at. We could hit a shovel blade at seventy-five paces. We were that good, yaw, sir. Aiming my Henry, I followed one man running for the boat. Just as he stepped on the gangplank, I fired and watched his hat sail away, spinning through the air. Kyle and I laughed so hard; funniest thing I had ever seen.

Then, alongside the second monster, five doors not big enough for a man to walk through flopped open. Before we knew what was going on, we were staring down five cannon barrels.

Kyle and I looked at each other in shock. Our eyes got as large as saucers as those barrels move out those doors into the open.

I shouted to no one in particular, "Oh, hell no!" Without another word we scrambled to our feet ran into the woods. My finger scraped furiously against its neighbor thumb. Behind us we heard a loud boom followed by four more in quick succession.

The forest around us erupted. Trees the size of my body splintered to nothing. Pieces of trunks lifted out of the ground and flew past as if we were standing still. I would have wet myself then and there, except I was too busy trying to outrun the blast.

The explosions from the cannons caught up to us and knocked us off of our feet, throwing us through the air to land on our faces in wet leaves. Great mounds of dirt and rocks rained down around us as we lay there dazed.

Silence settled in except for the sound of cracking limbs. I slowly raised my head and spit out a mouthful of muck.

I spotted Kyle ten feet away, sitting up, leaning on one arm, looking dazed. He glanced my way, pointed at me, and fell back onto the wet ground and laughed. I couldn't help myself, I was so glad to be alive, I laughed too.

Trying hard to hold back the laughter, we looked in the direction of the river. Noise in the forest carried a long way and we didn't want the Yankees to know we were still alive. We didn't want them to reload and use the cannons on us again.

Kyle walked over to give me a hand to my feet. After helping me up, we dusted leaves and dirt off our clothes and hunted for our rifles. Didn't take long to find them and get back on the road to the fort. We had enough fun and needed to report back to Captain Randolph about the second Yankee gunboat.

By the time winter was upon us, the dam the Yankees were building was almost finished as were our two forts. We were told that a third fort was in the planning for the following spring, if we could get the men and material to man it.

This time of year, everything was slowly winding down to a standstill. Nothing was going on at the forts. All manual work had stopped and we focused on surviving the winter, staying warm, and waiting for spring.

Chapter Thirty

WITH THE DAYS getting shorter, Kyle and I now rode to check on the Yankees in darkness. Each day we'd leave the fort before the sun came up and come back well after sundown. As we rode along in silence this particular morning, I held my reins loosely in my hand and let Sally pick her own way. She had traveled this trail so many times over the past months that I just let her go. I figured she could find her way just as well as I could.

I pulled the old blanket I was using as a poncho closer on my neck to keep the cold, slow rain out and tugged my hat down on my head. Bored, I rested my eyes as Sally plodded, not paying any attention where she was going or anything around me.

The forest was almost as silent as a church on Monday. The only sound made was our horses as they trotted along; rustling the leaves under their hooves as they made their way through the soft, wet ground. That-- an occasional outburst from an irritated squirrel high up in the trees above us; cussing for disturbing his territory. Every now and then a woodpecker would start his tapping, drilling holes, somewhere nearby.

Letting Sally take the lead, I rested my chin on my chest and tried to catch a nap. Although we traveled quietly through the trees, Kyle and I still kept our ears alert, listening for unusual noises. We had never had any problem on our daily journey to see what our friends the Yankees were doing and we didn't expect any trouble today.

The dam was finished and the water in the river slowly rose each day. Soon it would be deep enough to open the gate and float their ships pass the rapids. We needed to know what day that would be. We reported each day to our captain on how high the water had risen and if the Yankee boats were moving closer to the dam's gate.

Alert, Kyle pulled sharply on his reins, stopping his horse. I halted Sally and turned to him yawning. "Anything wrong?"

He held his hand out to me. "Shhh."

Kyle stood in his stirrups, looking around. We sat, listening. The woods were totally quiet. After a few more minutes I gave Kyle a questioning look.

He shook his head and said, "I thought I heard some'um." Kyle shook his head, looking over at me he shrugged. We touched our heels to the horses' flanks, moving forward again.

We continued on our way quietly. Letting our horses pick their own path through the woods again. Several minutes later, a twig snapped behind us. We both stopped and turned our horses in the direction of the noise.

A loud crack of rifle fire echoed through the woods. Startled... a bullet buzz past me and exploded against a tree trunk next to where I sat on Sally. Sally screamed, rearing up, and dumping me onto the ground on my back side. She snorted and kicked with her hind legs, just missing my head and launched a short distance from me.

Cussing, I got to my feet as fast as I could, ran to my horse and grabbed my rifle from under her saddle. As soon as I retrieved my Henry, another shot echoed; the ground next to my feet exploded. Sally, not liking the thought of being shot, bolted.

I jumped at the explosion at my feet, dancing like I had stepped on a rattlesnake. I dashed behind a nearby oak tree. Breathing hard, my hand shook as I pressed my body against the bark of the tree. I looked around to see if Kyle was all right.

He had his shotgun and squatted behind another tree, looking into the woods to see who was doing the shooting. Did the Yanks finally wise-up to us?

I made sure every part of me was covered and tried my damndest to blend into the tree bark. Eyes wide, Kyle shrugged, looking over at me. "I can't tell where the shots came from."

We waited and listened. Shortly, a voice called out, "Hey, Riley! How ya doing, Private? Did ya get hit?"

I gave Kyle a questioning look and hollered back, "Nope... ya missed me."

The voice floated to us on the wind. "Well, that's too bad.

Say, why don't y'all come out in the open and let me try again?"

Was this Yankee an idiot? "No thanks. I'm fine right here. I think I'll wait behind this here tree until I'm good and ready to come out. Who... who is that out there?"

Two voices laughed. "Private Hillman, you're safe with us. Trust me, we won't shoot at you again, I promise. You can trust me, I wouldn't steer you wrong. So, what do ya think? Y'all want to step from behind that tree and talk about it?"

I called back, "Hey... I, I, I don't think so, naw sir."

The voice called out laughing, "Private, I *order* you to step into the open and stand at attention so I can see you."

"Hey... Who is that out there?"

"It's Lieutenant Atkins, you son of a bitch! Now get your ass out from behind that tree so I can shoot you full of lead!"

"Hey... I'm afraid I can't do that, Lieutenant Asshole. Y'all are gonna have to come and get me," I shouted back. Kyle's eyes got big as saucers and he snorted nervously.

Another shot rang out and the bark on the tree I was hiding behind exploded, sending splinters in all direction. Kyle said softly, "I see 'em now, but he's too far away for my shotgun."

I called back to Lt. Atkins, "Two things are gonna happen here, Lieutenant, uh... sir."

"What's that, Riley?"

"First of all, I'm gonna stay right here and wait 'til it gets dark enough and then I'm gonna slip away and run back to the fort."

After waiting for me to continue, he called back, "What's the second thing that is going to happen?"

I gave a nervous laugh, "Hey... That would be y'all coming over here and getting me yourselves, because I ain't moving from here."

I heard another voice in German. I shouted, "Hey... Is that you, boss man?" No answer came. I called out again, "You know... I always thought of you two as butt cheeks. You two rub together like you belong there and so full of shit!" Kyle busted out laughing as two more shot rang out. One hit the tree and the other zinged by striking branches as it passed.

Kyle raised his shotgun and I waved him off. "Hey... wait 'til they're close enough so you won't miss."

He nodded, repositioning his squat to keep watch. I slowly

cocked my Henry. A moment later, Kyle pointed with the shotgun, "They're moving around."

Another shot erupted, echoing back and forth between the trees as Lieutenant Atkins made a run forward for cover, sliding in closer, getting into position to cover the other man. He leaned around the tree, raised his rifle and took a shot while the big man lumbered forward, ducking behind another tree. They maneuvered back and forth, moving closer each time.

I waited for the next shot before I took a look around to see how close they were. I watched the overseer as he trudged through bushes, kicking up wet leaves to dive behind a fallen tree a short distance from where he broke cover.

Seeing me sticking my head out, the lieutenant shouted curses at me while reloading his rifle. I was glad neither of them brought a repeater rifle.

I took two quick shots back at them, knowing I could not hit them at that distance. I just wanted to put a little scare in them and slow them down a bit. It worked for they remained in their hiding place for a few minutes before they tried to move again.

I glanced at Kyle's cover and discovered not one shot had been aimed at him. I guess they wanted me more than they wanted him.

After the shock of the ambush wore off, I felt calm and collected like at Vicksburg. I thought rationally again and decided I was not going to die here in these woods by hiding behind a tree, naw, sir. If I was going to die, I wanted to take that miserable excuse for a human out with me.

I looked at Kyle, speaking softly and calmly. "You take the big man with your shotgun when he gets close enough, but leave the lieutenant to me, all right? He's mine." I growled the last part.

"You got it," he said smiling to me before placing the butt of the shotgun snuggly against his shoulder, looking down the barrel, aiming where the giant was hiding. Kyle waited for the goliath to break and get closer before he would shoot.

He didn't have to wait long. Another shot rang out and the big man got up and scrambled, running for another tree. He made such a large target for Kyle with his heavy weight slowing him as he ran across the clearing.

Lieutenant Atkins ran as soon as the big German rose up and fired from his new position. While the German reloaded, I stepped from behind the tree, trusting in God that the lieutenant was a bad shot. I saw the smile on his face as he raised his barrel, then the flash as his rifle fired.

The big goliath glanced at the lieutenant expecting him to reload before running for a new place to hide. He jumped up in plain view of Kyle.

My friend rose up and emptied his shotgun into the giant. The look of surprise shone on his face just before his large body stopped mid-stride and flew backward, landing and skidding on his back in the wet muck.

Lieutenant Atkins shot barely creased my neck, breaking the skin. The pain was sharp and stung like hell. I felt blood running down my neck as I looked into his eyes. I didn't have time to worry how badly I was hit or how much blood I was losing. I concentrated on taking careful aim, squeezing the trigger slowly.

As soon as I fired, I saw a small limb above his head snap off. I missed. Lt. Atkins looked up to where the limb fell from. He smiled while he franticly worked on reloading his rifle. I guess he'd forgotten I had a repeater because he stood in the open. I cranked the leaver, putting another shell into the chamber. This time I didn't miss.

I saw a look of shock and wonder light up on his face. He stood still for a moment as I worked the lever-action on my rifle, getting another shell ready. He looked down and suddenly dropped his rifle and fell to his knees, holding his chest.

He stared first at a red spot expanding on his jacket before giving me a strange look. He gawked down at the blood and then back at me, his mouth working but saying nothing.

Kyle got to his feet and we went to check the bodies. Lt. Atkins finally fell face first and remained still. I nudged him with my boot-- Dead. I gathered all the saliva I could muster and spit on the side of his face. "Fuck you, you bastard!"

I looked at Kyle standing over the body of the giant. The hole in the German's chest was big enough to stick Kyle's fist in, and smoke rose from the wound.

Kyle turned towards me. He was not happy. "Now how in the hell are we gonna explain this to Captain Randolph? Can ya tell me that, Riley?"

I shrugged and joined him by the dead giant. As I stood next to him, looking at the big man lying at our feet, I said, "Hey... I guess we could leave 'em where they lay and let the buzzards take care of 'em."

Kyle looked at me with revulsion on his face. "That's just plain mean, Riley. I couldn't do that to a dog."

"Well, I guess we could take 'em back to the fort and see what happens."

Kyle grabbed me by the arm. "Are you crazy?! They'll hang us for sure, even though it ain't our fault. They came after us. We weren't out looking for trouble. Why were they after us in the first place, Riley?"

"It was personal between me and him." I nodded towards the body of the Lieutenant. "Hey... ya don't have to say a word. I'll tell the captain they were after me, not you. You didn't have any part in this except by happening to be riding along with me. Nothing personal on your part. You just happen to be the wrong man at the right time. That's all."

Kyle shook his head. "I don't know, Riley. We killed an officer and I don't think they'll care one way or the other who shot who. We could run. Texas is not that far away. Maybe we could go to Mexico and join up with General Smith. The war's almost over. We could wait there before coming back."

Looking down at my feet, prodding a small pinecone around with the toe of my boot, I thought of Lucinda. What would happen to her and the children if I left and ran off to Texas? What would she do? Where would she go? She couldn't follow me. I think she would want me to stay and take my medicine.

"Naw, I can't do that, Kyle. I can't go and leave Lucinda again and my little girl. What will they do? How will they live if I ran? Besides, she is gonna have another child in a few months. No, I couldn't do that to them. Hey, you go. I'll stay and take care of these two."

"Then let them lay where they are and if anybody asks, we never saw them." He looked my way hopefully and then his expression changed as he dropped his head down looking at his feet.

"I clean forgot about your neck wound there. Does it hurt

much?"

"Naw... it's fine. It's just a scratch. Kyle, I can't go back and act like nothing happened. Too many lies to remember. I'll have to tell 'em the truth. It's the only way. You go on to Texas if you want. I'll go back to the fort alone."

Defeated, he mumbled, "Well... let's see if we can find their horses and get them loaded up."

We searched the woods for about ten minutes, looking for the animals, before we heard one of them snorting and stomping the ground. They were tied to a small tree not too far away.

We parked one horse next to the lieutenant's body. The other we led to his friend, the German in the leaves with his arms outstretched and mouth opened wide. I grabbed his arms and Kyle grabbed his legs and together we lifted with a loud grunt. Nothing moved.

His legs and his arms lifted but the bulk of his body never budged. We tried again, lifting and struggling with the dead weight, trying to get his heavy body off the ground.

After several attempts, we gave up. The man must have weighed over three hundred pounds, which was more than both of us together. "His poor horse-- The burden it must have barred; carrying all of that weight," Kyle said, shaking his head slowly from side to side. Then a smile broke out on his face and he began to laugh, knowing he shouldn't make fun of the dead like that. I tried to keep a straight face but I, too, found it hard. After a moment we were both standing over the dead body, laughing until tears ran down our cheeks.

Gasping for air, I said, "Hey... to heck with this, Kyle! You and me ain't never gonna ever get this gall-darn body upon that horse. I say leave it for the birds. There's enough here to keep all the forest creatures alive through the whole dang winter."

Kyle leaning over with his hands on his knees, fell onto the ground next to the dead man, curling up in a fetus position, laughing hard enough to pee his pants.

I thought about what I had just said and started laughing too; visualizing the scavengers of the forest feeding on the dead body well into spring. Yep-- pretty gruesome.

After we got our laughing under control again, I said more seriously, "Hey... maybe we can send a wagon back later and get some help from the fort. We can take the lieutenant back with us, he don't weigh that much."

Kyle nodded and got to his feet. We took a bedroll off the back of a saddle, laid it on the leaves, and rolled the lieutenant's body onto it. We tied it securely before both of us lifted the body and laid him over the saddle. We took another rope off the horses and tied him securely.

Kyle hopped onto the other horse and rode out to find our mounts. He came back in a little bit with both our two horses in tow. I climbed onto Sally's back and we headed to the fort, leading both spare horses and the lieutenant's body slung over the saddle behind us.

Chapter Thirty-One

WHEN WE ARRIVED at the fort, we walked the horses and baggage toward the command hut. Along the way, we picked up a sizeable crowd of onlookers who stopped what they were working on to follow. Questions were thrown at us. The men were curious who was tied on the horse. Ignoring the men and their questions, we rode on. The noise from the onlookers got louder and louder as we picked up more people.

By the time we arrived at the main post, we'd gathered quiet a large crowd. The spectators stood outside the command shack and talked amongst themselves, making their own judgments as to what had happened.

After waiting a few minutes, the door of the command post opened. Captain Randolph, Lieutenant Buhlow, and the first sergeant stood just outside the doorway facing us.

As soon as they appeared, we saluted and started to dismount. The captain raised his hand to stop us. Captain Randolph came over and laid his hand on my saddle and looked up at me. He glanced at the neck wound. "First Sergeant, would you be so kind as to see who that is under that blanket?"

I opened my mouth to say it was Lieutenant Atkins but the captain, still looking at me raised his finger to stop me. The officer trudged over and lifted one edge of the wet blanket. As soon as he saw who it was he looked up at me, surprised, and then at Kyle before walking back to whisper into the captain's ear.

Captain Randolph without any emotion in his voice said calmly, "We'll discuss this inside. Sergeant, get a detail together and take ... take the body and bury it." Turning to the crowd that had gathered, he said in a louder voice, "There ain't nothing here that concerns y'all. Get back to whatever you people were doing. Lt Buhlow and I will handle this. You people are dismissed." Then to me and Kyle he growled, "You two... inside, now."

Capt. Randolph motioned to us. "Let's get inside away from prying eyes so we can talk. I want to hear what you two brave heroes have to say for yourselves."

Kyle and I eyed each other as we dismounted our horses and followed the two officers. Kyle and I marched up to the desk and snapped to attention and waited.

We didn't know what to expect as we stood there. We knew we were in trouble but we didn't know how badly. We had killed an officer and there were no witnesses to say if it was self-defense or murder.

Now that I had time to think about it, it didn't look good... not good at all. We stood before the commander's desk, at attention, and waited to tell our side of the story.

The two officers conferred in private in one corner of the room with their heads turned away from us. Kyle leaned over and looked in their direction. Seeing him look, I turned my head slightly and looked at him.

The first sergeant seeing us as he walked in slammed the door with a loud bang. Kyle and I both jumped. He snarled loudly, "Eyes forward, you two ninnies!"

We snapped back to attention, eyes focused on the wall in front of us. After another minute both officers left the corner and walked back to the desk. Lieutenant Buhlow stood, arms folded, expressionless.

Capt. Randolph sat at his desk. Folding his hands in front of him, he sat for a long moment, quietly looking at his folded hands, thinking. The only noise in the one-room building was a fly buzzing around the wound on my neck. I wanted to shoo it away, but I knew better than to move.

The lieutenant shuffled his feet, finding a more comfortable position to stand. My eyes cut to him as he moved to the back wall. The lieutenant's action seemed to break the spell the captain was in. He suddenly sat up straight and took a deep breath and snapped at us, "Well... what do you two heroes have to say for yourselves?"

Kyle and I began talking at the same time. The captain

held up a hand, stopping us. He said, "Sergeant, you first." Then looking at me, smiling, he continued sarcastically, "I can't wait to hear your side of the story, Riley."

I tried to swallow the saliva in my mouth, my thumb rubbing nervously along my fingers down by my leg. I wondered just how much trouble I truly was in.

Kyle stood at attention, eyes forward. The captain didn't let us relax, made us stand at attention the whole time.

Kyle said, "Sir, Private Rile... uh, Private Hillman and I were on patrol when we were ambushed by Lt. Atkins and his friend that overseer feller. You know who I mean--the big feller." He motioned with his hands lifting one high over his head.

Capt. Randolph nodded in understanding. Lt. Buhlow unfolded his arms and looked at the commander giving him a head jerk.

The captain asked Kyle, "Where is the other body; I only saw one? The body of Lieutenant Atkins's associate, I didn't see it outside."

Making an apology, Kyle said, "We had to leave him out there. We tried to bring him back but he was too darn heavy for us to lift onto his horse."

Lieutenant Buhlow choked back a laugh as he tried to turn the subject back to Lieutenant Atkins. "What exactly happened out there, Sergeant? Did you four get into an argument or a fight?"

Together, we both said, "Naw, sir!"

Capt. Randolph slapped his hand down on the desktop and shouted, "Shut up, Private. We are talking to the Sergeant here. You'll have your say in a minute."

Hurt, I said, "Yessum."

Kyle shook his head vigorously and continued, "Oh naw, sir! We didn't know who it was... not until Lt. Atkins started baiting Private Hillman here, calling him to come out into the open so he could get a better shot at him."

Capt. Randolph, trying to hide a smile, probably visualizing the gunfight looked quickly at me and then looked back at Kyle. He motioned with his hand, nodding, "Go on, Sergeant... continue."

"Well, sir, it was like this... they kept shooting at the Private here. Never took a shot at me the whole time. Private

Riley and me waited behind a couple of trees for them to get close enough before we shot back. Private Hillman here was nicked in the neck and we just happen to be better shots then they were.

"When all of the shooting was over, we tried to bring both of the bodies back with us, but we couldn't lift the other one... the overseer. Naw, sir, we couldn't get him up off of the ground, ya see? He was so big and heavy. Well... he's still out there where we left him; lying there on the ground where I shot him. We'll have to go back tomorrow and bring a wagon with us if we are gonna bring him back to the fort. It's gonna take some good strong fellers to lift his body and get it into a wagon... yaw, sir, mighty strong fellers."

Capt. Randolph sat quietly, listening and studying Kyle's face as he told his story. When Kyle was finished the captain continued to study his face while piddling with a pencil on his desk, thinking. After a few moments, he laid the pencil down and looked at me. "You got anything you want to add or say in your defense?"

I looked straight ahead and said, "Naw, sir, I ain't got nut'en to say, Sgt. Cloud here said it all, sir."

Capt. Randolph pushed his chair back from his desk and stood. Placing both hands behind his back, he walked over to the map hanging on the wall. Out of habit, his fingers flicked nervously.

Lt. Buhlow followed him with his eyes, remaining by the desk.

Captain Randolph stared at the map as he spoke more to himself than to anyone else in the room, "What in the devil am I gonna do with you two boys? It seems like every time I turn around, one or the other of you is getting into trouble." The captain turned and asked the lieutenant, "What do you think?"

The lieutenant gave him a bored look-- shrugging. "That's for you to decide, sir. You're the commanding officer here... not me."

The captain said, "Huh... Thanks." He rubbed his chin with his hand and called to the sergeant who was now seated at his small table in the far corner of the room. "First Sergeant!"

The man stood and said, "Yaw, sir?"

"Tell me, what do you think of the story we just heard?"

Standing at attention he said, "Sir, regulations says if an enlisted man strikes or kills an officer, it's an automatic death sentence. No pardon, no appeal, sir!"

The blood drained from our faces. My legs suddenly felt like rubber and I tasted bile rising in my throat. It looked like there was no way I was going to talk my way out of this one. Naw sir; no way I could figure. What was I going to do? Lucinda and the children would be devastated if I was shot.

The captain walked back over to stand in front of us, watching the expressions on our faces. "Death by firing squad... no appeal." He turned back to Lieutenant Buhlow. "How do you stand, Lieutenant, on regulations?"

Lt. Buhlow looked down for a second before answering, "Law is the law. Regulations are regulations, Captain. Have to live by 'em or you'll lose your authority over the men. Society, or the army, in this case cannot survive without its regulations and laws. It seems very clear to me, sir."

The captain stood directly in front of me, eye to eye. "Clear to me, too... So, which one of you two sharp-shooters shot Lieutenant Atkins?"

I swallowed hard and said in a shaky voice, "Hey... I guess, I did, sir."

"You? You Private Hillman? It was you who killed an officer of the Confederate army?"

Holding back tears of frustration knowing I was dooming myself by saying so, "Yaw, sir, I did. I had to. It was either me or him. He gave me no choice."

"I see. Sergeant Cloud," he turned to Kyle, "seems like you are off the hook, Sergeant. Private Hillman here is taking responsibility of shooting an officer."

"Yaw sir. I thank the captain, but, sir... I stand with the private here in this matter. He had no choice. He had to kill him or be killed."

Angry, the captain said, "You could have wounded him or taken him prisoner. Did either of you two think of that?"

I cut in and said, "Hey... I'm not that good of a shot to just wound him, and he was not going to be captured, sir."

"First Sergeant? What's your opinion on this matter?"

The sergeant walked around to stand in front of us. He snapped to attention and said, "Sir, I don't have an opinion on what's happened. The lieutenant was an officer. My superior, sir."

"No, you miss understand, Sergeant. Man to man-- civilian to civilian." He pointed back and forth between the sergeant and himself. "What kind of man was this Mr. Atkins? I never got a chance to know him while he was assigned to me."

The first sergeant looked uncomfortable and thought for a moment.

Capt. Randolph, prompted the sergeant, "Truth being, Sergeant, you knew him better than the rest of us did. You worked with the man day in and day out. So, what kind of man was he?"

The sergeant shuffled from one foot to the other looking unhappy. Finally he spoke, "Sir... I--I'd rather not say. I ain't saying nut'en against any officer."

"Sergeant, you can talk freely in this room. I want to know what kind of man Lieutenant Atkins was. Was he a good officer?"

The first sergeant said nothing, just looked straight ahead, eyes fixed on the wall.

"Sergeant, I am waiting."

"Sir... if I speak the truth, y'all ain't gonna like it and I might get myself in trouble, too."

"Tell me."

"No retribution if I speak the truth here, sir?"

"No retribution-- none whatsoever. I promise you. You have my word as an officer and a gentleman."

The first sergeant gave each of the officers a wary look. He remained quiet for a moment. I could see him thinking by the way his eyes shifted, weighing something in his mind. Finally he said, "Sir, I trust you. Your word is good enough for me, but could I have it in writing anyway and have it witnessed by the lieutenant here? Just to be on the safe side so if it comes back to me, anything I say cannot be used against me."

Captain Randolph glimpsed at the lieutenant and back to the sergeant. "Sergeant," he leaned over the desk and started writing on a piece of paper. "Sergeant, did you study law by chance?"

"Naw sir."

"When this war is over, I highly recommend you do so. I

think you will make a hell of a good lawyer."

Lt. Buhlow snickered.

Capt. Randolph handed the paper to Lieutenant Buhlow. The lieutenant bent over the desk and scribbled on the piece of paper and then handed it over to the sergeant. The sergeant looked it over; reading it in detail. When he finished, he folded the paper and tucked it inside his jacket pocket.

"Now that little bastard and his henchman are dead and out of the way," he patted his jacket pocket, smiling, "I can tell y'all what's been going on around here. The man was the devil himself-- swear to God. Him and his friend there were blackmailing me and a number of other fellers in the fort and stealing from the government, too. He was a profiteer and a scoundrel in the worst way and that big man there with the bullwhip was his muscles, backing him up."

Surprised by the outburst and accusations the first sergeant spewed, Capt. Randolph sat and motioned Kyle and I to a couple of chairs to sit while we listen to the first sergeant go on about Lieutenant Atkins and his low handed ways.

When the sergeant finished his angry rendition on the dead lieutenant his face was flushed with anger. The rest of us listened, fascinated. None of us had any idea as to what the lieutenant and his partner had been up to all this time.

Capt. Randolph looked up from his resting hands on the desk and said simply, "Thank you, Sergeant. I had a feeling something was going on under my nose. I just didn't know who it was. Every time Lt. Atkins was in my presence, Private Hillman's name here always came up in the subject." He motioned to me and I squirmed a little in my chair, uncomfortable my name was mentioned often. I didn't like to be the topic of any subjects.

The captain took a deep breath, absorbing all he had just heard. He let the air out slowly as he spoke, "You boys don't know how lucky y'all are. It would have been a shame to have wasted our precious ammunition on your firing squad. But don't look so cheerful about it; I still have to come up with some punishment for what you two heroes did out there. I can't let that go unpunished. If I did, we might have gun fights everyday out there."

Kyle and I, still in trouble, were very happy not to be

shot. Whatever it was, it couldn't be as bad as facing a firing squad. Naw sir.

Capt. Randolph, scowl on his face, waved his hand dismissing us. "You two get out of my sight before I change my mind. And you there, Private," looking at me, shaking his finger in my direction, "Get yourself over to the infirmary and have a doctor take a look at your neck-- Dismissed."

We stood and snapped to attention, saluted together and got out of his office as fast as we could. Once outside, I left Kyle and went home. I was not going to see an army doctor. My wife could do a better job than the infirmary. I'd seen how hospitals worked when I was at Vicksburg and I promised myself I would never put my trust in one of those.

Chapter Thirty-Two

As SOON AS I walked into the house, Lucinda took one look at me and planted herself in the center of the room. She pointed to a chair next to our table and said, "Sit." She went to a small cabinet I had built on one of the walls and picked up her sewing kit and grabbed her special ointment along with a pan filled with water and clean dish rags.

She never asked what happened or where I had gotten hurt. She motioned for me to remove my shirt. I took my shirt off and laid it on the table while she dipped one of the dishcloths into the basin and squeezed out most of the water. Taking her time she leaned against me and cleaned the wound on my neck.

Let me say right now that when a beautiful woman leans against you to clean a cut or a wound, you tend to forget about the pain because you are thinking of other things. Yaw, sir-ree. I was feeling real good as she leaned up close cleaning my wound. She smelled pretty good too-- Awfully good. I placed one hand on her hip and she quickly slapped it away giving me her 'not now' look.

I shrugged and smiled. She never smiled back but leaned closer and went back to work on my neck.

When she was finished and had salve applied, she threaded her needle and squeezed my neck pulling the skin tightly together. I winced, pulling away. "Owww... hey, take it easy there, honey. That hurts."

She shushed me grabbing my neck between her two fingers again, pinching the wound closed. "Hush." She took the needle and thread and sowed the gap as I gritted my teeth. With clean gauze, she wrapped the wound to keep it clean and protect it from being irritated by the collar on my shirt.

I didn't bother to tell her what happened or that I had killed a man today. She was so into her religion that she would not have understood that sometimes a man just needed killing. Lieutenant Atkins was one of those men. I just happen to be there at the time of his death. The world was better off without him... truly better off. If it hadn't been me, it would have been someone else, so I kept it to myself.

That night, after I blew out the light from the lantern, I crawled into bed. Lucinda moved closer to me, laying her head on my chest, placing one leg over mine, holding me close with her arm around me. She snuggled her rounded belly against my side and whispered softly, "Riley?"

Smiling in the darkness, I whispered back drawing out the word, "Yes?" I was starting to feel frisky again. I liked it when she got close and whispered in my ear.

"I'm glad you didn't get hurt too badly. I'll pray for you."

I suddenly lost the urge and put my arm around her, patting her on the shoulder and rested my jaw over her head and whispered back, "Thank you, I love you."

She then rolled back over, her back to me and said, "I know, I love you too."

The next morning I met up with Kyle at the command post. We had gotten a heavy frost overnight and everything was white with ice. It was the kind of morning where the air was still, but crisp and your breath came to life in front of your face. Kyle, on his horse, waited with a wagon. Two strong men sat upfront, waiting for me.

Kyle called to me as I rode up, "You remember Hendricks and the Swede. They are gonna help us with the body."

The men on the wagon looked at me and nodded, not saying a word. I tipped my hat back at them. Kyle smiled and shook himself. "I love mornings like this where it's frosty. It makes me feel alive."

No one else said a word, so he continued, "Well, now that the introductions are out of the way, let's get to it. Follow me." Turning his horse, he led the way.

We found the body where we left it the day before. His chest had crystallized into red flakes of ice where the blood had frozen. The Swede jumped first off the wagon and knelt next to the body to examine it. He looked back at the three of us and said, "Ja... Goot-n-stiff. He should be easy to move-- ja?"

I looked down at him and asked, "Hey... you've had a lot of experience with frozen bodies?"

"Ja... back in my country ve have real vinters there where everything freezes and lots of snow."

Kyle nudged the body with the toe of his boot. "Yep... frozen stiff. All right then... everybody grab a limb and let's get lifting."

Hendricks jumped from the wagon and I dismounted Sally. We gathered around the body and together we got down on one knee and Kyle said, "On the count of three. One... two... Three..." Everyone grunted as we lifted the frozen corps. The body snapped and popped a few times but never sagged. It remained stiff as a board while we struggled with the body; hauling it over and laying it in the bed of the wagon.

I looked at the other three men and said, "Hey... That wasn't so bad, was it?" They nodded and climbed back onboard. I took my blanket off of my horse and covered the body, then mounted and we made our way back to the fort.

Kyle and I received one week in the stockade where we were to live on bread and water. Not to mention whatever food my wife could sneak in. For entertainment, we cleaned and dug latrines and cut brush starting to grow around the two forts.

Chapter Thirty-Three

LATE FEBRUARY, THE rains came, flooding the river. The water rose, turning the forts into islands. We waited and prayed that the Yankees didn't come. I guess our prayers were answered. A week and a half later the water was back within its banks and no attack.

During the latter days of April, Kyle and I had managed to stay out of trouble since our gun fight in the woods. About that time we received the worst news of the war. Robert E. Lee had surrendered his army at a place called Appomattox, Virginia. We took this news badly. We refused to believe it, thinking it was a Yankee ploy to get us to surrender our forts without a fight. Now, they had a whole squadron of gunboats parked just out of range of our fake guns.

They never could get close enough to tell if our artillery was real or not, and none of them wanted to take the chance to find out. They knew the war was coming to its end and this was the last of the forts the Confederacy had. Nobody wanted to be one of the last to die or be wounded in this war as it was winding down. They were happy to just sit up river and wait us out.

On the first week of May we received reinforcements by way of a Confederate Ironclad warship named Missouri that anchored itself next to our two forts for support. Now we had the full extent of the Confederate Navy at our disposal, not to mention we increased our fire power three times over. But with the ship's arrival, came more bad news.

The official word arrived with the Ironclad that General Lee did in fact surrender his forces in Virginia on the ninth of April to General Grant. Him again. I had enough of him at

Vicksburg. They said he treated General Lee's men well when they surrendered and sent them all home. Whether it was true or not, General Grant was not here and we didn't know how we would be treated when and if we surrender. Being the last forts, they just might hang us all.

By the end of May the river had receded to its normal size. Roads were a quagmire of mud. Wagons lay abandon, muck up to their axles, waiting for the weather to dry the roads enough to get them unburied.

The insect population flourished with the heavy rains. The mosquitoes and Louisiana heat competed to see which would rule the land. My vote went to the mosquitoes.

At the beginning of June, Lucinda heavy with child had been walking around for the past few weeks having labor pains that came and went all the time. On this particular Sunday, her prayer group had their hands busy. This was the day she gave birth to a strapping young boy with lungs that could almost have belong to an adult. It was my, uh... our first son and in honor of the man I credited for saving my life, I named him Charles, but I called him Charlie.

It was a wonderful time for the both of us. The wails of the baby boy sounded so different than it did with our little girl. His cries were loud and masculine, so manly it made me smile with pride each time I heard him.

Yes... June turned out to be a wonderful month for me here in central Louisiana. As with all good things, they too must come to an end.

Captain Randolph called all personnel to gather inside the fort for a message. We heard that Lieutenant Buhlow did the same at our sister fort, just up the stream from us from where he commanded.

Rumors around the fort spread like wildfire. Some said we were going to attack the gunboats before they had a chance to attack us. Other said the Yankees were giving up on trying to run pass us and were leaving. Still other rumors said the Yankees called our bluff and would attack with everything they had, not leaving any man alive.

None of the rumors were to my liking. I'd had enough of this war. I wanted to go home, be left alone to raise my family on my farm. It seemed like another lifetime since I last worked those fields-- to get up in the morning and walk the freshly plowed ground. To smell once more the plants growing in the garden or walk rows in fall when the corn was tall and ready to pick. Yaw, sir. I was ready. I didn't want to throw my life away for any lost cause, but it seemed at the time I was trapped like a rat in a cage. Like it or not, I had to see this war to its bitter end.

Inside Fort Randolph, I followed the other men to where the captain stood on top of the ramparts waiting for everyone to gather. I saw Kyle standing off to one side and made my way to him.

The captain raised his hands to silence the soldiers. "Men," he said, looking down at us, "you've heard the rumors going on around the fort. You know the war has gone badly for us here in the south. Now with the news of General Lee surrendering and our president captured in Georgia... Well, I'm afraid I have more bad news."

The men standing around us started murmuring to each other; their mummers getting louder and louder by the second. I looked down, thinking; *please don't tell us we are going to fight those Yankee warships.*

The captain raised his hands again. Everyone quieted. "We... uh Lieutenant Buhlow and I, have been notified by what's left of our government that General Buckner, the commander of the Trans-Mississippi army has surrendered his forces in Texas. With this news, we have contacted the Union Navy parked just upstream from us to discuss terms for surrender of the two forts."

More murmuring broke out and quickly died back down. "Men..." He looked around at the faces below and stopped when he spotted Kyle and me. "Men... This is an official notification. The two..."

We heard cheers off in the distance coming from the direction where Fort Buhlow was located. All heads turned, wondering what was going on over there. The captain also looked for a minute before returning his attention to the men before him.

"As I was saying... This is an official notice that our fight for state rights has come to an end. The day after tomorrow we will turn the two forts over to the United States government. I tell you this now so you married men can get your families packed up and away from here before we surrender.

"I don't know what is in store for us once we do surrender. We have to wait and see. No matter what they do, at least we will be able to get our families to safety... uh, just in case. Men..." He looked around tears now running down his cheeks. "Men... It has been an honor and a privilege to have served as your commander this past year or so. This will be the last time we will gather before the surrender so God bless each and every one of you. Thank you for your service to the Confederacy. You married men are dismissed until seven o'clock Saturday morning when we will all meet here again to stack our arms for the last time."

When he finished, he turned to the river, away from the faces of those he led. As the men dispersed, there were no cheers. Unlike the other fort across the way, these men were silent. Some, like me, tried to hide the tears. Others like Kyle breathed a sigh of relief. Kyle and I grasped each other's hands tightly lest we wake up and discover it was all a dream.

I left Kyle and caught a ride to the livery stable where all the wagons, mules, and horses were kept. I picked Sally out of the corral and harnessed her to my wagon. I tipped my hat to the owner of the stable and headed for home. I didn't tell him he was about to go out of business, I thought I'd let him find out on his own.

I parked the wagon in front of our little place and set the hand brake, securing the reins to the handle. As soon as I jumped down, Lucinda was at the door. She held Charlie in her arms, his mouth pressed against her bare breast, noisily suckling. Rachel, my little girl, stood next to her mama holding onto her skirt, grinning up at me.

I smiled down at her and gave her a wink. She smiled and twisted from side to side, still holding onto her mother. Lucinda had a worried look as she stood in the doorway. "What's happened, Riley? What's going on? What are you're doing here with our wagon?"

I opened my arms to hold her tight to me. With tears streaming down my face I said softly against her hair, "The war... it's over, Lucinda. It's over at last." I pulled away and said, "We will be surrendering the forts, Saturday. But before we do, I need to make sure you and the children are safe. Let's pack the wagon and get you on the road for home. If I'm lucky and they don't hold us here too long at the fort, I should be able to join y'all in a week or so. If not... well, I need to get you and the children to safety."

We quickly gathered everything. There wasn't that much to pack. After loading what we had, the wagon was still half empty.

Once ready to go, I lifted Rachel upon the wagon seat to make her comfortable. I looked around and saw wagons lined up all down the narrow road. People were busy, hurriedly gathering household items and packing.

I took Charlie from Lucinda while she climbed onto the seat next to Rachel. When she was comfortable on the wooden bench, I lifted Charlie to her and she tucked him into the well under her seat. As she was making Charlie comfortable, she noticed my rifle and hand gun tucked under the seat and looked down at me. "Won't you be needing your guns at the fort?"

I shook my head. "Naw... I want you to keep them safe for me. I'm sure the Yankees will confiscate all firearms once they take over the forts and I don't want to lose them."

Still looking down at me; her eyes full of fire and determination, she said, "I'll camp and wait three days for you where the road splits... about ten miles west of here. If you don't show up by then I will go on over to the Moore's place in Slagle."

Thinking I knew where she was talking about, I asked to be sure, "Where that big cypress is shading the small stream there?"

She nodded. "That's the place."

"That'll be good. Good fishing and clean water. I'll come as soon as I can... if I can."

Wasting no time on farewells she grabbed the reins off of the brake handle and flicked them getting Sally to move on. "I'll pray for you, Riley" were the last words I heard from her as she drove off.

I held up one hand to wave. I watched her until she got to the end of the row of houses and turned onto the main road that led west. With nothing more to do here, I walked back to the fort to see if I could find Kyle.

The next two days passed slowly. Everyone at the fort was worried over what they thought would happen when the Yankees took over the two forts.

Wild speculations flew around like coal-oil poured over a fire. Some said they were going to give each man a mule and twenty dollars in gold to go home and start their life again. Another rumor running around was that every third man would be shot or hung.

Some of the men, the ones who had money, mostly the worthless Confederate money, buried it in mason jars so they could come back later and dig it up. I didn't have anything of value that needed to be hidden and if I did I sure as hell would not have buried it near the fort.

Kyle and I listened while some of the men talked of sneaking out and running off to Texas. Someone had heard there were other Confederate soldiers forming a new brigade somewhere around Waco. I said to Kyle, "Let 'em go. I don't care. Now this war is over, I'm going home."

Kyle nodded in agreement. He was ready to go home, too, and see if Mr. Moore's daughter, Mary, was still waiting for him.

I didn't believe any of these rumors except maybe the sneaking off and heading to Texas, but Kyle and I had no plans on going to Texas.

Saturday morning arrived. It was the Third of June, Eighteen Hundred Sixty-five. The sun rose over the ramparts of the two forts that sat near the banks of the Red River. Anchored close, blocking the river rested the one Confederate Ironclad warship. No flag flew over either fort or the warship.

The weather promised to be a hot and sticky day. Lots of heat and humidity to go along with the flies and mosquitoes as the men from the two forts milled around inside their dirt walls waiting for their commanders to make their appearance.

After a few minutes of waiting in the sweltering heat, the commander of the fort slowly made his way through the crowd of men, stopping now and then to shake a hand or pat someone on the back. As soon as he reached the main gate to the fort he did a military about-face and called the company of men to attention.

The soldiers, nearly all wearing civilian clothes, snapped to attention with their rifles resting on their shoulders. One group of men forming a color guard squad, carrying our two flags moved forward.

One flag was the white flag of the Confederacy with the

crossed stars in a red field in the corner and the other was our own state flag with several rows of blue, red, and white stripes with a red field in the corner carrying one gold star in its field.

The first sergeant called out, "Form up in your companies!" We scrambled around searching for our sergeants. After a few minutes we were called to attention again and shouldered the rifles we were issued. This time our rifles rested with the butts of the guns in the air, holding the tip of the barrel with our right hand. The gates to the fort opened and the command was given to march. We stirred up a dust cloud with our feet as we headed out of the fort as proudly as we could to the waiting Yankees outside.

Once everyone was outside we were called to halt by the first sergeant, letting our dust cloud drift away with the morning breeze. We were told to line up by squads and one at a time stack our weapons on the backend of a wagon and then fall back into companies, empty handed, facing the Union soldiers.

Our eyes followed Captain Randolph as he handed over the state flag and then the flag of the Confederacy. The flag of our state was rolled up on its pole and placed on the floor of a wagon. The flag of the Confederacy was ripped from its pole and stuffed in a sack. As the flag was thrown into the wagon, men around me began to weep openly of shame and despair. I too cried to see our wonderful old flag given up like that in surrender.

Lastly Captain Randolph bowed his head and presented General Sheridan his sword. The general accepted it and passed it on to an aide with no emotion showing his face. The two of them, General Sheridan and Captain Randolph stood for a moment, not speaking, just looking at one another. Then Captain Randolph, not finding anything else to say, stood at attention and saluted the general. General Sheridan would not return the salute so Captain Randolph, clearly embarrassed by the situation, made an about-face to face his men.

General Sheridan, a small man of stature with a giant ego and reputation, moved forward and called out to us, "You men of the fort stand at ease. As you know, the war is over, has been since May twenty-sixth. Your General Buckner surrendered the rest of the Trans-Mississippi forces at that time. You people are the last."

He stood silent for a moment before continuing. "You know... if I had my way I would hang your officers and march the rest of you off to prison for treason!" He stopped and gave us a cold look of disgust; sweeping his eyes around the defenders of the fort standing before him. "But... our supreme commander-in-chief has *ordered* me... ordered me to pardon each and every one of you scoundrels." He glared at us. "I don't want to see any of you people ever again. Do I make myself clear? So get! Get out of here and never come back, because if you do... orders or no orders I swear I will hang every one of you I can find and I'll burn this whole state to the ground. So go! GET OUT OF MY SIGHT!"

We broke ranks, some running others walking. We couldn't get out of there fast enough to suit me. Kyle and I joined up and on foot headed for the road that led west toward home.

Late that afternoon, as the sun was sitting, we met up with Lucinda at her campsite. The first thing she did was to hand Kyle his shotgun, pistol, and gun belt. I then noticed his horse and saddle amongst our things. I looked at him and then gave her a questioning look.

She smiled and said, "I came across him as I was getting onto the main road heading towards our place after leaving you. He left his guns and horse with me for safe keeping."

"Oh-- well okay. Hey-- how's the baby and Rachel?"

"They're fine. Both sleeping in the back of the wagon. Come on, both y'all and get something to eat. We have a long day ahead of us tomorrow," she said as she led Kyle and me to her little campfire.

The End

Author's Note:

Riley's stories were told to me by my father when I was a child. He would tell me of how Riley Hillman (his grandfather) had been at Vicksburg and how he had swam the Mississippi River in order to go home. Riley is listed at Vicksburg as "Wiley Hillman" of the 27th Louisiana Regiment, Company "C". I don't know why his name was listed as 'Wiley' instead of Riley, but it was.

After Vicksburg, he returned home to find out that his wife had been deported to the Indian Territories in Oklahoma. He had to travel there to bring her home. Paroled at Vicksburg, he served the remainder of the war at one of the forts that were being built on the Red River in Central Louisiana.

All events in this book are not necessarily true facts. The story is based on tales my father told me of his grandfather. The characters in this book are mostly fictional. The only real people in this book are Riley, his wife, and the officers and sergeants at Vicksburg. No one else is a real person.

Made in the USA
Middletown, DE
12 November 2018